DEDICATION

To every one who fell in love and had to fight for it!

DEDICATION

Kelly

Love is like
pieces of heaven

Natasha
Madison
XOXO

Prologue

Mick

I'm sitting here on a stool in this old, run-down, dead bar called Molly's. The smell of stale cigarettes lingers on the walls, having soaked in over the years, way before they were banned.

I swirl the brown liquid in my glass, thinking about how I got here, how much I could fuck up, even my own life.

The stool next to me moves, scraping across the floor, but I don't take my eyes off the glass.

I don't have to turn around to see who is sitting next to me. I know Fred, the bartender, called him. It's what he always does when he thinks I've gone over the edge.

I think this is my worst bender yet, and trust me, I've had a lot of fucking benders. How could I not?

I've been here for the past five days, each day coming in at around noon, not leaving till past midnight. A couple of times I even passed out on his dirty, old couch in the office, waking in a puddle of drool with cat hair on my tongue.

Just another phase, they thought. Just another bad time. If only they fucking knew.

"So," I hear Jackson talk. "How long is it going to last this time?" This is not our first rodeo. Jackson is the only one who has been there for me over the years.

I shrug my shoulders, not even sure of the answer myself.

"Is it Marissa? Is it Lori?" Just the mention of their names is like a stab to the heart. The pain is so unbearable I grab the glass and drink the amber liquid, hoping the burn will overpower the pain.

"Gone," is all I say, all I can muster up.

"Gone where? Bella just spoke with her," Jackson says.

"Sandie's pregnant." The thought alone makes the liquid I just swallowed down begin to climb back up.

The shocked look on Jackson's face mimics mine when she told me.

"Had heaven in my hands and I let it go. Fucked it up. Now I'm living in hell."

With that, I close my eyes, remembering the day I actually touched heaven.

One

Mick

The alarm is blazing somewhere, but my hand can't seem to find the button to turn off the horrid sound.

Fuck, my head is pounding, my tongue is dry, and my stomach is rumbling. I peer one eye open. I'm never fucking drinking again.

I reach out only to touch a naked leg. What follows next is a moan that I don't think I've heard before.

I raise my head to take in the room. Lavender walls with white trimming greet me. Definitely not my fucking house. The floral duvet is the second sign that I'm not in Kansas anymore. Turning to peer at the naked body next to me, I throw my head back, cursing all the saints above.

I knew going out to shoot pool with the boys wouldn't end well. The fact that I got my ass handed to me by Thomas was the first sign to go home.

The blonde who came slinking up to me when I tried to sink the eight ball was the second sign.

The blowjob she gave me in the bathroom twenty minutes later was the fucking flashing billboard saying abort mission.

Continuing the party at her house wasn't a good idea. Fucking her on every single surface was an even worse one.

Getting up, I try not to make a sound to wake her. Searching around the room, I don't see any of my clothes, but it's no surprise because she undressed me at the door. Tiptoeing out of the room, my cock lets me know he's not on board with this plan.

Once I step foot into the living room, it looks like a tornado has passed through it. A bottle of tequila is empty on the floor. Body shots are what she called it. The couch cushions are scattered everywhere.

I find my boxers under a cushion along with a shoe, and then I scan the rest of the room and find my shirt hanging on the lamp in the corner. Snagging it off the lamp roughly as it teeters on the table, I manage to grab it right before it crashes to the floor.

"If you're looking for your jeans, they are in the kitchen near the fridge."

I turn to see the blonde leaning against the doorframe, naked in all her glory, her fake tits rimmed with fingertip bruises from the assault I gave them last night.

"Oh, um." It's all I can say while I use my shirt to cover my junk. I mean, I know she's been intimately introduced to him.

"No need to cover up. I got my fill last night. Just close the door on your way out." Turning to step into the bathroom, she closes the door, effectively dismissing me.

I make my way into the kitchen, snatching up the rest of my clothes before hightailing it out of there.

My car is parked right at the curb, so at least I'm not running around looking for it.

I head home and park in the driveway. Before I can even turn off the ignition, I see a car pull in right behind me. Sandie.

I take a deep breath. This is going to be another episode my neighbors probably don't want to see.

The car door is ripped open and lo and behold Sandie is there, filling the space with her scent of flowers. I used to love that fucking smell. Now I can't stand to even look at flowers.

"Did you fuck another woman last night, Mick?"

I stare at her. Her blond hair is perfectly coiffed, and it's just barely 8 a.m. Her makeup is also tasteful and perfect. Just like she thinks she is, but I know better.

"You are asking me that question when you sleep next to another man, day in and day out." I push her away from the door, trudging

4

inside my house.

She says nothing to me while she follows me in, slamming the door after her.

"You know I don't fuck him." She still follows me while I approach the coffee machine, slipping the Keurig cups into place to wait for the smell of coffee to fill my senses.

"No. What I know is that nine years later, you're still taking his cock and mine. Sweet deal you got there, babe." I sneer while I take a sip of the coffee that has just finished brewing.

She walks up to me, rubbing her hands up my shirt, wrapping them around my neck. "You know you're the only one I love." She kisses my neck, the sensation making my cock stir to life. Bastard has a mind of its own when it comes to her. "You know I'm just organizing things so I can finally leave him." Her hand palms my cock that is straining to come out.

"I've been listening to your excuses to leave him for the last seven years." And before I say anything else, she pops the button of my jeans open and drops to her knees.

Taking my cock out, she draws me into her mouth. I have to give it to her. The woman knows how to suck a cock. She's like a fucking Hoover.

I know what mood she's in. She hates when I fuck other women. She gets territorial. She wants my thoughts on her and only her, so she's erasing thoughts of the last woman and replacing them with thoughts of her.

I know she's going to want it rough, too, and I'm pissed enough to give it to her exactly how she wants it. I'm one of Pavlov's damn dogs when it comes to her, and she fucking knows it.

I place my coffee down, grabbing her head in both my hands, pulling her hair.

I fuck her mouth, not stopping when she starts to gag. She loves this shit. She's already got her skirt up and is working on herself.

That is the thing with Sandie. She keeps coming back for more because with me she can be the dirty girl she wants to be. With me, she can be fucking filthy, and those are things she just can't be or do at home.

With me, she knows I won't turn her away. But tomorrow...well, maybe tomorrow I'll try. .

Two

Mick

My eyes roam the ceiling in my room before slowly closing. I hear Sandie get off the bed and start running around the room.

"I'm going to be so late picking up Jason Jr.," she says while trying to shimmy her panties up.

I rise up on my elbows to watch her. The years have been good to her. Even after having Jason Jr., her body is tight just like when we were in high school.

"I guess this was a fuck visit?"

Her head snaps up. "I need to make sure everything will be okay with Jason Jr. when I finally leave Jason." She climbs on the bed to straddle my waist.

"It's been seven years. How much more do you need?"

"You know I can't just leave, baby. I have no money. Everything is in Jason's name."

"I told you I would take care of you." I put her hair behind her ears.

"You know we have to be careful." She kisses me on the lips, my hand snaking around her waist.

"Whatever, Sandie." I push her off me. I was the stupid idiot who fell back into bed with her the minute I laid eyes on her almost one year after she gave birth and married Jason.

"Close the door on the way out. It's been fun," I tell her while I shut the bathroom door, locking it, and then finally wash off last night and today.

I step out of the shower and wipe the fog off the mirror with my hand. My eyes are still bloodshot. My mouth still tastes like ass, no matter how long I stand here brushing. I lean down to rinse out my mouth. As I wipe my mouth off, I look at myself again, and I wonder how the fuck I got to this place.

It all started when we were fifteen years old after I transferred from the public school to the private one.

I didn't have any money. Shit, my mother was a stripper, and we lived in the projects. We barely had food in the fridge, but I had a natural talent throwing that football. So they gave me a scholarship.

The first day I walked into homeroom, my eyes landed on hers. She was the ultimate pinup girl, with blond hair, a nice rack, a mouth that was made to suck cock, and a juicy ass. It took two days to find out who she was.

Head cheerleader, Sandie, dating the other quarterback on the team. I laughed at the irony.

Every single time she tried to corner me, I walked away from her leering looks and pretended I didn't see her. She kept waiting for me after practice, and I kept leaving out the back door just to avoid her.

I wasn't second string to anyone. Until she cornered me in the locker room one day when I left the field to go grab something I had forgotten.

That was the first time she gave me head, and I didn't give a shit if people found out. I wasn't wrong about those lips.

From then, we started sneaking around. She always said she was forced to date Jason. Their parents were country club friends. She had no choice. It was just for show.

So during the day she would hold his hand, but at night, she would come over and fuck me.

It was a good thing my mother worked nights. It went on for two years, and every single time I would tell her we were done, she would come over that night and profess her love for me. I hate to admit it, but she got under my skin. I loved her, too.

Until that one day, she came over with tears streaming down her face.

"I'm pregnant." Those two words changed my life. It changed hers.

"It's okay. I can get a job, and we can finally be together." It didn't even dawn on me that we always, always wore condoms.

I didn't even pick up the fact she was fidgeting with her hands. "It's Jason's, Mick."

I jumped away from her, starting to pace around my small, two-bedroom apartment. "What do you mean, it's Jason's? You said you were never with him!"

"It was one time, that night we got into that stupid fight because of Jenny. I thought you were going to date her. I went home. He was there. One thing led to another." She looked up at me. The beautiful face of the girl I thought I would wake up to every morning, the beautiful face of the girl I thought would have my kids, the beautiful face of the girl who made me feel like I was worth something. The beautiful face of a liar.

"Please, Mick, don't hate me," she whispered.

I had never hated anyone more than I hated her in that moment. Sitting on my mother's ratty, flowered couch where we first made love, I vowed, right then and there, to never ever give my heart away again. To anyone.

I went on to training camp, did my own thing. I thought of her from time to time. One night while out at a bar, I saw her. Our eyes met across the room. She walked right up to me, and we started talking. It was like no time had passed. We caught up on life, and soon she was touching me any chance she got.

Now, here we are seven years later, and I'm still just her fucking toy.

I'm the man who wants to believe her empty promises. I'm the man who wants the girl to finally pick him, and I'm the man who wants to believe that love conquers all. What the fuck is wrong with me?

Three

Mick

I spend the good part of the morning in the gym near the precinct. Nothing makes me feel better than beating the shit out of a punching bag. Eminem blasts in my headphones, while the sweat pours off me, my muscles nearly seizing up every time my jab strikes the bag.

By the time I shower, get dressed, and head into work, my mood has changed from frustrated to semi-irritated. I start thinking of the caseload that we just got so my mind isn't on Sandie.

I jog up the steps to my office, and I'm greeted by my partner, Jackson. His broody mood is bouncing off the walls. I sit down at my desk, which is right in front of his.

"Good morning, sunshine!" I lean back into my chair, waiting for his eyes to come to mine. When he doesn't say anything but just grunts, I know it's going to be a great day.

"I thought Kendall came over last night? Yet here you are ready to blow up?"

He glances at me. We've been partners since the beginning. We entered the academy at the same time, both of us with chips on our shoulders, both hoping to change the world. I'm trying to get scum off the street, and he's making sure every runaway is found.

"Shut the fuck up, Mick, not today." He looks down at the file in front of him. Another runaway kid who seemingly disappeared into thin air. I hate everything about this case.

He lifts his gaze, pinning it on me. He doesn't need to say anything. I already know what he's thinking.

"I met my neighbor this morning," he tells me while I squeeze my stress ball in my hand. "She had bruises on her arm, a couple faded ones on her face." He closes the file in front him, tossing it on my desk.

I open the folder to see the picture of the latest runaway.

"So now what?" I ask him, but I know the answer even before he tries to answer.

"She's running from something. I don't know what or who, but there was real fear in her eyes. There was the kind of pain that breaks a person," he tells me while he starts typing into the database.

"You can't save everyone, Jackson, you know this. It's like you're constantly chasing that same ghost." I lean forward, putting my arms on the desk.

"I don't want to save her." He shakes his head to clear his thoughts. "I just want her to know she's safe."

"What the fuck are you doing?" I ask when I see him start typing in Nan's name.

"I need to know what her story is, Mick." Right before he can pull up anything, I call his name.

"It's her story to tell, Jackson. Not yours to find out. If she is the way you say she is, there's no way in hell she's going to be cool with you looking into her before she's had a chance to tell you."

He shrugs at me, not ready to admit I'm fucking right.

"Yeah, I know you aren't going to stop searching till you find out those answers. You want to keep her safe." I pause, cocking my head to the side. "Who is going to keep you from yourself, Jackson?"

"I have no idea, but something is pulling me to her, something I can't even explain. I've got to get home. I promised to mow her lawn."

"Which lawn we talking about?" I duck when he throws a balled up piece of paper at me. "How are you going to explain Kendall?"

"There is nothing to explain. We're friends, just friends, from now on." He grabs his keys off his desk, not interested in finishing this conversation.

"I hope you know what you're doing, for both your sakes," I tell him right before he walks out of the room.

I stare at the case file in front of me. A young girl who just up and vanished with a guy no one knows about. I don't know what it is but something in my gut tells me this case isn't what it appears to be. My instincts tell me we won't be closing it any time soon.

I read over the notes a few times, trying to find some kind of clue.

Having done all I can do for today, I get up to leave. I make my way out the door and head home to my empty house, my empty fridge, and my empty fucking life.

The next day Jackson and I decide to hit the streets to find out if anyone knows anything. We may be looking for a needle in a haystack right now, but we need something, anything, to go on.

"No one is fucking talking, Mick. Plus, all the people we want to talk to are probably still sleeping it off," Jackson says right before he puts his water bottle to his lips.

"We should come back down tonight, catch them in action. You up for it tonight? Or are you still nursing your sour mood?"

"Kendall and I have run its course. It's over. Been a long time coming." He places his hands on his hips, waiting for my snarky comments.

"It's about time you set her—and yourself—free. I've been waiting for this. There was nothing anyone could have said to make her turn around and walk away from you. It was always going to have to be you who pulled the plug. She's a good girl. She'll be just fine." I turn to walk to the car. "What was the last straw?"

"I can't really pinpoint one thing," he tells me while getting into the car. "I got home, she was on my couch watching television, and it just felt wrong. Then my neighbor dropped off cookies, and my head wasn't there. She sensed it, we had a conversation, and now we're just friends, without benefits."

I pull out into the street, making my way back to the precinct.

"Your neighbor brought you cookies? That threw you off?" I turn around in my seat, taking off my sunglasses to look at him, thinking he has lost his mind over cookies.

"Leave it be."

I relent, knowing he'll talk when he's ready.

"What time do you want to head out tonight?"

"I think around ten should be good."

We make it to the precinct, and he nods his head. "I'll pick you up tonight. I'll get an unmarked car."

"Sounds good. I'll be at home if you need anything." I open the door, leaning into the car. "Hey. Bring me a cookie tonight." And just like that, I close the door before he can reach over and smack my head, belly laughing the whole way to my car.

Four

Mick

I finally get the last of the groceries put away when the doorbell rings followed by a knock and the door pushing open.

"Baby?" I hear Sandie's soft voice calling.

I open the beer in my hand and take a long pull. I don't have to answer. I know she'll find me.

She walks into the kitchen, dropping her purse down on the table. She looks like she just stepped out of a fashion magazine. Everything matches, right down to the jewelry she's wearing. She has some kind of complicated scarf around her neck that drapes over her stylish shirt that coordinates perfectly with her flowered skirt, all leading down to a sexy pair of wedge sandals. Hell, her outfit probably cost more than my couches.

She walks up to me, snaking her hand up my chest to wrap around my neck. "Hey, baby, I missed you." She leans in, kissing me on my neck.

"Yeah." I find it very hard to believe that she missed me. "My cock maybe. But me? That's debatable."

"You know I miss you. I sent you a text." She places both arms around my neck.

"Really?" I ask. "I didn't get anything."

I can see the fucking lie on her face. I'm a detective, for Christ's sake. Doesn't she realize I can see right through her?

"You know, I've been thinking, Sandie." I take her hands from around my neck, pushing her away gently. "How much fucking longer is this shit going to go on? Aren't you fucking tired of leading a double life?" I pick up my beer, taking another pull from it. "I know I'm about fucking done. You're never going to leave him, and I'm tired of being that other guy." I place the beer back down and assess her. Tears are welling in her eyes.

"I just finished filing divorce papers. He is being served tomorrow. It's time we start *our* lives." She comes to me again. "It's time I show the world that I'm yours and you are all mine."

These are the words I've been waiting to hear for seven years, words that make my heart beat faster, words that make me feel *wanted* for the first time in my life.

"Promise?" I ask her, not sure if I should take the bait, if I should get my hopes up.

"Promise, baby," she says right before she smashes her lips on mine, and we spend the next few hours fucking in my kitchen.

Lying on the couch with her on top of me, I hear my phone ringing from my jeans that are heaped in a pile on the kitchen floor.

I run to them to see Thomas's name flash on the screen. Fuck!

"Sup?"

"Hey, Mick, it's Thomas. Got a call from a woman named Marissa about her runaway daughter, Lori. Captain says it's your case."

I put the beer that I was just about to open down on the counter. "Yeah, it's our case. What you got?"

"Kid called home, mother was hysterical. Good luck with that one. I texted you her address."

"Thanks. I'll check it out and take care of it." I hang up, looking at the text at the same time I'm dialing Jackson.

"Yo," he answers, his voice tight.

"We just got a call from that girl, Lori's mother. She got a phone call from her today. She is freaking out. Called the precinct looking for you, but they called me first."

"I can be ready in ten. Where should I pick you up?"

I hear him rushing around, knocking shit down.

"Um, how about I just meet you at the station in about thirty minutes?" I look over at the couch where Sandie hasn't moved.

"Station, eh? Should I even ask where you are or are we not getting into it now?"

"I'll see you in thirty." I hang up without acknowledging his question.

By the time I make it outside, I'm already running through the details of the case. Lori, age seventeen, started hanging with the wrong crowd, and then one day, she just didn't come home. Her mother hasn't seen or heard from her since. Until today.

Friends say she's been in touch with them. The thing is, she's seventeen, so it's hard not to consider that this might be a case of a teenager just wanting her freedom. Her mother said that lately she'd become more distant than usual, and her grades began slipping. When she confronted her, they had a big argument that ended in Lori storming out of the house and not coming back.

I make it to the precinct at the same time that Jackson pulls up. I wait for him to get out of his car before I leave mine.

"Your shirt is buttoned wrong."

I look down at my shirt and see that my shirt is, in fact, buttoned wrong. After hanging up the phone with Jackson, I was too busy rushing to get out of there, placing a kiss on Sandie's head with a promise to text her later.

"Fuck." I go about righting my shirt. "I wasn't expecting to be called in. I was…"

"You don't have to explain yourself to me. I just hope you know what you're doing." He makes his way over to our unmarked car.

"I know what you're going to say, so we can just skip this whole bullshit conversation right now." I pull into traffic, heading toward the center of town.

"I wasn't going to say anything. You're a grown ass man. You know what you're doing." He stares straight ahead.

"She says she's leaving him. I have to believe her," I say to the windshield, instead of turning to look at him.

"She said that last time, too, didn't she? Strung you along for four months before she told you she couldn't do it right then. Then there was your birthday, when she showed up and spent the whole weekend telling you she left him, only to go back home on Monday. Trust me, I remember. It was me who found you after you lost yourself in the bottom of a bottle of Jack. It wasn't pretty." He isn't fucking wrong. It's been a fucking roller coaster, to say the least.

"She said it's finally time. She loves me."

He shakes his head, knowing this is a game Sandie is playing with me. He knows she's been stringing me along for the last seven fucking years now.

"I want nothing more than for that to be true. You know this. But it shouldn't be this hard, Mick." He wants to continue, but knowing that he's going to start sounding a bit too much like Dr. Phil, he backs off and continues staring out the window.

Five

Mick

When we pull up to the address on the text that Thomas sent me, Lori's mother's house, I'm instantly on alert because we're now in the projects. The five matching apartment buildings are known around here as Welfare Avenue.

A couple teenagers on the corner try to be intimidating and let us know we're on their turf, puffing out their chests and taking us in. Right in the middle of the group is the leader of the pack. The two I suspect are his seconds are right beside him, chewing on toothpicks, sizing us up with their cell phones in their hands.

We open the door, unsurprised the lock is broken, allowing anyone to just walk in. The hallway is dark, with just a few lights working, while most are broken and a few are flickering. I bring my hand to my nose to block out the burning sensation from the stench of urine. We get to the third floor and make our way to the door with the number five on it.

Jackson knocks on the door twice, taking a step back while I look over his shoulder, making sure we aren't going to be ambushed.

We hear the locks clicking open, but neither of us is prepared for the sight we are met with.

A tiny girl, maybe all of five foot one, opens the door, wearing tight booty shorts and a tank top that has seen cleaner days. Brown hair that is at least clean sits in a messy bun on the top of her head. Her face is free of makeup.

"Are you the cops?" she asks, her voice soft, yet trying to be hard.

"Yes, ma'am. Are you Marissa, Lori's mom?" Jackson says, flashing her his badge. "May we come in?"

I don't bother with mine since she moves to the side holding on to the open door, ushering us in. I look around once I get in, and I have to admit I'm kind of shocked. Inside is completely neat and clean. The furniture looks almost new, and a television sits in the corner. There is a small kitchen with no table, just two stools.

Two bedrooms open to the living room, both rooms looking clean with beds and a few other pieces of furniture. I can tell one is obviously a teenager's from the posters hanging on the wall.

"Please have a seat. Can I get you anything?" She's nervous. I know this because she is wringing her hands.

"We're good, thanks," Jackson answers her while he goes to sit down, and I stand by the kitchen, leaning against the wall. I'm letting Jackson take the lead with this one.

"So you called in saying Lori got in touch with you?"

"Yes. I got a call on my cell phone sometime after ten a.m. I was asleep, but the minute I heard her ringtone I flew out of bed."

"What did she say?"

"She said she was fine and to call off the dogs." She looks between Jackson and me.

"You weren't here when she went missing, right?" I ask her from my side of the room.

"I was here when she left, but it was when I got home from work at three a.m. that I noticed she hadn't returned." She looks down at her hands. "I was working. She usually just texts me, but since we got into a fight the night before I just thought she was pissed off."

"You're a stripper, right? Is there any way she got ahold of your drugs or saw something she shouldn't have?" As the words come out of my mouth, even I'm shocked. I have never ever assumed the worst of anyone in my life. But the fact that she is a stripper is hitting pretty close to home.

My mother was on the same road as Marissa here. When I lived with her, she was in and out of the house at different times of the day and night. Sometimes high, sometimes not, usually with a different guy. If she kept a roof over my head and food in the fridge, in her mind that was her being June fucking Cleaver.

Jackson whips his head around to glare at me with a clear 'what the fuck' expression on his face.

Marissa's shoulders go back like she is gearing up for a fight. "Yes, I'm a stripper, but no, I don't do drugs. If you want, we can take a piss test right now to ease your mind, Detective." Her sassiness comes out full force.

"Won't be necessary," Jackson cuts in.

"A seventeen-year-old sees her mother as a stripper. You don't think she'll follow in your footsteps?" I won't give in that easy, so I just continue.

"I don't know, I think her knowing you have to work for things isn't such a bad lesson. Considering her father left me with his bookie debt of eighty grand and the only way the guy he owed the money to wouldn't take it out on us was if I agreed to work for him. I think showing her you don't run from your obligations, like her weasel father did, but instead you keep fighting and working to earn the things you want is good. So, if you came here just to pass judgment on me and my job while not taking my daughter's disappearance seriously, I think we've both wasted our time." Marissa goes to stand up, her hands shaking.

Jackson grabs her wrist, stopping her, making me stand up straight with the need to rip it away from him. I make a mental note to go and research the douchebag who left her and his daughter to clean up his mess. I'm not sure what it is about this chick that's getting me so riled. It's confusing as fuck, especially considering I just met her five minutes ago.

"I'm going to apologize for my partner and his mood today. Please know finding your daughter is very important to us."

She looks, or rather glares, at me, waiting for me to say something, but I just shrug my shoulders. I'm afraid my voice will deceive me if I open my mouth again.

"I asked around at work and there's a new guy who has been coming in. I don't have his name yet, but he's been in a couple of times. He is also in scumbag Bentley's crew. Owns a pawn shop, isn't fair, and sells whatever you bring to him to the first person who wants to buy it before you even get a chance to get it back yourself. He also doesn't care how you get his money just as long as you do."

"I need you to not try to do anything on your own and let us handle things."

"Oh, yeah, it looks like you guys are really handling things. She's been missing for a week," she whispers, and a tear escapes her eye, rolling down her cheek.

I want to reach out and catch it. Instead, I push my hands into my pockets to stop myself.

"We are working on it, Marissa, but if you're interfering, it's just going to create extra work for us. So please, if you hear anything or see anything, call us first. Don't just go charging in, call me first." He takes out his card and hands it to her. "My cell number is on there so you can call me whenever you think you need to."

I just barely manage to stop myself from snatching it out of her hand and throwing it back in his face. I shake my head from the scene in my head.

She wipes her cheeks with the back of her hand. "I'm doing all of this for her. So I didn't uproot her and take her away from everyone and everything she knew."

He stands up, for sure making notes in his head about this fresh new face out there. We must be thinking the same thing; that we need to pay Bentley another visit. It'll be the fourth time this week.

"Thank you for calling us with this update," Jackson says to her.

I barely get through the door into the hallway before it is shut right behind me, almost bouncing against my head.

"What the fuck was that bullshit in there? Since when did you become such a judgmental asshole? Spewing bullshit like that to a victim's mother, what the fuck, man?"

I don't even answer, I just walk away.

I storm to the car without saying anything. Jackson doesn't even have the door closed before I peel off from the curb and slap my hand down on the steering wheel twice.

"FUCCCKKKK!" I pull over one block down. Whipping the door open, I jump out and slam it shut before I kick it in.

"I'm going to go out on a limb here and say your head isn't in the game today," Jackson says while he's standing in the open car door one foot still inside, while he places a hand on the roof of the car.

"That was fucked up. I'm on edge about Sandie, and I totally let that poor woman have it. Jesus, I'm surprised she didn't try to have me killed before I got to the car."

"We have a whole night ahead of us. Why don't we head over to see the pawn shop dealer, Bentley? Let's hear what he has to say about this new player in town. But you pull that shit again"—he points back in the direction we came from—"I'll fucking kill you for her."

I nod as I get back into the car. The rest of the night is a blur of us chasing a ghost. From one side of town to the other, all empty leads, all leading back to this new guy.

It's a long night and when I get home, Sandie isn't there, just a note saying she'll call me tomorrow.

I shake my head, knowing once again I got played. But this time it's the last fucking time.

Six

Mick

I'm just about to line up my winning shot when my phone rings. I lean the pool cue on the side of the pool table and pull my phone out. It's been two weeks since shit went down with Sandie.

The day after she told me she was leaving her husband, I went into work and searched for her divorce case. Not surprisingly, nothing was filed.

The next thing I did was to call a locksmith and have my locks changed. Then I sent her a text.

You played me for the last time.

The minute I pressed send, I had my number changed. It didn't stop her from showing up at my house the next day. But she wasn't expecting to be stopped before her foot could even touch my step.

"What are you doing here?" I asked from my front door.

She wasn't expecting me to do this scene in the front lawn, especially in the middle of the day.

"I think we need to talk, don't you?" She looked around, seeing some of my neighbors outside, some looking over at us. "Privately."

"Nope, I have nothing to say to you, in public or in private. Sandie, do me one last favor and get back in your car, and go home to your husband. Forget me, forget where I live, forget about my cock. Jesus, just please, leave me alone already and fucking move on." I crossed my

arms over my chest.

The tears welling in her eyes did nothing to me anymore. Kind of like the boy who cried wolf, I was at the point now where I didn't give a shit. She was never going to pick me, not back then and not now.

"Baby—"

I held my hand up, stopping her from continuing. "Aren't you fucking tired of this song and dance? I sure the fuck am. Just fucking hire someone to fuck you right if he doesn't do it for you, because I'm done."

Before she could even reply, I quickly turned and walked back inside, closing the door and locking it behind me.

It didn't take long before I heard her car start and drive off, peeling down the street. Seven years we'd been doing this dance, and I was just done with it.

"Jackson," I say into the phone, giving Thomas the one-second finger to step away to take the phone call.

"Got a call from Marissa. Said Lori called her again. I'm on my way to Manny's Jug House."

My hand clenches the phone hard. The thought of her stripping just pisses me off. I've been making up so many excuses in my head about why it pisses me off so much that I'm not even believing them.

"I'm on my way, leaving McHugh's Brews & Cues. For the record, I think it's a big waste of time." Walking back to the table, I tell Thomas that I have to go and give him a quick update about the case.

I'm barely in my car when Jackson calls me back asking for my ETA because he's already there. He must have gunned it.

I get to the club just in time to see Marissa run straight into Jackson's arms. I've never once had a violent thought about my partner, but right then and there, I want to kick his ass.

"She's hurt, my baby is hurt. I can tell. I heard it in her voice," Marissa says before she starts sobbing.

I get out of my car and approach them, taking in Marissa's 'work' attire. She's wearing a micro-miniskirt, and I'm using the word 'skirt' loosely, seeing as it barely covers her ass cheeks. Her tube top is white and practically see-through. I can see that she has little star stickers on her nipples. Her 'uniform' is completed by a pair of sparkly, six-inch, platform, clear acrylic heels.

I take off my jacket and toss it to her. "Jesus, cover yourself up. You're almost naked." I then look around to see if anyone is leering at her.

I'm so fucking agitated by this whole scene that I don't even wait for Jackson to ask the questions. I have no idea what is going on with me, why I'm so angry with this woman. "So what happened now, Marissa, that you couldn't wait till tomorrow before calling us?"

"Lori…she, she called again. She called my cell." She hands me her cell phone, which I take and start looking through it.

"Unknown number. We can't do anything." I hand it back to her.

"She said she wants to come home. She just can't get here." She looks back and forth between us with panicked, teary eyes. "I have to get her home." The tears start to run down her face, taking her mascara with them. "Help me find her."

"Did she tell you anything? Where she was? Who she was with?" Jackson asks her as she is rapidly shaking her head.

"Nothing. The call lasted maybe twenty seconds, but I asked her. I told her to tell me where she was and I'd come get her. She just kept saying she wants to come home." She wraps her arms around her waist as her body starts to shake.

Jackson leans in, taking her in his arms just as she starts to fall to the ground.

"How did you get to work? Did you drive?" he asks her right before a skinny black man approaches us.

"I don't pay you to come outside and turn tricks. I pay you to shake your ass and show off your tits. Now get back in there and do what I pay you for." He looks back and forth between us. It's the last fucking thing I need to hear before I snap.

I go toe to toe with him. He may be the same height as me, but I have a good sixty pounds of muscle on him.

"I would watch your fucking tone, man. Can't you see the lady is crying? Instead of making sure we aren't forcing ourselves on her, you tell her to get back to work. Disgusting."

"Ain't no one need to force her to do anything, she does that shit for free."

The minute he says that, my fist flies faster than a lightning bolt, popping him right in the jaw. The man is knocked to the ground, but

I pick him up by his collar and get right in his face. "Talk to her like that again, I'll have you eating through a fucking straw for a month," I growl out menacingly as he pushes me away.

Jackson grabs my arm before I can do anything more.

"Marissa, you get your ass back in there now or you look for something else."

"She fucking quits, asshole," I say as I turn to her. "Go get your shit. Now."

Marissa is either still in shock or just scared of the rage that I'm sure is shining in my eyes, but she nods and hurries inside.

"We are giving her five minutes. If she is not back, then you go in and get her," I tell Jackson while I shake my fist, which is starting to swell. Just great. I need a fucking ice pack.

"Mind telling me what the fuck is going on there, partner? You talk to her like she's trash one minute, and then you step up like a knight in shining armor the next." His question is a valid one, but I can't admit something I myself don't even understand.

Before he has a chance to press me more, Marissa comes out dressed in jeans and a shirt. A huge bag of clothes is in her hands.

"I have no idea how I'll pay my next month's rent, but I guess I'm done with this shithole," she says quietly. Her face is cleaned of the black streaks that were running down her cheeks, and she looks much younger without all that makeup on. Almost angelic.

"Did you see anyone out of the ordinary come in tonight?" Jackson asks her.

"No one. It was really slow which is why I had my phone on me. The minute I felt it ring, I jumped." The tears start to fill her eyes again. "I need to find her."

"We are doing everything we can right now. If she calls you back, you tell her to tell you anything. Preferably where she is, but if she doesn't know then ask what she sees, what she saw on her way there, anything that can lead us to her."

"I'll take you home, see if maybe there is anything there you might have missed," I cut in before Jackson makes the suggestion.

"I have my own car. I don't want to come back here," she says to me while handing me my coat back.

"Fine, I'll follow you. Jackson, I'll send you a message if I find anything or if Lori calls again."

He has nothing to say to me, just nods his head in agreement, but I see the questions in his eyes, and I know I'm going to have to call him the minute I'm done.

I wait in my car right across from Marissa as she gets into hers, and I follow closely behind her as she drives home.

She parks, and I pull in right behind her, killing the engine and getting out of my car just in time to grab her bag from her.

"You don't need to babysit me. I'll be fine," she tells me while trying to snatch her bag out of my hand.

"I'll carry it up, make sure you're safe." I walk ahead of her to the door, holding it open for her. "After you."

Now normally a woman would say thank you for the gesture, but not Marissa. She shoots me such an angry glare that a lesser man's balls may have shrunk up in response. Me? I bite back a chuckle because she's fucking adorable.

I do smile, though, knowing that she won't take any bullshit from anyone else.

She leads the way up the steps with me following behind her, my eyes glued to her ass. Images of my hands on her ass flash in my head, causing my cock to wake up.

She stops in front of her door and unlocks it, then turns around to grab her bag, obviously intending not to let me into her apartment.

"Thanks for following me home, but I'm fine now," she says while trying to wrestle the bag out of my hand, but I'm not letting it go.

"Marissa, let me come in and put this down. Maybe make you a drink to settle your nerves."

"Why?" She looks me straight in the eyes as she crosses her arms over her chest. "Why the sudden desire to make sure I'm safe? The last time you were here, you threw my job in my face and asked if my kid took my drugs. So tell me, Detective, why the sudden change?"

I like the fact that she didn't let the last time slip, but I'm also pissed at myself for being such an asshole. I have to say, I'm really liking that she's so direct. With Marissa, what you see is what you get, there is no bullshit with her, and it's fucking refreshing.

"I'm sorry about last time, okay? I was an asshole, and you did not deserve that shit I served up. The whole situation...it just hit a little close to home. That's it, I swear." I move closer, our bodies almost touching. I can practically feel the heat coming off her. "Let me come in and make sure you're okay, Marissa."

She sighs heavily, nods her head, and pushes the door open.

I walk in after her and wait as she turns on all the lights. I place the bag of clothes down on the couch and sit next to it.

"Did you eat?" I ask her as she pulls a bottle of water out of the fridge and opens it, making her stop midway.

"Okay, that's it. I've had enough crap happen to me today. I need some normalcy here, and right now my only option is for you to go back to being an asshole."

The way she just called me out again makes me snicker to myself. "Fine, I'm out of here, but"—I take her phone off the counter, calling myself so I have her number—"if you need anything, give me a call." I emphasize me, hoping that I'll be the one she calls, not Jackson, if something comes up.

Placing her phone back down on the counter, I salute her with two fingers as I walk out of her apartment.

Once I'm in the hall, I hear the lock click shut. It brings me out of my head. I have no idea what the fuck just happened. I have no idea why I would even bother to do that.

I feel this inexplicable pull to her, and I have no idea why or what it means. I know that she doesn't need—nor want—me. I don't know, maybe that's the draw. Maybe I'm just predisposed to want women who don't want me. God, I'm so fucked up.

Making my way to my car, I do something I suspect I will regret tomorrow.

Seven

Mick

I wasn't wrong when I said that phone call would have made me hate myself. The minute I sat in the car looking down at the phone, the number of a girl I used to hook up with just waited for me to push the call icon. I came really fucking close. Instead, Marissa and that pull to her I don't understand made me throw my car into drive and head to my usual watering hole where I sat my ass down and drank until I couldn't feel anything, let alone that pull to Marissa, anymore.

I don't remember anything after my first round at the bar. The night before I got there, though, plays in my mind like a movie reel on a continuous loop. Marissa's face when she almost collapsed, her face when I tried to help, and her eyes, those tear-filled eyes, brimming with her fear, sadness, and worry for her missing daughter. I remember feeling helpless, like there was absolutely nothing that I could have done to make any of it better for her. Nothing, and I think that's what killed me the most. All I could say was 'I'm so sorry' over and over.

By the time morning rolls around, I have a headache that could rival the pounding of ten lumberjacks hammering away in my head. My mouth is drier than the scorched earth of Death Valley but God dammit, my bed is empty and I'm alone, so I'm still counting last night as a victory.

After taking a shower and drinking four cups of strong, black coffee,

I get dressed to head out to Phyllis's Diner.

I park and head inside, not taking off my sunglasses. The sun is just too bright for my bleary eyes and aching head today.

The jingle of the bells as I open the door takes me right back to when I first met Phyllis.

She was our next-door neighbor. Even though she hated my mom, she looked out for me on the nights mom went to work.

I spent more time with Phyllis than I did with my mom, and soon I was always at her house. She was more like a grandmother to me.

I clear my throat, and she whirls around to face me. The ever-present scowl on her face morphs into a megawatt smile when she sees me.

"Look at my boy, coming to visit me," she says to everyone within earshot as she places a pie in the glass stand on the counter.

The diner is fifties inspired and serves comfort food, all made from scratch from Phyllis's own recipes. She also gave me my first job—bussing tables—when I was eleven. *"It'll keep you out of trouble, boy,"* is what she said, not really giving me a choice, and I took it because not only did she pay me, but she also fed me like a king.

Walking behind the counter, I lean down and give her a loud, smacking kiss on her cheek. She giggles and then pushes me away. "You look like shit." There she is, my Phyllis never sugarcoating anything.

"Awww, thanks, you look like shit yourself." I give it right back to her.

She scowls at me again, right before she lets a deep belly laugh loose. "Sit down. I'll get you coffee."

She gets me a steaming cup of coffee, sliding it in front of me with a big piece of homemade apple pie. She's won numerous blue ribbons for this pie.

"So, what brings you here?" She leans on her hands on the counter.

I fork into the pie, chewing it before I tell her why I'm really here. "Need a favor." I don't take off my glasses nor do I look at her for fear that she'll see right through me.

"Oh, yeah? Since when does Mick Moro ask for favors?" Her question doesn't surprise me. She knows I don't ask anyone for anything.

"There's a first time for everything, right?" I drop my fork and take a sip of the hot coffee.

"What do you need?" She stands up, removing the plate from in front of me.

"Have a friend. She needs a job, bad. You have anything open?" I finally look up at her, my chest not moving because I'm holding my breath.

"You actually have friends?" She smiles at me, and I know that she is going to help me out. That is the way she is. That's Phyllis.

"She worked at Manny's Jug House. Her daughter ran away from home, and let's just say she can't go back there." I take another sip of the coffee before I say more than I want to.

"Oh my goodness! That poor thing! She can have any shift she wants. Money is good during the week in the mornings and at lunch. Breakfast and dinner on the weekends. You think she would have problems with that?"

I have to think about how she's going to be pissed at me for stepping on her toes, but in all honesty, I'm the reason she lost her job. I nod my head at Phyllis before taking my phone out of my pocket to text her.

Hey, are you there? It's Mick.

My phone dings a second later, and I know she's stuck to her phone, hoping that Lori calls her again.

What can I do for you, Mick?

I can practically see her eyes roll and hear her attitude through the phone.

You think you could come down to Phyllis's Diner in about twenty? HMMM let me check my calendar. Oh, that's right, I have no job, so my calendar is wide-open. Leaving now. I'll be there in ten. Order me a piece of pie, and keep the tab open so you can pay for it.

I laugh at her bossiness, throwing the phone down on the counter, and look over at Phyllis. "She's on her way. I should probably warn you she would rather drink acid than accept my help."

Phyllis raises her eyebrows questioningly.

"She pretty much hates me."

Phyllis crosses her arms over her chest. "Nothing new there, boy. Give it some time, she'll come around. They all do."

I almost choke on my coffee while she continues talking.

"I haven't ever seen you go out of your way to help anyone. So I know this one is different."

30

I put my hand up to stop her before she goes home tonight and knits baby booties. "It's not like that with her. Trust me. You'll see once you meet her."

She looks around us to make sure no one is listening before she speaks, "That bitch filled your head and your heart with garbage, and it's high time you flush it out of your system once and for all."

I don't have time to say anything before the door opens and the sound of bells fills the silence that has grown between us.

I turn and take her in, the sight of her knocking me for a loop. She is dressed much the same as last night, tight jeans hugging her small body, a black, V-necked T-shirt that molds perfectly to her breasts, and black flip-flops on her tiny feet.

There is not a trace of makeup on her face, and up close like this, I can see tiny freckles sprinkled over her nose. Her hair sits on top of her head in one of those bun things women wear. It occurs to me that she looks just like her daughter from the pictures I've seen.

She slides onto the stool next to me, giving Phyllis a smile. "Hi there," she says then turns to me, giving me a nod before turning back to Phyllis. "Did he order?" she asks as she reaches over and grabs the menu from the middle of the counter.

"He's just having pie," Phyllis says.

"I'll take a bacon cheeseburger, all the way, with fries, please." She flips the menu over, looking at the drinks. "And a chocolate shake. He's buying." Once she is done placing her order, she looks up and smiles.

It takes two seconds to realize this probably wasn't my smartest idea. These two are going to ruin me. Phyllis just smiles at her and walks back to the kitchen to put in the order.

"So, Mick, what did you want?"

"I'm going to introduce you to Phyllis, whom you've just met, by the way, and she is going to speak with you about a job."

Her spine stiffens, and she glares at me, the green in her hazel eyes deepening with her rising anger.

"Now before you go apeshit on me, it's my fault you lost your job last night, so just go with it."

She lets out a laugh. "Just go with it. I've heard that before." She shakes her head. "I could get my own job. You know that, right?" She crosses her hands in front of her.

Phyllis walks out with the chocolate shake in her hand. She places it right in front of Marissa, who leans forward and takes a big sip, groaning out in ecstasy.

The sounds of her pleasure over the shake have my cock springing to life.

"I haven't had one of these in three years. I haven't had a cheeseburger in over six months!" she says and then goes back to her shake.

Before I can ask her why, Phyllis does it for me.

Marissa shrugs her shoulders. "I was a stripper, so I had to keep my weight below a certain number. Now, though, that's not an issue." She finishes about half the milkshake before we hear the order pick-up bell coming from the kitchen.

"That sounds like your burger is ready. Now stop drinking that so you'll have room for real food," Phyllis says to her while walking away.

"You don't need to watch your weight, you look fine," I say before I can stop myself.

Before she can respond, two plates are plunked down in front of us. Phyllis looks pointedly at me. "You need some grease in your system to absorb all the whiskey that is seeping out of your pores."

Marissa doesn't wait for me before she bites into her burger, ketchup gathering in the corner of her mouth. Her tongue slides out to lick it away, and that innocent gesture has my cock knocking on my zipper.

She dips a fry in ketchup. "Is that what that smell is? You should have showered."

I glare at her, taking my own bite of my burger.

Right before I answer, Phyllis cuts in, "So, Mick mentioned he got you fired from your job last night."

Marissa just nods her head since she has so much food in her mouth, she looks like a chipmunk.

"Lucky Jolene gave her notice last night after I found her on her knees in the supply closet with Becky's husband. The same Becky who was sitting in a booth, waiting for him to finish in the bathroom."

Marissa's eyes practically bulge out of their sockets.

"So if you want the job, it's yours. I don't tolerate tardiness, it's rude. I also don't tolerate my waitresses giving head to the customers, especially the married ones, in my supply closet."

Marissa swallows her mouthful, wiping her hands in her napkin. "I would love to work for you. I haven't been late for a single shift, not one, *ever*. I'm kind of focused on getting my daughter home right now, so I have bigger things going on in my life. There'll be no blowjobs given out by me. And just so you know, I don't tolerate being talked down to or disrespected. Some people will come in here, and all they'll see is the stripper, not the woman. I won't allow anyone to treat me like a whore, because I'm not one."

The thought that people actually judge her because she's a stripper makes my blood boil. My fist clenches open and shut while I try to get myself to calm down. Then I realize I was that fucking asshole once or twice also.

"I like you," is all Phyllis says before looking at me then back at Marissa. "Can you start tonight? I know it's last minute, but I'm really stuck."

"Yup, I can start right after I finish this and that piece of pie"—she cocks her head in my direction—"he's going to buy me."

Phyllis lets out a laugh. "Oh, this one is going to work out just fine," she says before going back in the kitchen.

"I like her," Marissa takes another bite. "She'll be cool to work for."

This might have been a mistake, but just seeing Marissa smile I know that I would do it again. Smiling to myself, I pick up the coffee cup and drain what's left. "I believe you now owe me one."

My comment makes her stop mid chew, and with one of her famous glares, she says, "It's your fault I'm here to begin with." She doesn't even care that she is talking with her mouth full.

I know I shouldn't be doing this, shouldn't even be thinking about this, that this is going to end fucking badly for *everyone*. But I just don't care right now, not one fucking bit. My heart beats just a tiny bit faster because of her, and I don't think it's done that for anyone but Sandie, ever. That is reason enough to not walk away from her. This thing between us has a mind of its own. This pull is real, it's strong, and I'm already tired of trying to fight it.

"I'll make you dinner," she whispers softly, hunched over her plate, pushing her fork around what's left of the pie. "But just so you know"—she takes a huge breath before continuing—"I'm not going to sleep with you, not now, not ever. No matter what people may think, I'm really not that kind of girl."

The words that come out of her mouth shock me. Yes, I judged her at the beginning, and yes, I thought the same thing. But five minutes with her and I knew that wasn't what she was about.

"Good to know. You can come over on Friday after you finish your shift here." I don't say anything more, but I take in my hands. One is clenched in a fist, and the other is gripping the coffee mug so tight I think I might shatter it.

I get up, tossing some money on the counter before Phyllis comes back because she wouldn't let me pay for anything. "I'll text you my address."

Once I'm in my car, I realize that the tightness in my chest has loosened up, just a touch.

Eight

Mick

"Eat all your food. Momma has someone coming over and you can't be walking all over the house," she told me while piling more mac and cheese into my bowl, a cigarette hanging from her lips.

I didn't say anything, just shoveled the food down. It was a good thing that Jimmie lent me the new comic book that he got. "Okay, Momma." I didn't have time to say anything else before there was a knock on the door.

She quickly threw the pot into the sink that was already overflowing with dirty dishes, throwing her cigarette in another one while she turned the water on to soak the pot.

She really fixed herself up today. She was wearing her 'good' clothes, so I thought whoever was coming was someone important.

Walking over to the door, she fluffed her hair before she opened it. "Baby," she cooed softly. The man whom I couldn't see stepped in.

When he did, I saw that he was wearing a suit like my principal wore at school for picture day, clean-cut, clean shoes, his hair short with a beard.

He closed the door behind him before grabbing my mother around her waist. "Marla," he said before kissing her on her cheek.

"Is that any way to treat the mother of your kid?" she asked him, and my head snapped up. What was she talking about?

"Marla, we have been over this many times before. You can't keep saying things like that." He didn't even notice that I was now standing right behind my mother.

"Who is this?" I asked them both, wondering who would answer me.

The man looked at my mother and then at me. *"I'm an old friend of your mom's. We went to school together. You can call me Billy."*

My mother didn't say anything, just rolled her eyes at him. *"Yeah, we went to school together."* She placed her hands on her hips. *"Now, Mick, go to your room and close the door. Bedtime is at eight."*

I didn't say anything to her or to him. I just nodded and walked back to my room, closing the door behind me.

It didn't take long before the moans started. You would think I would be used to this, but I wasn't. Grabbing my headphones off the side table, I put them over my head, hoping that this time went quicker than it did when other guys came around.

I mean, my mom tried her best, but she missed love. At least that was what she told me. I didn't have a grandma or a grandpa. They told her to leave when she was pregnant with me. So it was me and her against the world, she said. That is until one of her boyfriends came over, and then it was just me against the world.

I didn't know how much time had passed, but when I took off the headphones there was no more noise, so it was my chance to sneak out and go to the bathroom.

Opening my door softly so as to not make any noise, I peeked my head out but didn't see anyone in the living room.

Billy's jacket was still on the couch, so I knew they were somewhere there, probably in Mom's room.

When I tiptoed to the bathroom, I saw Mom's door was slightly open. That Billy dude was sitting at the edge of the bed while my mother was standing in front of him, naked.

"What do you mean you aren't leaving her?"

"It's more complicated than you think it is. I can't just go in there and tell her I'm leaving her. I work for her father at her father's company. I'm going to have no job. How the hell do you expect me to keep giving you money if I have no job?"

"You said you were leaving her when we found out I was pregnant. You promised if I kept quiet, you would leave her when I gave birth."

"I know what I said, honey, but now isn't a good time," he said *while trying to grab her hand to pull her closer. She didn't make him work hard, and she was standing in between his legs while he grabbed her ass in his hands.*

"She's been depressed ever since she had the baby. She isn't strong like you. She's weak. I'm telling you, she's going to snap soon, and then I can put her away and have you and Mick finally move in with us." He kissed her right between her breasts. "I love you, always you."

She sighed deeply. "Yeah, right, you love me. You love to sink your cock into me, always have. I'm tired of the promises, William, tired of being your dirty little secret, tired of being the mother to your bastard son."

"I promise you, this will be over soon, and then I can claim Mick as my own, give him my last name, and we can be a family."

"I really hope so, because I think I'm pregnant again," she told him, and he pushed her away from him.

"What the fuck are you talking about? You said you were on something, and now you tell me you're fucking knocked up again?" He pushed past her to get his pants off the floor. "I can't fucking believe this shit. I have one knocked up at home, and I have you knocked up here. What the fuck?"

My mom's face turned white. "She's pregnant? I thought you said you were leaving her. This is why you didn't leave her yet? Because you fucked her and got her pregnant?"

Billy's hand flew out so fast, my mom didn't see it coming. Her head snapped back, and she fell to the floor. I rushed in to try and save her right before he kicked her while she was down. "Fucking bitch trying to trap me again."

"Leave my mom alone." I put myself in front of her.

"You can have her. Cheap bitch spreads for everyone." He put his shirt back on. "Don't try to say this one is mine, too. You know I'll fucking bury you before the results come back." And with that, he stormed out of the room.

I looked over at my mom, who was curled up in a ball crying. "It's okay, Mom, I'm going to get you water." I ran back into the kitchen, grabbed a glass and water, and then walked super slow so I didn't spill any.

What greeted me when I returned to the room was my mom in a puddle of blood pooling around her bottom. "Mom? Are you sick, Mom?"

Her eyes were closed, and the blood just didn't stop. My hands were all covered in it now.

"Mom?"

My eyes flash open, the sheets tangled at my feet, my chest heaving, the bile slowly rising. I barely make it to the bathroom before everything ejects from my body.

Bending over the toilet is not the way I wanted to wake up this morning. After rinsing my mouth and brushing my teeth, I head downstairs to start my day at four-oh-four in the morning.

"Fucking great," I say to myself as I wait for my Keurig to finish brewing my coffee.

I sit and peer out into the dark night, so quiet and peaceful. I bought this house because it had a backyard that led to a lake.

Looking out over the calm lake, my mind wanders back to the blackest days of my life.

I called 911, not really understanding what was happening but knowing I had to get my mother help. Mom suffered a miscarriage right there in her bedroom. She was never the same after it. As soon as we got back from the hospital, she packed up all our stuff, and we left that little apartment, the only place I ever had good memories of my mom.

That's when everything spiraled out of control. The drugs, the stripping, the men. It was a fucking revolving door. Once when I was sixteen, she was high and drunk, and I picked her up off the couch and brought her into her room. Her whispered confession that night were words I never forgot, words that still haunted me. "I try, Mick, but it's just so hard. It's so hard loving you when all you do is remind me of him."

I didn't have to ask her who 'him' was—I knew. In that moment, I realized that love wasn't unconditional, and my mother definitely loved me with conditions.

Pouring milk into my coffee mug, I go sit outside near the water. The sounds of crickets and frogs fill the silence. I make up a list in my head of things to do, but my mind inevitably drifts to Marissa. Her expressive green eyes that hold so much sadness and so much heart.

I watch the dark night sky slowly turn to orange as the sun makes its way over the horizon. Leaning my head back, I close my eyes, hoping to just rest. The sounds of the water rolling over the rocks at the edge of the lake and the cry of the crickets lull me back to sleep. I wake a couple hours later to the sound of a school bus honking.

Grabbing my coffee mug, I head back inside for my gym bag and head there, where I'll knock the shit out of the heavy bag, beating the old memories of my mother, that night, and the guy whose blood runs through my veins out of my head.

Nine

Mick

I make it inside my door right as the sun is setting. My body still aches from the beating I gave it this morning at the gym. My feet hurt from walking the streets trying to chase down leads on a guy who everyone seems to have seen but no one really knows.

I barely make it into the kitchen before there is a knock on the door. Throwing my head back, I run my hands over my face and groan. I'm sure it's fucking Sandie. She has been blowing up my phone for the past two days. Ever since she showed up at the station and pretended she got a new phone and all her contacts got erased. I could kill fucking Chris for giving her my new number!

When the soft knock comes again, I hope it's not her. I throw the door open and stare, mouth hanging open, at the person on the other side.

"I wasn't going to come, but Phyllis said I at least owed you a meal, so here I am." She shrugs her shoulders. "She also gave me your address, so I don't want you to think I'm stalking you, because I'm not."

I take her in. She's wearing a pair of flip-flops, faded jeans, a tight top, and a pale blue, zip-front hoodie.

I don't say anything. I'm stuck on the fact that she's here to do something nice for me. No one has ever done something like this for me.

"This is stupid. I'm stupid." She thrusts the bag in her hands at me. My hands reach out to grab it, still not saying a word. She turns around to walk down the steps, and I snap out of it.

"Marissa, get your ass in the house so we can eat dinner."

She turns around, letting her head fall to the side. "Is that any way to talk to someone who slaved over a hot stove to make you dinner?"

I peek at the containers in the bag, knowing damn well Phyllis gave them to her. "I don't know." I raise the bag in my hands. "Did you actually cook this?" My lips are fighting to hold back the smile that wants to emerge.

She throws her hands up. "Okay, fine, I didn't actually cook it. But I did box it up, and I sure as hell paid for it, so it's almost like I cooked it." A slow smile starts to creep across her face. "Now, are you going to be a bit nicer and let me share it with you?" she asks as her hands fall to her hips.

I don't reply. I just turn toward the kitchen, leaving the door open behind me. I don't have to wait long before I hear the click of the front door shutting.

"Do you want to eat outside or inside?" I place the food on the counter.

"Outside would be great," she responds. "Here." She grabs the food. "I'll bring this out. You bring out the plates."

I open the cabinet and pull out two plates and then I grab forks, knives, and two glasses. I don't even finish gathering everything before she's back inside to help me carry it all out. "What do you want to drink?" I ask her as she takes the plates from me. "I have beer and water."

"Wow, those are some tough choices. I'll take water, please. Do you want me to bring out anything else?"

"Nope, all good. I'll be out in a second." I turn back to the fridge to grab the drinks. I also take a moment to talk my cock into calming down. It seems that he is very interested in our sudden dinner guest.

I walk outside to the table that sits just to the left of the porch. I flip on the light switch, and the little white Christmas lights I have strung up all around the yard turn on, casting a soft glow over the space.

I look at the table and find that she has already taken off her flip-flops and has thrown herself into a chair that looks out onto the lake.

"It's beautiful out here, Mick."

I nod in agreement and sit in the chair to the right of her. She stands up, opens the bag, and pulls out one of my favorite meals. Chicken fried steak with garlic mashed potatoes. She dishes out my portion onto my plate and then opens the container of gravy, pouring it over the top of them. My stomach lets out a huge growl, letting her know she did well.

She throws her head back as she lets out a huge laugh. "Well then, I guess I made the right choice?" she asks while she serves herself a small ass portion. I think Lilah, Jackson's step daughter, eats more than she does.

"Phyllis didn't tell you that this is my favorite meal?" I ask her while I cut a piece of chicken, dipping it in the potatoes.

"Nope. She suggested the seafood chowder. I thought you were more of a meat and potatoes kind of guy," she tells me while she pushes the food around her plate.

"Are you going to eat any of that or are you going to just push it from one side to the other?" I ask her while cutting up the rest of my chicken.

"I've got a lot on my mind. I haven't heard from Lori again, and my stomach is in knots. I'm so worried and scared, Mick." She shrugs and looks up at me with clearly troubled eyes. "I keep replaying her last call, the sound of her voice, over and over in my head." She drops her fork on the plate and grabs a napkin from the center of the table to dab her eyes.

When she looks back up at me, I see tears swimming in them. The green has turned bright. "I did all this to show her you don't run from your problems. You stay and clean them up."

I finish chewing my food, and before I can stop myself I'm asking her, "What's your story, Marissa?" I don't know why I'm asking. I'm not even sure why I care. I just know that I do.

"Oh, good God, where the hell do I even start? I got pregnant at sixteen. My parents kicked me right out of their good Christian home, crossing me off the family tree forever." She grabs my beer bottle and takes a large pull before continuing, "My boyfriend at the time, Lori's dad, was in a band. They were good, and they were making the rounds and playing the clubs. He was eighteen, and he was going to make it big." She laughs and shakes her head.

"The only thing big he made was an ass out of himself. I walked in on him and another guy in the band having a threesome in our bed. I packed my stuff and left. I had one thousand dollars in my account, I was six months pregnant, and I was homeless. I got myself a one-bedroom apartment in a shithole building with a scumbag landlord who didn't ask questions as long as you could pay your rent, in cash preferably, and you could put down the deposit. The place was disgusting. Filthy, roach and rat infested. You name it, it crawled next to me while I slept. I got a job as a waitress and worked until I couldn't anymore. Lori was a big baby, almost ten pounds. I swore I would never have another child after her. The minute I had Lori, he came back. He said he changed, and he promised me the world. So I gave him another chance. While I was busting my ass waiting tables, and he was getting wasted every night when he went to his 'gigs', little did I know he was betting everything we had all the time. He would bet on horses or fucking dogs, football, basketball, hockey. You name it, he bet on it at that time, and he managed to rack up bills all over the place and then one day he up and vanished, leaving me with an eighty thousand gambling debt that they were going to collect even if it wasn't from him."

"Eat a few bites of your food, please." I don't want to interrupt her, but she hasn't touched her food other than to move it around on the plate.

She takes a bite of the chicken, chewing it slowly. "What's your story, Mick?" she asks while she takes another bite.

I don't usually talk about myself, but if it makes her eat, I'll fucking sing my story.

"My mom was a stripper. My father was a scumbag who had another family, his real family, and my mom was just his action on the side. Phyllis was the only person who actually gave a shit about me. I was on track to pursue a career playing professional football until my throwing arm was injured during what was my last touchdown pass ever. A rotator cuff injury in the last game of high school. All my dreams of playing college and the professional ball went down the tubes. That was that. It never healed quite right, and my career was over before it even began. I spent two years getting wasted every night and feeling sorry for myself. Phyllis had to come bail me out of jail one night. I was picked up after I almost got ran over by a police car while walking home intoxicated. The next day, she packed my shit and sent me to boot camp. Didn't even give me a choice. Just said you go and don't fucking come back until you sort yourself out and do something with yourself we can be proud of." I shrug my shoulders. "I met my best friend and my partner, Jackson, there. I did what Phyllis said. I sorted myself out and became someone she could be proud of." I look up to see her staring very intently at me.

"Is that why you hate me? Because you think I'm like your mother?" she asks, dropping her fork on her plate with a loud clatter. She pushes herself out of the chair, throwing the napkin down onto her plate. Turning, she slides her feet into her flip-flops.

It takes me a second to realize that she is leaving. I push myself out of my chair and round the table to wrap my arms around her waist from behind. The action stops her in her tracks. Her spine stiffens at the intimate hold I have on her, but she doesn't try to get away.

I lean down to whisper in her ear. "You are not one thing like my mother." I feel her lean back into me, and I know she's listening, so I continue, "You are out there working hard and doing right by your daughter. You're so strong, baby, something my mother never was. Don't let anyone tell you otherwise."

She turns in my embrace and wraps her arms around my waist. "That is the nicest thing anyone has ever said to me." She tilts her head up as mine comes down, and I take her lips in a kiss. As soon as our lips touch, my world is knocked off its axis.

I feel the kiss all the way down to my bones, the memory of it searing itself into my mind. My tongue licks along her bottom lip, and she opens her mouth, tangling her tongue with mine. We come together through this kiss, and it feels like it's something we've been doing forever. I pull her closer to me, wanting to devour her. I cup the back of her head to deepen the kiss. I don't want to stop kissing her. I can't stop.

Her hands slide up my neck and into my hair, her fingers twining themselves into the strands. She tightens her grip on my hair, giving it a slight tug. The little bite of pain races through my body and settles in my cock. I pull her closer, pressing my hips into her belly, and she groans.

Knowing that if we don't stop I'm going to fuck her out here on the patio, I slow the kiss to nips and nibble at her lips before I break it. I place my forehead to hers, and we both try to catch our breaths. Chests heaving, her tits are pressed tight to me, and I already know my cock is not going to be happy with me.

"Why don't we bring in the dishes and go make out on my couch?" I ask hopefully as I grab her hand that has now fallen from my hair to her side.

A little dazed, she just nods and takes the plates to bring them inside. I'm just coming through the door when I hear an unfamiliar ringtone. Marissa grabs the phone from her back pocket, her eyes lighting up when she sees that it is an unknown number. "This is Lori."

She presses the green button and rushes out her greeting. "Hello?" Tears immediately fill her eyes and spill over as she continues, "Baby, it's me. Baby, where are you?"

I spring into action. "Ask her to look outside and tell you what she sees, anything she can see." All the while I'm sending a text to Thomas, telling him that Lori is on the phone again. His response is back within a second, telling me they are starting to trace the phone call.

"Baby, I want to come and get you, but you need to tell me where you are, honey." She starts to shake, my hands going around her to hold her up. "Please, baby, stop crying and look outside. You need to tell me what you see, so I can find you."

I grab the phone from her and put it on speaker so I can hear, too, and I almost wish I didn't. What we hear next chills me to the bone.

"I can't move, Mom, I'm chained. The guy fell asleep on the bed, and we got his phone." We hear the clinking of chains in the background. "So tired, Mom. No more drugs, please."

I hear groaning in the background right before she clicks off.

"Lori? Lori, baby? Lori?" Marissa is yelling as the phone's screen goes black, telling us the call has ended.

"NOOOOO!!!" Marissa sobs. Overwhelmed by her despair, she collapses onto her ass in the middle of my kitchen.

I don't have time to grab her up off the floor before I hear the sound of the front door open and close. Confusion is etched on both our faces.

Marissa looks at me, wondering who it could be. I don't even have time to think about it myself because of the sound of shoes clicking on the hardwood floor.

"Baby, I have a surprise for you." Sandie enters the kitchen, her jacket open, completely naked, showing us everything she has to offer.

She doesn't care that someone is in the kitchen next to me. Her hands go to her hips. "What the fuck is this?"

I put my hand over Marissa's eyes, not even sure why. "What the fuck are you doing here, Sandie?" I ask her, surprised she would be here during the night. Usually, she's home with her son.

"I came to surprise you. You always love my surprises." She doesn't even try to cover up her body.

Marissa slaps my hand away from her face. "I'm going to go." She gets up to her feet, wiping the tears from her face, and walks right past Sandie, knocking her arm away from her waist.

I follow Marissa to the door while she is grabbing her shawl. She doesn't even try to put it on, just opening the door. She rushes to her car with me on her heels.

"You shouldn't drive in your condition. Your head isn't there."

She looks at me. The tears from two minutes ago are gone. In their place is a look that could knock me down. The look that will haunt me in my dreams. "You shouldn't be giving me the wrong idea, Mick, when you already have someone warming your bed." She shakes her head, her green eyes shaded.

Opening the door, she climbs in, slamming the car door shut. I try to open it, but she locks it and rolls down the window. "Step away, Mick. Go back inside. Your girlfriend is waiting." She doesn't wait for me to answer. She just rolls the window back up.

She starts the car, and I have no doubt in my mind that she would run me over if I didn't move, so I step up on the sidewalk, watching her pull away, watching the red lights of her car fade away till there is nothing left for me to stare at.

I rub my hands over my face, grabbing my hair, pulling it as I yell, "Fuck!" Right before I completely lose my shit, I get a text from Thomas. The call wasn't long enough to be traced. It is the last straw that breaks me, shatters whatever control I have on my anger.

I return inside to the kitchen where I left Sandie. She isn't there. Just her jacket is lying on the floor in a puddle.

I bend over, picking it up, and start for my room. She is exactly where I thought she would be, spread eagle, her hand buried inside of her.

"What took you so long?" she asks, her eyes closed while she

46

continues to pleasure herself.

"GET THE FUCK OUT!" I roar at the top of my lungs. Her eyes snap open, and her hand stops moving. I throw her jacket at her. "Get the fuck out of here, and for the last time, stay fucking gone."

I don't wait for her to respond. Instead, I walk over to her, grab her arm, and get her off my bed. Grabbing her jacket up in my other hand, I drag her out of my room, down the stairs, straight to the front door. As soon as I'm about to open the front door, she yanks her arms out of my hand.

"You're really going to choose that other bitch over us?"

I throw my head back and laugh at her. "Us?" I ask her, practically sneering. "There is no fucking us. But"—I lean in close to her—"she is a million times the woman you could ever be."

Not one to be told that she isn't the top of the chain, she snatches her jacket out of my hand, mumbling as she puts it on.

Before she takes one step down, she turns to me. "If you let me leave now, I won't ever come back!" She waits for me. Waits for me to change my mind or call her back. But after that kiss with Marissa, I know I won't. I haven't felt like that in a long fucking time, and I want more.

"Just remember your promise," I tell her while I slam the door in her face. Walking back into the kitchen, all that goes through my mind is Marissa.

I get my keys off the counter and head to my car where I find myself driving to Marissa's apartment. I have to make sure she made it home okay. Once I get there, I check for her car and find it sitting alone in its parking spot. Looking up at her apartment, I see that her window is dark.

I take my phone, noticing that I have twenty-seven missed calls. Ignoring them, I pull up her number and text her.

I'm outside. Just want to make sure you're okay.

I wait a couple of minutes and when nothing happens I send another one.

I just want to know if you're okay. I'm not leaving till you answer me.

Nothing, not a peep, not a text. I have radio silence.

I'm coming in if you don't answer.

As soon as I send the text, it vibrates in my hand.

I'm not your concern, Mick. Go home.

With that I know in her mind it's over, it's over even before it fucking started. It's over even before we had a chance to explore it. I punch the steering wheel, turn on the car, and peel away from the curb.

I return home, where I see that Sandie's car isn't anywhere. I stop into the kitchen, not turning on a single light.

Dark, dark like my soul, dark like my life. I take a swig of the whiskey and throw myself on the couch, replaying the night in my mind.

I take another swig, but this time it's bitter. So I get up to empty the bottle in the sink. Still in the darkness, I go to my room where I lie in the middle of my bed, staring out into the darkness of the night. The memories go darker. All I see are her eyes, all I feel is empty, hollow, broken, alone.

I hold my phone in my hands, hoping that she reaches out to me, hoping that she gives me a chance, just plain fucking hoping. My eyes close shut. All I see is Marissa's face watching me, smiling at me, crying out for me. I'm afraid to open my eyes for fear she will go away.

I feel her hands on me. I feel her kissing me. It's a fucking dream I don't want to wake up from. It's a dream that I just want to keep dreaming about. It's like she's here with me.

And I fall deeper into a daze, sliding faster down the spiral slide that is my life.

Ten

Mick

When the sunlight hits my face, I slowly peel my eyelids open. It feels like my mouth is full of cotton balls. I can't even swallow.

When I make it to the kitchen, the dishes from last night taunt me. I pick them up and throw them all in the garbage. I'm going to get new plates, a new table, a new bed, sheets, fuck it all.

Jumping in the shower, I stand under the water till it turns ice cold. And even after that I stay till I can't feel my fingers anymore. I stay till my heart slows to a calmer beat, till all the memories of everything that Sandie put me through are purged from my body. I stay till I feel whole again. I stay till Marissa's smiling face makes me realize there are things worth working for, things worth fighting for. I stay till I know I'm worth it, and I'm going to fucking show her that she is worth it, that we are worth it.

Once I get in my room, I throw the towel down, put on my boxers, and run downstairs to see that I missed a text from Jackson.

What happened with Marissa?

My first thought is that she told him something. I know I pushed the envelope the minute my lips touched hers, but I won't fucking apologize for that. I reply back fast.

Nothing happened with her. Why, did she say something did?

I pick up the phone, checking to see if maybe she texted me also, but there is nothing there.

Where are you?

This is obviously a conversation better had face-to-face.

On my way!

I walk into the station to see Jackson smiling behind his desk. I haven't seen him look calm in the longest time.

"Looks like you got that situation taken care of!" I tell him while I slide into my chair across from him. Our desks are connected in a small corner of the big office.

"So what's the story?" he asks me, not even bothering to take the bait on my greeting.

"No story, nothing." I lean back in my chair, folding my hands over my chest.

"Where is she now?" he asks me, knowing I know exactly who he's talking about.

"Got a job waitressing at the diner across the street. Phyllis owed me a favor. I cashed it in."

"You cashed in a favor for someone you don't even like?"

"It was your fault she got fired, so technically I cashed in a favor so your ass wouldn't feel guilty." I point at him. "You're welcome."

"It's my fault that you punched her boss?" He turns the subject around.

I just shrug my shoulders, not ready to get into it with him.

"Lori called again?"

"She did, almost same MO as before, except this time she said she was chained. Crying, asking for help, begging to come back. Lasted maybe a minute. Then nothing." I sit back up, placing my hands on the desk. "I don't like this shit. I think there is more than meets the eye here. Something else is going on. I just can't pinpoint it," I say, and he doesn't have to say anything for me to know that he agrees with me. This isn't just another case of a teen running away to be with friends, there's more to it. We just can't see what it is yet.

"Where was she when she got the call this time?" he asks me, and I can see him trying to see if maybe there is some other similarity to the last call, hoping to find a dot to connect.

"My house, having dinner."

His eyebrow shoots up. "Your house having dinner? Do I have to say thank you for that one also?"

"Don't make it out to be more than it is. She came by to thank me for getting her the job and putting in a good word with Phyllis." I break eye contact and start pulling papers out of a pile as I pretend to be looking for something.

"Okay, so she came over to thank you. Did you fuck her?"

My head snaps up. I glare at him angrily.

"Watch it! I didn't fuck her. She brought me food, we sat down, and she got the call. She obviously freaked out and wore a hole in my rug trying to get Lori to talk to her. The call ended, she calmed down, and then she left."

"Just like that, she left? I saw her the last time Lori called. She couldn't stop shaking. How long did it take her this time?" He is fishing for something.

"Sandie showed up. Ten minutes after the call." I finally let out the breath I've been holding. Shaking my head, I continue, "Raincoat, naked. Marissa saw and bolted, okay? There, now you got the story. She hasn't talked to me since."

"You know we need to go see her, right? You know we need to follow up?" He doesn't need to tell me this shit, but he does anyway.

"I know," I whisper. "I didn't touch her. We just ate dinner. That's it."

"You don't have to convince me of anything. I don't think you would cross the line."

"There was another girl who went missing two nights ago." I thrust the paper at him. "Name is Jessica, seventeen. Divorced parents. One week with the mother, one week with the father. Started hanging with a new guy on the scene. No one knows him. Just his name. Robbie. Met in secret every time. Not even her best friend knows him or what he looks like. Mother found a bag of weed, punished her for the week. She left to go to her father's, but she never showed up there. He didn't notice until she didn't answer her mother two days later. Mother called the father. He said she texted him saying she was staying at her mom's for a couple extra days. Phone goes straight to voicemail, and it appears the SIM card has been taken out since she had the 'find my phone' app open and now no one can trace her."

"What about school? Any leads there? Did she start hanging with a different crowd?" he asks while he checks all her details. Five foot seven, one hundred seven pounds.

"Nada, best friend said she met this new guy at the mall when she went shopping. Was smitten, started texting like crazy. From that moment on, all her time was spent with him. All Jessica told her was that he was older, drove a car, and 'was hot as fuck,' which, by the way, was a direct quote in case you're wondering."

"Any connection with Lori?" he asks.

"Just the fact they both met a mystery guy no one else has met. I'm going to take off and go check the gang unit. See if they have any leads there. Something might be there. At this point we need anything," I tell him while walking out of the room.

I spend the rest of the day going through the database, running different parameters, searching different names to see if maybe someone else is also working on the case. I call up the gang unit again to see if maybe this is gang related. I come up empty.

After sitting and staring at the computer for more than seven hours, Jackson looks over at me. "Maybe we're looking at this the wrong way."

"What do you mean?"

"Maybe they didn't run away at all. What if they were taken?"

I shrug. "At this point, it could be anything. We have nothing, not even a fucking description of what the guy—or guys—looks like. It's like we're chasing a fucking ghost."

"What about the cameras from the mall? I know it's a long shot, but maybe we can catch a glimpse of him so we have a visual of who we're looking for."

"Good idea. I'll contact the security office in the morning. I know the exact date they met because she sent a text to her best friend going apeshit over him."

"Sounds like a plan. Any leads on Adam?" he asks me, knowing he isn't supposed to.

I look around, making sure no one is in earshot before I speak quietly. "Nothing. He's gone. I doubt he's going to come back."

"I still want to know where he's living."

"I know."

He gets up, not saying anything else before shutting down his computer. "Don't stay here too long, yeah?"

"Yeah, I'm going to take off soon," I say while typing in some notes in the system in case a lead comes in during the night.

Once I finish, I close off my own stuff and head downstairs for my car, my stomach rumbling while I walk outside.

I know I should give her space, that I shouldn't throw myself at her. You know what they say, you get knocked down, you dust that shit off and get back up. She knocked me on my ass yesterday, but I'm coming for her again, this time not ready to dust myself off.

Eleven

Marissa

The bells over the door ring every single time someone walks in. I've been on edge ever since I got in this morning. Lucky for me it's been non-stop people coming in, so my mind hasn't been able to wander to Lori.

Now that it has been quiet and I'm filling the salt and pepper shakers, my mind wanders. It wanders to my baby girl, who is somewhere out there begging to come home. The sound of her voice plays in my head on repeat. My hands start to shake, so I close my eyes and sit down on a chair before my knees buckle.

I blink away the tears threatening to fall over, my heart starting to beat so fast I hear the echoes in my ears. A plate of meatloaf, mashed potatoes, and gravy is shoved in front of me. Phyllis's eyes greet me when I look up.

"Eat that and then go home. You are done for the day. You've been here for fourteen hours."

I look over at the clock hanging behind the counter that reads 8 p.m., realizing she's right.

"I'm just going to finish filling the shakers then I'll take off." I know she's about to argue with me when the bell over the door rings again, making us both look up.

His eyes find me right away. My heart that was starting to calm down is now speeding up. I focus on my meal, cutting a piece of meatloaf and dipping it in the gravy before popping it into my mouth. I try to ignore the heat of his stare, try to think of anything but him and that naked woman from last night. His girlfriend. I was so stupid to think that he would actually want me. I'm a used up stripper whose daughter ran away from home. I'm the opposite of what he wants or needs.

The chair in front of me is filled with his big frame. The scent of his aftershave, of cologne lingers around us. Musky, rich, and woodsy. It's the smell that has seeped its way into my memory along with the way his lips felt on mine. The way that I just fit, like I was made for him. I blink away the memory, looking up at him.

"All the seats in this place are open and you sit in front of me?" I ask him before scooping up more food. I didn't notice how hungry I was till I started eating.

"You didn't text me back." His voice is hard, his muscles tight, his jaw ticking.

I take out my phone. "Oh, I put the do not disturb on under your name. Maybe that's why."

My phone is snapped out of my hand in a blink of an eye. "What the fuck?" I see him touching the screen angrily and turning it off.

"You know you're doing that for nothing since I can turn it on again?" I finish off my whole plate, making my stomach hurt since it's the first thing I've eaten since last night.

"What if I had information on Lori?" Bulls-eye, hit straight through my heart. He must see the color drain from my face as I realize that I fucked up. I'm not going to admit it to him, though.

"I don't have Jackson's number blocked, and he would have called me." I shrug my shoulders, picking up my plate to bring it to the gray bussing bin.

Walking over, I wipe down the table right when Phyllis comes out from the kitchen.

"There you are! I have your order ready. It's being boxed up. Did you want dessert with that?"

His eyes never leave mine. "No, that's okay. Thanks, Phyllis."

I grab my phone from him, putting it in the front pocket of my waitress pouch. "I'm taking off. My feet are killing me. See you tomorrow, Phyllis."

I don't wait for her to say anything to me before I walk out the door to my car. Turning it on, I drive home, determined not to give Mick another minute of my thoughts. Just one problem with that plan, though. No one mentioned to my head that I wasn't thinking about him because his eyes flash in my mind, the hard lines around them. The sorrow that is buried there, the sadness that he thinks no one sees but is there, if you look long enough.

I make my way into my apartment, taking my shoes off my throbbing feet at the door.

Walking into the kitchen, I take out the tips from my pocket and count them out. Three hundred and seventeen dollars. Two hundred of that is going to that damn debt that I'm still paying off. I can't fucking wait till it's over. I walk over to Lori's room like I do every single night, turning on the light to see if maybe something has been misplaced or moved.

I've put scotch tape on the drawers to alert me if they've been opened, but it's still intact. I've labeled her clothes hanging in the closet by number, and I count them, seeing that none have been taken either.

The bed is exactly how she left it. I crawl into her bed and grab her pillow, breathing in her scent. Tears run down my face, seeping into the pillow. This has become my nightly routine. I sleep here so I'm closer to her. I lie in this bed, talking to her. Telling her about my day, praying that she calls me again. I tell her stories about when she was small, about the day they placed her in my arms. The tears never stop. It's like an endless river.

The soft knock at the door has me raising my head. Walking slowly to the door, I look through the peephole and see that Mick is in the hallway. His hands are braced against the doorframe, his head hanging down.

I place my forehead on the door, take a deep breath in, and open the door. His eyes land right on mine. The tears continue to roll down my cheeks, right off my chin on their way to the floor. He brings his thumb up to my chin, catching them.

"Marissa," he whispers, and it's all I can do before I collapse into his arms, sobbing. Begging. Pleading with him to bring her back to me.

He picks me up and carries me inside. Sitting on the couch with me curled into a ball in his lap, my tears soak his shirt. I'm so exhausted from the fear, stress, and worry. I'm just too tired to move.

"I'm a good mom," I whisper to him. "I was tough on her only because I wanted better for her. Wanted her out of this life. Wanted her to be something." My hand lies on his chest, the beat of his heart pounding against my palm.

"I know, baby, I know."

I don't say anything more. I just continue to soak up the feeling of his heart beating as it calms me. My eyes droop, and the exhaustion drags me under.

I don't move from this position all night. I wake the next morning with the same heart beating against my hand.

Twelve

Mick

I know the exact moment she wakes up because her body goes stiff. I feel her eyes blink open, her lashes making my shirt move. Just a touch.

"Morning." My hands circle her waist while I bring her closer to me.

She stills for a moment before she wiggles free from my embrace, mumbling that she has to pee. I let her go and take a moment to will my cock into calming down. If she squirmed against me any more, I might have gone off in my pants.

I pick up my phone to look at the time. Four thirty-nine. I hear a flush from the bathroom, and I get up to make some coffee for us. I open the cupboard, and I notice it's pretty bare. Four cups, four plates. Everything seems to be in fours.

I open a few more cupboards as I look for the coffee, and I find that they're almost empty as well. The bathroom door slowly opens, and I hear her pad into the kitchen. Her eyes take me in as I continue opening the cupboards.

"Lori and I usually do all the shopping together." A tear escapes one eye, which she quickly wipes away before it can land on her cheek. "It was our thing. She even uses coupons, which drives me nuts." Her voice starts to drift off.

"What time do you start work?" I ask her, leaning back on the counter, crossing my hands over my chest.

"I'm going to go in for six a.m. so I can help her set up."

"Okay. Go get dressed, and I'll drive you over. We can eat there before you start."

She shakes her head. "No, I'm not doing this, Mick. I'm not doing this with you, not now. Actually, not ever. You have a girlfriend. A girlfriend who is comfortable enough that she doesn't even think twice about showing up at your place naked." She places her hands on her hips but doesn't stop her rant. "You need to leave now. There is no need for you to contact me unless it has to do with Lori. This"—she indicates with her finger moving between us—"is never going to happen again."

I stare at her for a second, taking her in. She's tiny, so tiny, yet she thinks she's a beast. Her eyes are tired but proud, and her makeup free face is showing the pain that she is carrying from all of this. I take it all in and decide that those eyes will shine again. No more dread will darken them as I vow to work until they're shining with happiness. I'll do anything, fucking anything, for her. She'll never want or need for anything if I can help it. I take in her face and decide that I'll be the one who makes sure that she smiles for the rest of her life.

"We need to get some things cleared up. I don't have a girlfriend. I never did." I look at her, waiting for my words to sink into her head. It obviously doesn't since she huffs out and rolls her eyes. I rein in my desire to pull her into my arms, because this is important. I have to make sure she gets it. "We had a thing, but we don't anymore. I'm not going to go into Sandie now. You don't need that shit in your life. Fuck, I don't need that shit in my life. But if you want, one day, when this is all over, I'll tell you all of it. With that said, this thing"—I point between me and her—"it's fucking happening. I'm not fighting it anymore, and you aren't going to fight it either. We both deserve to be fucking happy." I break down at that point and take her face in my hands. "Let me make you happy. Fuck, let me be happy, too." My thumbs gently stroke her cheeks. "Please," I whisper my plea, hoping like hell she gives in to the inevitability of us.

Her hands move to my wrists while I hold my breath, hoping she doesn't rip my hands from her face. I move in closer to her, watching her eyes gazing up at me. "I've never depended on anyone for my happiness. I've just created my own. I don't know what it is, but something is pulling me to you."

The minute she says those words, I don't hold back. My hands fall from her face, landing on her ass as I pick her up, her legs automatically wrapping around my waist. Her arms curl around my neck, and our eyes meet at my eye level.

"If we do this and I find out that this chick shows up naked again... two things may happen. One, I end up in prison, and I would hate that because I don't care what they say, orange is not the new black. Or two"—she leans in and whispers in my ear—"I will give Lorena Bobbitt a run for her money. We clear?" she asks, a little smile playing across her lips.

"Clear. And just so you know, my dick is trying to crawl back into my body at the mention of knives and him."

She throws her head back and lets out the sound that is music to my ears and a bolt of electricity to my body: her laugh. The minute she stops, I take her mouth and claim her like I've never claimed anyone else.

I slip my tongue into her mouth, and my heart slowly calms down, my body recognizing this woman as mine. The way our tongues tangle has me unleashing the growl that I was holding back. I turn my head, taking the kiss deeper, and she brings one hand up to hold my face while she clings tighter to me. My hands grip her ass, bringing her in closer. I'm almost ready to throw her down on the floor and shove myself into her in one strong thrust, when the alarm on her phone sounds, echoing loudly in the room.

"I need to get ready." She kisses my lips softly, then my cheek, the underside of my chin, and finally my neck. My poor cock is ready to bust through the zipper of my jeans.

"If you don't stop that, no one is going to work today," I tell her while her legs tighten around my waist.

"Then let me go, so I can get dressed and we can eat something before I start my shift."

I don't want to let her go, but I have no choice. She unwraps her legs from my waist and slides down to her feet.

"I'm going to go get dressed. You can go to the bathroom and take care of that." She chuckles as she points to my cock, who is making it known he's up.

She turns around and walks back into her bedroom, closing the door softly. I look at the ceiling, placing my hands on my hips, trying to think of anything to get me out of this predicament. My thoughts go straight to Marissa and the way her ass fit in my hands, the way her tits are the perfect size, the way it's going to feel when I sink inside her for the first time. The thoughts running through my head aren't helping my situation at all, so I walk into the bathroom and turn on the cold water, splashing some on my face. One, two, three times, before my cock starts to deflate.

Grabbing the towel hanging on the bar, I wipe off my face and return to the kitchen. Marissa walks in wearing a flowery skirt and a white tank top. "Bend over," I tell her, my voice tight.

She stands tall, or as tall as she can given her small stature, and folds her arms over her chest. She doesn't say anything to me nor does she do what I asked. She just levels a raised eyebrow glare at me.

"I want you to bend over so I can show you something," I tell her again, not giving up.

She turns around and bends over. Her skirt rides up but doesn't show anything. I don't let this opportunity go, though, as I walk over to her and run my hands under her skirt. She whirls around and pokes me in the chest.

"Don't you start this shit." She pokes me hard for someone so small. "I don't need you to tell me how to dress." She keeps poking me. "I'm old enough to know what to wear." She puts her hands on her hips. "Do you get what I'm saying right now?"

I reach out and pull her to me, burying my face into her neck. The smell of strawberries fills my nose and makes my mouth water. My mouth goes right to her neck as I trail my lips, nipping and sucking, up to her ear. "No one gets to see what's mine." I nip her ear as her body responds with goose bumps. I suck her lobe into my mouth, and my fingers playing along her neck feel her heartbeat pick up beneath them.

"You know I was a stripper, right? People have seen me naked. Many of them come into the diner," she tells me as she grips my shirt while I continue to assault her ear and neck. She tilts her head to give me more access to her neck and continues her tirade. "You do realize my uniform was a thong?" She waits a second before she pushes herself from me.

My hands fall to her hips.

The look in her eyes is guarded, almost fearful, and she drops her hands from my chest. "You need to decide before we go on if this is going to be a problem."

I look at her, watching the different ways that her eyes change with each emotion that she is feeling.

"I get it if you're going to be embarrassed to..." Her voice trails off. "Be seen with me." She looks down at her hands that no longer grip my shirt. "I just need to know."

Placing my forefinger under her chin to raise her face so I can look her in the eye, I take in tears that are beginning to well before she blinks them away. "I will gladly hold your fucking hand in here and out there. I will walk proudly by your side. Head held high." I lean in and kiss her on her lips gently, almost like a whisper. "Now let's go. I'll drive you to work."

"Umm, no, I'll take my car in case I finish before you can come and get me," she tells me while trying to look away.

"I can come get you."

"No," she says while trying to get her purse and keys.

"What's the secret, Marissa?" I eye her, my body going rigid.

"No secret, Mick."

I stare her down till she finally puffs out a huge breath.

"Fine, okay, you win. It's Friday. I go down to the shelter and ask around for Lori, see if anyone has seen her. I know that she might not be there since she called and she's being held, but maybe, maybe someone has seen her."

"How long have you been doing this?" I ask her, furious that she would put herself in danger like that.

"Since she has disappeared," she says softly, her voice almost cracking,

"It's not safe."

"Don't make me choose between this and you. I will choose her every single time. She is the air I breathe, the reason for everything that I have ever done." The tears that she was keeping at bay finally break free, and she swipes the back of her hand across her cheeks.

"I would never ask you to choose between me and your daughter. Not now, not ever. But, and this is a huge but, you go out there tonight or any other night and I'll be really fucking pissed."

She nods her head.

"I need to hear you say the words, Marissa."

"I hear you, Mick," she whispers.

"Good. Now let's go. I'm fucking starving," I say to her while walking to the door, pulling her hand so she follows me.

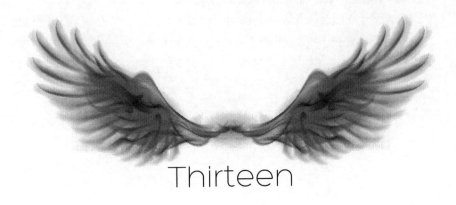

Thirteen

Marissa

As we walk into the diner hand in hand, Phyllis smacks hers down hard on the counter. "I knew it! Roy, you owe me fifty," she yells while walking into the back to speak to the cook.

Mick shakes his head and laughs as he walks around the counter to grab himself a coffee.

"Well then, I guess that cat is out of the bag," I tell him as I round the counter and reach under it for my apron.

Leaning against the counter, he drains his coffee. "Never planned on keeping it a secret."

Phyllis comes back out with three plates and places them on the empty table.

Sitting herself down in front of one of the plates, she forks up some eggs. "Are you two going to watch me eat or join me?" She throws a glance at the clock, which reads 5:45. "We open in fifteen minutes. Let's get some fuel in us."

I join her at the table and take the plate opposite her. The remaining plate is obviously for Mick, with three eggs, pancakes, sausage, bacon, Canadian ham, and toast on the side. "Are you going to finish all that?" I ask him as I dunk my toast into the egg yolk before biting some off and chewing it.

"This is only number one. Once I'm finished at the gym, I'll grab another," he says while shoveling down half the plate in the time it takes me to finish one piece of toast.

"You're going to get fat," I say with a smirk at Phyllis as I glance at him.

He lifts his T-shirt, displaying his tight eight-pack. My mouth goes dry, and my fingers itch to touch him. "I think I'm good," he says before dropping his shirt.

"Meh, I've seen better." I take a sip of my coffee. "Right, Phyllis?" I bring her in on this when I see the smile in her eyes.

She nods her head. "Seen better and had better," she agrees with a wink.

Mick smirks at her as he curls his arm around my chair and strokes my shoulder with his thumb.

"So what is this thing between you two? Am I going to have to replace my best waitress or my best boy?"

We both look at each other. "This has nothing to do with my job. What happens between Mick and me will never, ever come to work with me."

Phyllis grabs her plate, smiling at us before she trains that too wise gaze of hers at Mick. "Don't make me poison you," she says in warning before she walks away. "Roy, I'm unlocking the door in five!" she yells through the food service window while putting her dirty plate in the bin.

I get up, taking my plate and Mick's with me. "Let the party begin," I tell him before heading behind the counter.

As I place the plates in the bin, I feel him come up behind me. He rests his hands on my hips like he's done it a million times before and says, "I'll be back tonight. What time do you finish?"

Turning in his embrace, I place my hands on his and peel them from my hips. "I have no idea. Why don't I send you a text when I'm almost done?" I lean up on my tippy toes to kiss him lightly on the lips.

The bells over the door chime, alerting me to my first customer. "Now you need to leave so I can make some money." I turn to start another pot of coffee.

I don't see him leave since I was busy serving the two tables that came in. By the time the morning rush finishes, it's ten and I'm gearing up for the lunch rush. I grab my phone out of my pocket.

Seeing that I haven't missed any calls or texts, I then open Facebook and check my notifications. Scrolling through, I notice it's all garbage. Doing what I always do, I click over to Lori's page to see her pictures, to see if something has been added or if anything has changed.

Last thing on her wall was a message from me asking her to call me and then another asking if anyone has seen her. I start scrolling through her photos, noticing how she changed from a happy, smiling kid to a sullen one with troubling friends. I can't help but wonder where the fuck I went wrong.

Grabbing a glass of water to calm the tears clogging my throat, I click on Facebook Messenger and send her another message.

I miss you so much, and I want you to come home. I'll come and get you, just tell me where you are.

I press send and see that all my other messages to her haven't been read. I still can't help but hope that she'll see them. Hope that she sees them and calls me, that I get her back.

"Oh, isn't this just fucking cozy?" I hear said from behind me. I turn around on the stool, and I'm face-to-face with the naked woman who showed up in Mick's kitchen. This time she is actually wearing clothes. Nice, fucking fancy clothes. Tight jean capris that probably cost more than my entire wardrobe. A beautiful peach-colored shirt hangs off one shoulder, with thick bracelets on one wrist while the other is adorned with a Rolex and a diamond tennis bracelet. Her big wedding band nearly blinds me.

"Excuse me?" I ask her, noticing that Phyllis practically came running out from the back with Roy on her heels.

"You heard me. So you think because you work for this woman you can worm your way into Mick's life?" She sneers then laughs. "Honey, do you know how many poor waitresses have been in and out of his life?" She crosses her arms under her breasts, the movement pushing them up high on her chest.

"I have no idea who you are, and I have no interest in knowing you. Now, if you'll excuse me, my break is over." I try to walk past her when she reaches out and yanks my arm sharply, causing my head to jerk back.

"You listen here, you white trash bitch," she says as I rip my arm out of her hold. "He's mine. Has always been mine, always going to be mine. So you should know you are fucking with the wrong person. I'll make your sad, sorry life even worse."

Having heard enough of the shit she is spewing, I pick up my warm coffee and throw it right in her face. I hear gasps from all around the diner. I didn't realize that we had an audience. An audience that also now consists of Jackson, who just walked in.

"What the fuck?" she screams as she grabs napkins to clean her face off. She turns to look at Jackson. "Did you see what she just did? I want to press charges." She demands while wiping her chin before any more coffee can drip onto her shirt.

I shrug my shoulders at Jackson. "I was testing a theory," I tell him.

"A theory? What theory? That you're crazy and assaulting me?" she shrieks.

"The theory was to see if you would melt with hot water." I move closer to her. "I can see that my theory was wrong. My bad."

She lunges toward me, but Jackson stops her in her tracks, looping his arm around her waist.

"You bitch!" she screeches while trying to squirm her way out of his hold.

Looking around, I see many of the regulars trying not to make eye contact with me. I've always been the outcast, but not this time. "I may be a bitch, but you're straight up crazy. What did you think would happen when you came in here? Did you expect me to slink away? Did you think I'd be scared of the likes of you?" I laugh humorlessly to let her know that she hasn't gotten to me. "I may be white trash, but you, well, you're just plain fucking trash. Yesterday's garbage. You want to press charges? Do it. But who do you think is going to pay my bail?" I ask her so she sees where I'm going with all this. "Oh, yeah, I see you're getting it now. That's right, honey, Mick will bail me out. My knight in shining armor. The same guy who tossed your naked ass out to the curb when you showed up begging for his attention."

"He didn't toss me anywhere. I can call him right now. Who do you think he'll choose?" She breaks free of Jackson's hold as she smoothes her hands down to straighten her now rumpled outfit.

"I could kill fucking Chris for giving her my new number!" Our heads both whip toward the door to see Mick standing there. His breaths come in harsh pants, almost as if he ran here. Looking past him through the window to the parking lot, I see that he didn't even close his car door.

He walks straight to me, his eyes raking me over to make sure I'm okay. They stop briefly on my hands as he notices they're shaking. His nostrils flare, and his angry eyes burn furiously as he turns to her. "What the fuck is wrong with you? Have you lost your mind?" He seethes.

"Bab—" she starts before Mick raises his hand to silence her from saying anything further.

"Jackson, I want this on record that she came in here to harass Marissa. I want to get witness statements," he says, and Jackson nods in affirmation. He looks back at her, totally disregarding the crocodile tears running down her face. "This is the last time you breathe the same air she breathes. You see her, you walk the other way. You don't come into her life, or mine." His tone is serious and leaves no room for discussion. She doesn't miss how he takes my hand in his and intertwines our fingers as he brings my hand to his lips. The shaking stops as I soak in his strength in this moment.

"This isn't over, Mick," she spits out like a spoiled child. She whirls around to grab her bag and then stomps out of the diner.

My eyes scan the room quickly before I look down at the floor. It takes Phyllis two beats before she claps her hands and calls out to everyone in the diner. "Drinks on me! Who wants more coffee?"

"Are you okay?" Mick asks me, worry obvious in his voice.

"I'm okay. I'm just going to need a few seconds." I leave for the bathroom. Before I can close the door, a hand covers mine, preventing me from shutting it. Mick's gray eyes greet me.

"Mind if I join you?" Not waiting for my reply, he closes the door and locks it.

"Can I say no?" I ask him as he leans against the door.

"You can, but I won't take no for an answer. I'm so sorry, honey." He reaches out to tuck some loose hair behind my ear. "So fucking sorry that I brought that into your life, into your job." His hand gently cups my face, and I turn it slightly to kiss his large, calloused palm. "I swear I will do everything in my power so that she never does that to you again."

"It's not your fault, Mick. I mean, other than dating a fucking psycho but, hey, we all make mistakes, right?" I attempt a joke to lighten the moment.

He laughs at me. "Yeah, she is one mistake I wish I could go back in time and undo." He wraps his arms around me and pulls me in close. "Did you really throw hot coffee in her face?"

"It wasn't hot, just warm," I tell him sullenly as I face-plant into his chest, his calming scent filling my nose and working its magic. "How did you know?"

"Jackson had me on speakerphone the whole time."

"Great. Three days on the job, and already people think I'm trash. I should just quit before they take it out on Phyllis."

"You will do no such thing. You'll go out there with your head held high because you did nothing wrong."

I draw in a deep breath and slowly exhale. "I guess I have no choice now, do I?" I shove him away from the door and make my way out, seeing Phyllis and Roy quietly talking. "Phyllis, I'm really, really sorry about that. I promise I will pay for any damages."

"No need to pay me for anything, honey. In fact, you just got yourself a raise. Been wanting to hit that woman for a long ass time. I think that was even better." She smoothes down her apron. "Now go on out there. You have customers waiting to be served. And you"—she points to Mick—"better take damn good care of what you have here." She looks pointedly between the two of us.

He doesn't reply verbally, just nods his head, and follows me out.

The rest of the afternoon and early evening pass uneventfully, thank God. I get through the rest of the day on the knowledge that I get to search for Lori tonight.

Fourteen

Mick

I stand back and watch Marissa do her thing. As soon as we got back to her place, she went straight into Lori's room. She walked around, inspecting things, checking to see if anything was out of place. I can see how much she hopes for this search to be different, for things to be out of place. Her shoulders droop in disappointment when she realizes that everything is exactly as it was the last time she checked. Watching that hope in her eyes quickly fade back to sorrow guts me.

Looking up at me with tears brimming in her eyes, she quietly says, "She hasn't come back yet."

"I'm going to get her back to you." It's not like we haven't been trying, it's just been one dead end after another. One minute we think we have something, only for it to turn out to be nothing. She nods her head.

"I'm going to change and then we can go," she says as she walks past me, leaving me in the room by myself.

I walk around, taking in all the little 'booby traps' that she set up. The scotch tape on the drawers, the picture frames with strings attached to them, all in the hopes that she'll come home and realize that Lori had been there. I can't even imagine what that constant level of worry and devastation would do to me. I never really thought that I would be the kind of man who cared so much about children, but Lilah changed that for me. She really is the perfect kid.

Walking the room once more, I notice that her clothes haven't been washed. She doesn't want to touch anything. I'm about to sit on the bed and see if maybe there is something here that we've missed when she walks into the room.

"I'm ready," she tells me, and I take in her outfit. Gone is the skirt she wore to work, and in its place are tight blue jeans that mold to her body with a bulky sweater that gathers at her waist. The look is finished with a pair of black Chucks. Her hair is tied high on her head in a ponytail, and her makeup free face makes her look like she's a teenager herself.

"Can I say something before we leave?" I ask her, waiting for her nod. "We get out there, the minute I feel something isn't safe, I'm stepping in. I don't want you to get all huffy and puffy. I need you to trust me, trust my instincts and my experience. I want to find something that leads us to Lori just as much as you do, but I'll do it without compromising your safety." The minute I say that, her head cocks to the side, and she crosses her arms over her chest. I don't give her a chance to give me attitude before I continue. "You get me?"

"I can take care of myself."

"I have no doubt that you can, Marissa, but now you have me to help with that. So just give me this, yeah?" The question hangs in the air for a couple of minutes before she finally gives in.

"Fine, I'll give you this," she says. "But you can't scare these people off. If you go into cop mode with them, they won't talk."

I walk to her, grabbing her face in my hands. "We are going to get her back. I promise you."

She nods her head as I lean down and kiss her lips. I was going for a soft kiss, but the minute she leans into me, my body takes over. One arm wraps around her waist as my mouth opens to tangle her tongue with mine. Our tongues dance together, both of us trying to get the upper hand over the other.

She pulls back from me and breathlessly says, "We should go." She licks her lips before walking to her purse and pulling out two pictures along with her keys.

"Ready." I follow her out the door, watching as she locks it.

We walk out of her building, and I guide her to my car with a hand on her lower back as I take in our surroundings, making sure that no one is watching us. I hate that she lives here, but I know that she isn't going anywhere till Lori comes back. I don't even have to ask her to know that if Lori never came back, she would stay there her whole life waiting, just in case. But I make a mental note to discuss it with her when I bring Lori back.

"Where to first?" I ask her while starting the car and merging into traffic.

"I usually start at the soup kitchen down on 5th Street. If there aren't that many people there, I go to the homeless shelter down the street before doubling back to the soup kitchen. After that, I go to the alley behind the bodega on 7th Avenue—"

The second she says it, I lose my shit.

"Are you fucking telling me that you've been down to pier warehouse next to the alley near the bodega? By yourself? AT NIGHT?" The thought of her down there at night by herself sends chills down my spine. Homeless men, women, and junkies gather there, many of them getting drunk or high. It's fucking dangerous down there, even for me, and I'm a fucking cop with a weapon and experience. I get that she's worried and feels like she has to do something, anything, to help bring her daughter home, but I am furious that she is so reckless with her safety. I need to take a few calming breaths so I don't lash out at her.

"What if one of them saw her? What if she was there? I have to do what I have to do. If you have an issue with this, maybe you should just drop me off so I can get what I need to do done." She continues, "You think this is the first time I've done this? I've been on these streets every day since she left. I don't have enough energy left in me to argue with you right now. So are you driving me or not?"

I don't answer her. I'm still deep breathing. Instead, I start making a list in my head. Change the lock on her front door, follow up on Lori's Facebook page, and investigate all of her friends, turn her ass pink before fucking her raw. My mind lingers on that last item on my to-do list. Thoughts of her lying across my lap, her ass in the air, pink from my hand, and her drenched pussy ready and waiting for me has my cock springing to life and throbbing in my pants.

"Okay, Mick, just spit it out. What's on your mind right now?" she asks as she turns her body in her seat toward me.

"Honestly?" I ask her, not sure she really wants to know. She glares at me, her eyes practically shooting daggers at me. "I was thinking a couple of things. First, I need to change the lock on your door. It can be picked open easily with a spoon, that's how weak it is. Then I was thinking about digging deeper into Lori's Facebook friends. Finally, I was thinking about how pink I'm going to turn your ass if you ever go back down there without me again." I pin her with my own glare before I turn my eyes back to the road.

"Turn my ass pink?"

"Turn your ass pink. With you laid across my lap, I'll use my hand to turn that perfect little ass a pretty shade of pink." I stop at a red light and assess her. A second more and I would have missed the pink of her cheeks, the hitch of her breath, the way she pressed her legs together tight. "Right before I fuck you," I say, and even I can hear the huskiness in my voice.

"I haven't had sex since Lori's dad left," she says without meeting my eyes. My mouth hangs open as she continues, "Which was a long, long time ago."

I don't say anything because I hear a honk behind me. Looking up, I see that the light has changed to green.

"Just so you know, if you thought that I slept around, I don't." The last part is whispered softly as she turns in her seat again to stare out the window.

I pull over into an empty parking lot, reach over to unbuckle her seat belt, and pull her into my lap. "Look at me, Marissa, and hear what I'm saying. I was a dick when I first met you."

She places her hands on my chest, her thumbs stroking it gently.

"I can't take that back, but what I can promise is that I will always treat you with respect. I will treat you like a queen, my queen, because that is what you deserve. You deserve that and so much more." I kiss her on the tip of her nose. "Let me in, Marissa," I ask her quietly, holding my breath as my heart pounds so loudly, I'm certain she can hear it. "Let me in, baby, so I can do all of that for you and more."

"Lori is my life. The reason I never dated was because I didn't want her to see a revolving door of men. I wanted her to know that love is special and something worth waiting for. Something that should be cherished if you've been lucky enough to find it. But mostly I wanted her to know that she came first, always. She's my baby even though she's almost an adult. So I can only tell you that I will try, but I can't make you promises till she comes home. Till I hold her in my arms again. I can't let you into my heart because it's shattered. It's in pieces and the longer I'm without her, the harder it will be to put the pieces back together. Because you, Mick, you deserve my whole heart, and I can't give that to you yet."

"Let me be there for you, Marissa. Let me hold your hand, let me hold you, let me guard the pieces of your heart till she comes back. I'll take them, one piece at a time, until I have the whole thing."

She doesn't say anything else to me, just rests her cheek on my chest and nods. She pulls back and kisses me on the nose. "Can we please go and see what we can find out about my girl?" She climbs back into her seat and buckles her seat belt. "Chop chop! Let's go, Moro!"

I let out a laugh, feeling lighter than I have in a long fucking time. I buckle my seat belt and put my car into drive, heading straight to the first stop on her list, hoping and praying that tonight is the night we get a lead.

Fifteen

Marissa

I'm immediately disappointed when we enter the food bank. I already know we won't get anything here since there are only four people in tonight. Walking to the counter, I see the same two volunteers I see every single Friday. Pulling Lori's picture from my pocket, I ask them if they've seen her lately. I get the same sad smile I've gotten from them every time along with the shake of their heads in apology. I take the picture back, looking down at it. Her smile is so bright, and I remember back to when it was taken. The two of us went to the local fair and stuffed ourselves sick with funnel cake, fried Oreos, and corn dogs in between rides on the Ferris wheel.

I see Mick talking to the only other people in there, both of them shaking their heads no. He pulls out his card, giving one to each of them. Walking up behind him, I hear him saying, "Tell your friends there is a five-thousand-dollar reward."

I grab his hand and pull him outside. "Why the hell would you tell them that? I don't have that kind of money!" I storm off in the direction of the homeless shelter two blocks down.

"Hey, wait a second before you go off half-cocked. You want your daughter back. I want to bring her back. The only way these people will keep their eyes open is if there is something in it for them. Not because you're cute, or you wiggle your ass, or that it's a sad fucking story,

but because that money can help get them out of the hole they're in."
I listen to him knowing that he's making sense, until he continues by
saying, "I'm giving this reward, not you."

"No. This isn't your problem."

"That is where you're wrong, Marissa. It's your problem, and you're
my woman, which makes it my problem. I have the cash. Let me do it."

"Fine, but I'll pay you back. I don't know when, but I will," I tell
him, making a mental note to add another debt to my growing list of
them. Grabbing his hand, we make our way to the homeless shelter,
stopping people we pass on the street and showing them Lori's picture.

When we approach the shelter door, the man standing out front tells
us that it's full for the night. I'm just about to turn around when Mick
pulls out his badge and says, "I'd like to go in there and ask around to
see if someone has seen her daughter."

The man just nods his head and tells us to check in at the front desk.
Once we're signed in, I follow the woman as she leads us into the room
with all the bunk beds. Looking at the layout and seeing that it hasn't
changed, I work my way from one bed to the next, not coming up with
any leads. Nothing. No one has seen her. After we asked everyone
there, and some people twice, we walk out into the cool night.

"Why can't we just catch a break?" I ask the universe.

"It'll come when we least expect it." He shrugs as he looks at his feet
and puts his hands in his pockets. He looks back up at me and says, "I've
been told God works in mysterious ways. Bella, Jackson's woman, tells
me that all the time. She's one of the nicest, kindest, strongest women I
know. You'll meet her Sunday."

"What do you mean, I'll meet her Sunday?" I ask him.

"Jackson and Bella invited us over. I said yes." He takes my hand,
leading us back to the car. "Where to now?" he asks, but he knows the
answer.

"The pier," I respond, looking straight ahead. I know that this time
of night it will be hard to see faces, so I check my phone, hoping I have
enough battery left to shine the flashlight app on Lori's face.

We don't talk as we head to the warehouse by the pier. I'm dreading
doing this with him. I know he knows danger, but he hasn't seen me put
myself in danger. He hasn't seen me leave there with my knees bloody
from being pushed down. He hasn't seen me walk away with scratches

and bruising from being attacked by a drunk old man thinking I was stealing his dried up fruit.

He turns off the car and looks at me. "Remember what I said," he warns before he gets out of the car.

We park on the side of the building where there are a couple of beat-up cars. You can't really see much since almost no light from the street is illuminating the area. Mick leads the way with me following him and holding his hand.

When we get to the open door at the side of the warehouse that people go in and out of, he opens it slowly, the creaking noise loud in the quiet night.

Once we make it inside the warehouse, I have to blink my eyes a couple of times to get them used to the darkness around us. The smell of urine and smoke makes my eyes burn a little. Looking over at Mick, I see him stand taller. It's almost like he's in a defense mode. I squeeze his hand a touch to make him look at me. The minute our eyes meet, my blood runs cold. Gone are the warm eyes that look at me, and in place are the hard eyes of someone who would shoot and ask questions after.

"We are going to seriously have a discussion after we leave here." His voice is tight, the veins in his other arm bulging with the force of the fist his hand has curled into. I don't answer him right now, afraid that he'll turn around and leave.

We walk farther in as I take in our surroundings. You'd think I would be prepared for this by now, but I'm not. The room is vast and open, with windows high up on the walls all around the room, some broken, some still intact. The walls are cinder blocks, the floor is cement littered with cans, papers, old pizza boxes, and other trash, but what is most shocking is the number of used needles lying around. Mick looks down as he makes his way over to the couple in the corner. They're lying on a thin, badly stained mattress with holes in it. The couple is laid out haphazardly, like they just collapsed on the mattress. The girl's ass is on full display, and the guy's pants are unbuttoned and barely covering him. If we had come in a few seconds earlier, no doubt we would have walked in on them going at it. The girl's blond hair is matted and dirty, her fingernails bitten down almost to the quick. Her face is streaked with dried blood from scabs that she must have been picking at. Mick kicks the mattress softly so they stir. Both of them groan.

"Have you guys seen Lori?" Mick's voice breaks up the silence of the room.

The girl blinks, and her dazed eyes open. "Baby, you want a blow job?" She looks straight at Mick, but her eyes lose focus, and her head lolls against the mattress as she lets out a groan and passes out again.

Not waiting any longer, he pulls me from that corner, and we walk to the next group of people, who are gathered around a metal garbage can lit with fire. Five men are standing around drinking from a brown bottle that is being passed between them.

"Hey, we were wondering if you have seen this girl?" I say, holding up my phone to the picture.

All five men don't even bother looking and just shake their heads. Mick pulls me away to the next group.

A woman with a cart full of what looks to be knick-knacks is lying on a blue tarp. Her clothes are tattered, and her shoes are held together with tape and look to be about four sizes too big. Socks are on her hands to keep her warm.

Mick squats down next to her. "Ma'am," he says, and my heart melts. The fact that he treats everyone with respect and dignity despite their circumstances is something I hadn't noticed about him before. The woman stirs and sits up. Her eyes open and tell the tale of a woman who has seen better days. Her dull green eyes appear almost gray.

"Have you seen this girl?" he asks her, grabbing the picture from me and showing it to her.

She looks at it for a good minute, making me hope that she has seen her, but she shakes her head no. Mick gets up and digs into his pocket, coming out with a ten-dollar bill. "Thank you for your help," he says as we head to the far corner of the room. The corner where my nightmares come from.

A couch is thrown up against the wall. Its cushions are missing, and burn holes are evident all over the couch. A squeaking sound is coming from it; probably some rats that have claimed it as their shelter. A man is sitting in the corner of the couch. A woman on her knees between his legs is sucking his dick. His head is resting against the back of the couch. The woman is wearing a filthy, faded, formerly white summer dress. Her breasts hang out of the top. The back hem of the dress barely covers her ass, and her flip-flops are a few steps from being worn out.

Mick clears his throat, hoping to get their attention. I turn my head to the side, taking in the chair beside the couch where another man is watching the show on the couch while he masturbates. At the sound of Mick's throat clearing, his eyes swing my way, and he smiles a greasy, rotten-toothed smile at me. I move closer to Mick. He clears his throat again, and the man finally opens his eyes.

"I paid for thirty minutes. It's not over yet," he says then tilts his head sideways to check me out. "How much for that bitch behind you?" he asks as his hand pushes the girl's head further down on his cock. The sound of her gags echo around us.

"You seen this girl?" he asks him, not approaching, just holding up Lori's picture for him to see.

"Shit, I fucking wish. I'd pay full price for that pussy."

The girl pulls her mouth off of his flaccid penis, spit still clinging to her chin. Her brown hair, stringy and oily, sticks to her head. Her eyes are sunken in, and old black makeup runs down her face. Her eyes are vacant, like she's not really there, and the track marks on her arms tell me that she probably isn't. She's maybe eighteen, if not younger. My heart breaks for this girl's family, who is probably looking for her and feeling the same worry that I feel for Lori.

While we wait for their answer, another man steps out from the corner. He's huge, well over six and a half feet, if not bigger. His short, blond hair is buzzed into spikes. His clothes are in pristine condition considering where we are. His blue eyes are cold and menacing. "You are disrupting my girl's work. Either pay for her time or move along." His tone is hard, almost as hard as Mick's.

"You her boss?" Mick asks.

"You a cop?" He shoots back.

"Just looking for my girl. Have you seen her?" Mick holds up the picture, but the guy doesn't even acknowledge it.

"You either pay for this bitch or move on," he says while lifting up his white shirt so we can see the gun that he has stashed there.

"Let's go," I whisper to Mick, who is staring at him.

Mick nods his head, grabs my hand, and heads to the door.

"But we haven't asked anyone else," I tell him as we walk out the door into the cool, night air.

He doesn't say anything as he shakes his head and heads to the car.

He opens my door for me and rounds the hood to get inside himself. "Marissa, five minutes. I need five minutes to calm down before I lose my shit."

If I thought his eyes were hard before, I was wrong. His eyes are harder and angrier than I've ever seen them, fury and rage churning in them.

I just nod my head and give him his five minutes in the hope that when they are up, my man, whose eyes are always soft and kind on me, is back.

Sixteen

Mick

I knew going into that warehouse would be hard for me. But for different reasons. She doesn't know that I've been in there more times than I can count, not just for work, but to get my own mother out of there.

The thought of her in there by herself the last couple of times is enough to make me want to blow the damn place up. The minute I saw that pimp come out of the shadows, I wanted to take him down. After all these years, he hasn't changed a bit. I was expecting his hair to at least turn white, that his face would show the signs of his hard life and his age. I really hoped that death would have claimed him in a painful way. He didn't recognize me, the man I've become. I wonder if he even remembers the boy who would beg for his mother. The boy who would sit next to her and wait for her to be sober enough to walk us home. I can't stop the awful memories of my childhood from running through my mind on a constant loop.

I make it to Marissa's apartment, the silence still looming between us after I demanded a few minutes to calm my thoughts. I turn the car off and look over at her, the defeat obvious in her eyes and her slumped shoulders. "We are going to find her. I fucking promise you. I won't stop till we do."

A big tear rolls down her cheek, and her bottom lip quivers as she softly whispers, "I pray every single night, Mick, but I don't think he hears me. Maybe my mom was right, maybe I am destined for Hell, because it sure feels like that's where I am now." She curls into herself and succumbs to her sobs.

I round the car, open her door, and reach in to lift her into my arms to carry her inside. I take the keys from her and open the door, flipping the lights on. I set her down, and she immediately heads into Lori's room to do her nightly check. Just like all the nights before, she comes up empty-handed.

"Nothing," she says as her stomach simultaneously gurgles loudly.

"Did you eat?" I ask her even though I know her answer is no. "You don't have any food. Can we go shopping tomorrow? Just to pick up some essentials?" I ask, and she just shakes her head no. I don't push it. "Fine. Let's order pizza."

"I'm exhausted, Mick. I just want to shower and go to bed," she says.

"So go. You working tomorrow?" I ask.

"Only the dinner shift. I'm off on Sunday," she tells me as she is startled by loud banging on her door.

I swing into action, placing her behind me as the banging starts up again.

"Open up, bitch, I know you're in there," a male voice on the other side of the door yells.

She walks around me, swinging the door open. "Jesus Christ, you scared the shit out of me!" she tells this man, who is leaning against the doorjamb, a toothpick dangling between his lips.

He's about five foot ten. He looks like a pimp in his fake leather jacket, black dress pants, dress shirt unbuttoned to his sternum, and his shiny dress shoes. Jesus, the guy's even wearing a freaking fedora, talk about stereotypes. His pock-marked face looks like the surface of the moon, if it were wrinkled and saggy, and the dark circles under his sunken, beady eyes only accentuate the fact that he is not a good-looking guy.

"First of the month came and went. Where is the money?" he asks her.

She goes into her room, bringing out a white envelope that is filled with cash.

"That is this month's and next, Ralph." She hands it to him, and he opens the envelope to count it.

"Word is that you got fired from Manny's Jug House. You going to turn tricks now?" he says, still counting what is in the envelope.

"Who the fuck are you?" I growl out.

"Who the fuck am I? Who the fuck are you, man?" He finally notices me and stands up tall.

"It's all there, Ralph," Marissa tells him while closing the door on him, turning around and leaning on it. "Jesus, when will this night end?" She rubs her face.

"Two seconds, Marissa. Start talking before I go after him."

"That's Ralph, the bookie/landlord/boss/asshole," she says as she walks into the kitchen and grabs a glass to get herself some water from the sink.

"Bookie?"

"Yes, my ex's bookie, who holds the debt that asshole left me with. He comes in person to collect from me. He promised to never touch Lori if I continued paying him." She brings the glass to her lips, her hands shaking.

"How long?" I ask her, hoping she answers me, but knowing I'll be paying Ralph a visit myself tomorrow to find out.

"I lost count." She finishes her glass of water and puts it in the sink.

I nod my head, knowing now isn't the time to get into this with her. She's had enough today. "Go shower, M."

"You're not leaving?" she asks me softly.

"Nope, and I gotta warn you, we'll be sleeping in your bed together tonight. Okay?"

"Ummm."

I see the questions in her eyes.

"Just sleeping, M," I tell her. "Go shower, and I'll run down and get my bag out of the car."

"Cocky much?"

"Not cocky. I just knew it was going to be a hard night—for both of us." I grab the keys from the counter and head out, locking the door behind me.

I make it outside, and I see Ralph leaning against the side of the building. His two goons are behind him.

"She's not worth it, you know?" he says while throwing the toothpick on the ground. "Sweet pussy, or so I've been told, but not sweet enough for any man to want to get in deep with her."

I watch him without saying anything, my thumbs in my pockets.

"Bitch has more problems than she has years left on this earth. I made it so she'll never be free of me. Never. Unless she wants to spread those fucking legs." He laughs. "Then I'll take off a good chunk of what she owes me. Fuck, I look forward to that day."

"Funny you should be here, Ralph," I say, leaning in, whispering in his ear, "or should I just call you Frankie?" I pull back to see his face that was grinning before is doing nothing but staring at me in shock. I look at his goons, who are trying to figure out what just happened.

"Go wait in the car," he yells at them. When they are out of earshot he turns. "You know shit." His tough guy act is only that, an act.

"Okay, let's say I know nothing. Let's say that I don't know that you really are Frankie from Hoboken. Let's say you didn't run down here twenty years ago and changed your name. Let's say that you didn't snitch on the Grilli family and they put a hit on your head. A hit that is still live in case you were wondering. Let's also say that you don't own half of the Manny Jug House, a club that makes some of their girls run tricks. A club that also deals in drugs. A front to the big poker club that you guys hold in the basement. Let's also say"—I put my hand on my chin—"that all this information falls in the wrong hands, say someone that knows Chris Jr. You know Chris, right? You guys went to school together. He took you under his wing, brought you home. Made you part of the family. The same family that you snitched on. Now what do you think that is worth?" I wait for him to answer the questions.

When I see his hand shake, I answer for him. "I'll answer for you. About fifty grand. Debt clear. And just to make sure you understand. I have numbers programmed in my phone ready to be dialed. Choice is yours. What do you say?"

"You have my word," he says and turns around, walking away.

I rub my face with my hands. I start to walk back inside, my bag be fucking damned. "Oh and, Ralph, you touch one hair on her head or Lori, one, I'll fucking gut you. You'll wish for death to take you before I'm finished with you." I lean in. "Trust me on this. One fucking hair." I see him finally try to swallow, his mouth probably dry.

I head back up the stairs and into the apartment. I hear the shower still running as I walk over to the couch and drop down on it. I sink further into it, resting my head against the back as I scrub my hands down my face. I feel a headache coming on. I close my eyes as I think back over this clusterfuck of a day.

I don't even hear the shower turn off or Marissa walking into the room and calling my name.

"Mick," she says softly, touching my hand.

My eyes peel open, taking her in. Her hair, still wet from the shower, is tied to the side in a braid. She's wearing little pink shorts and a black tank top with no bra. Her tits droop ever so slightly, telling me they're real. "Do you want to shower before bed?"

I pull her into my lap, guiding her hips to straddle me. The scent of strawberries swirls around us, filling my nose and making my mouth water. Looking into her eyes, I see that she is unsure how she should act, and I can practically see the questions running through her mind.

"My mother used to turn tricks in that warehouse," I tell her, not looking in her eyes, instead focusing on the end of her braid and how the hair curls. Her gasp is soft, almost a whisper, and I'm sure if I looked up, I'd see her wide eyes searching my face intently.

"He was her 'friend,' that man we spoke to at the end," I say with a humorless laugh. "I can't tell you how many times I went in there to find her."

She runs her hands up and down my arms soothingly to encourage me to continue.

"Mick, baby," she says as she gently strokes my cheek, "go shower so we can go to bed, okay?" Her unsure eyes have now been replaced with a soft look of understanding, kindness, and sadness.

I cup her face in my hands and bring her lips to mine, groaning when I feel her breath hitch as my lips claim hers. My tongue slides into her mouth, and she tilts her head to the side so I can deepen the kiss. Her hands wrap around my neck as her chest rests flush with mine. I can practically feel the heat of her pussy through her shorts and my jeans, right over my now hard cock. She grinds her hips down on me as this kiss starts to spiral out of control.

I snake a hand around her waist and flip her onto her back before coming down on top of her. Her legs circle my hips, locking at the ankles behind my back as she draws me closer to her.

I break the kiss, her chest heaving like she just ran a marathon. Her nipples peak into hard points under her top. I brace myself over her on my forearms as I say, "Fucking perfect, that's what you are, fucking perfect and fucking mine." I look into her eyes, hoping she sees all that I want to give. Hoping that she sees all of my own brokenness, wanting her to see my hope for us, willing her to see the love I want give her.

I kiss down her neck, my tongue trailing out as I work my way to her ear. I whisper into it, "Tell me yes, Marissa. Tell me." My heart thumps in my chest while I wait for her answer, wait for her consent to take us both to heaven.

"Yes," she whispers. One word, one word that is music to my ears.

I pull down one side of her tank top to take her nipple in my mouth. I stop right before I can bring her flesh to my lips when I see the barbell running through her nipple. "Jesus, baby, that's hot." I suck her nipple deep into my mouth, my teeth biting down gently but still enough to give her a little bite of pain before I flick the barbell with my tongue. Her back arches off the couch.

I rip the other side down and move to her other nipple, taking it in my mouth just as I did the other one. My forefinger and thumb roll the wet nipple I just left, the peak getting impossibly harder. Her hips buck, and her pussy grinds up against my now painfully hard cock. Her legs tighten around my back, pulling me closer to her. "Fucking hot," I tell her as I back up onto my knees and palm both of her tits in my hands. A fucking perfect handful. I squeeze them both at the same time, bringing the tips of my forefingers and thumbs to her nipples where I gently pinch then twist. She throws her head back and moans so loudly, I'm sure the neighbors can hear.

Her hips search for some form of friction, but with me on my knees, there's nowhere for her to rub against. I look down at her, at us. She's laid out in front of me, legs spread over my lap, me between them. Her hands are over her head, clutching on the arm of the couch. Her gorgeous tits are tight and high, nipples pink and peaked, her chest heaving. One leg has slipped off the couch and onto the floor while the other is pinned between me and the back of the couch. I gaze down at her still covered pussy and groan when I see the wetness seeping through her shorts.

I trail my hand from her nipple down her stomach to the center of her pussy. I run my knuckle right down her covered slit. She whimpers and tries to move her hips as my fingers continue to torture her. I start to circle her clit that I know must be aching, and she's almost desperate as she tries to work herself against my light touch.

I continue stroking and teasing her, applying a bit more pressure, when I feel something hard. "Baby, you keeping something from me?" I ask her while I peel her shorts down and take a look. I see her pink clit and puffy lips glistening with her arousal, but it's the little steel ring with a pink diamond pierced through her hood that catches my eye. "Fuck me." I groan out as my mouth comes down on her pussy. My tongue flicks the piercing before I give it a little tug with my teeth. Her back arches off the couch as her hands come to her nipples to tug them. She circles her hips against my tongue, frantically trying to find her release.

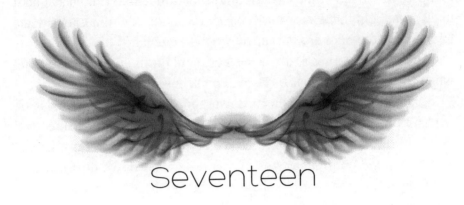

Seventeen

Marissa

Oh, God. I have either died and gone to heaven, or I'm having a really fucking fantastic dream that I don't think I ever want to wake up from.

His tongue continues to tease me with slow, soft licks all around my clit, his teeth playing with my piercing. Occasionally he'll drag his tongue down my slit and back up, licking and nipping at my lips. I peel my eyes open and prop myself up on my elbows to watch him. Fuck, what a sight.

My shorts are only pulled down enough so he can get to my clit. I raise my legs in the air and pull my shorts free with one hand. Bringing them back down, I spread wide for him, wordlessly telling him what I want. I move one hand into his hair as I continue to play with my nipples with the other hand. I'm panting and whimpering.

"Fuck, you taste like fresh fucking strawberries. Straight from the plant." He continues to lick and suck and tug until I think I'm going crazy.

I push down on his head, and he chuckles. I moan my frustration.

"Ask me real nice, baby, and I'll give you what you need," he says, his hot breath tickling over my engorged clit.

"Please, Mick. Oh, God, please make me come," I beg.

I can't say any more because he instantly gets serious. I've never come just from my clit play, but I feel my pussy start to pulse. He sucks it into his mouth as his tongue flicks the ring, and I feel his finger slip inside of me, the tip searching for that sensitive spot. He hones in on it and rubs it as he sucks my clit hard. I feel my back bow off the couch, and my eyes close. I see flashes of bright light behind my lids, and my entire body spasms with the intensity of my orgasm. He goes back to gentle licks and kisses as he brings me down.

I take a few moments to recover. Then with a surge of sexual courage I haven't ever felt before, I push him off of me, whipping his shirt off before he falls to his back. I'm on my knees between his legs, braced over him on one arm as I palm his rock hard cock through his jeans. "Your turn, Mick."

His breath hitches when my free hand unsnaps the button and drags his zipper down.

"If I came that hard from just your tongue, I can't even begin to imagine how hard I'm going to come with your cock in me," I whisper into his ear and then give the lobe a little tug with my teeth. I slide the tips of my sensitive nipples across his chest as his breathing picks up to a pant. I start by placing a soft kiss under his chin while my hand snakes its way over the tight ripples of his abs and over the bulge in his jeans. I run kisses down his chest as my hand works his cock through the denim. I think I feel the telltale bumps of Mick's own surprise in his pants. Fuck, I've never been with someone so fit. I've had two lovers in my life, the three-pump chump who took my virginity and then Lori's dad, who wasn't much to write home about either. I've had self-induced orgasms better than any of the ones he gave me.

I pull back to admire him, removing my hand to trace along his abs. I take a moment to take in all that is Mick. His shoulders are big and broad. His chest is muscular and defined, leading down to his eight pack abs that taper into a V-cut into his jeans. I trail my finger across his pecs and then down to his abs as I feel the ridges and bunches under his smooth skin. My exploration is clearly working him up since his breathing is coming out in puffs.

I open his jeans to reveal his white Calvin Klein boxer briefs, but before I can get any further, his hands grasp me under my armpits and he lifts me off him.

My eyes snap up to his as doubt creeps in. I'm not very experienced, and it's been a very, very long time for me. Maybe I read him wrong.

Maybe this isn't what he wants. "Um," I start to say. "Sorry, I just thought..." I don't have the chance to finish as he drags me up his body and shuts me up with his mouth.

His tongue invades my mouth, my taste on it. His hands reach my hips where he squeezes me. "I need a shower before we continue."

I'm afraid to answer him, so I just nod.

"Turn off the lights and wait for me in bed." He walks toward the bathroom.

I do so and lock the door. Making my way into my bedroom, I think about putting on some sexy lingerie, but all I have is what I bought for work, and the thought of wearing anything that is associated with stripping makes my stomach turn.

I turn on the bedside lamp that casts a soft glow to the room. I decide to just get into bed naked and see what happens. Pulling the covers back, I slide in, anxious for what I hope is to come. Is it like riding a bike? Will I remember what to do? Will he fit? Will I gag on his cock?

He steps into the room. And. Holy. Fuck. Me. A gush of wetness releases from my pussy with a throb. The sight of him in nothing but a white towel around his hips held in place with one hand is something to behold. Little droplets of water still run down his chest, and he looks like someone out of one of those fitness magazines. My mouth has now run dry, and I think if I try to say anything right now, it will sound weird, harsh, or I might just moan if I open my mouth at all.

"Water pressure sucks!" he says right before he looks up and takes me in. I'm sitting up now, the sheet pooled in my lap as I gawk at him. He stares right at my naked breasts and mutters, "Jesus." He drops his towel, giving me an unobstructed view of him. *All. Of. Him.*

Is he even going to fit? Should I just call it quits now? "You're pierced?" I point at him and can't believe that the words actually came out of my mouth.

"For your pleasure, baby," he says as he fists his cock in lazy strokes up and down.

Now it's my turn for my mouth to water. "Will it fit?" I whisper my question softly.

He smirks at me as he walks to the bed.

"I think we should talk about this a little before actually doing anything. Mick?" I look at him. "It's not going to fit. And I'm not even trying to stroke your ego a bit right now."

"I'm going to fit, baby, right down to my balls. I'm going to make it so good for you. I'm going to get you good and ready for me before I slide in." He plants his knee on the bed, and it dips.

"But, but," I'm stuttering at the size of his cock, because it's much bigger close up and naked and fully erect. His head is almost purple and angry looking, a bead of pre-cum filling the slit at the top. And those barbells running the length of him! My God! The girls at work always said fucking someone who was pierced was a whole different ball game. Being pierced myself, I didn't really get what the big deal was, but I can see it now.

"Lie back, Marissa, and spread your legs for me," he says while whipping the cover off of me, leaving me naked and for all of him to see.

He hooks his hands underneath my knees and drags me down to my back. I lean up on my elbows to watch him. He settles on his belly between my legs and looks up at me. "I could spend hours playing with this little ring, Marissa." He moans softly as he flicks it with his tongue. "Fucking perfect," he whispers while he opens up my pussy lips with his thumbs. "You're all swollen and glistening, baby, almost ready for me." Then his tongue darts into me.

This time, he's not fooling around. No longer teasing me, he starts working me over aggressively with his tongue, lips, and teeth. He runs his tongue from my opening to my clit, flattening it as he runs it up in one hot, wet swipe. He circles my clit, alternating with tugs of my piercing. Drawing it into his mouth, he slides one finger into me. I feel my walls squeeze him. "Fuck, so tight," he says as he slides in another finger and bites down gently on my clit. My hips buck against his fingers and mouth, and the feeling makes my toes curl.

"Oh my God," I say when he starts to rub my G-spot with the pads of his fingers. Curling them up a bit to apply a little pressure, the stirrings of an orgasm begin in my belly. The tightness builds, and I open my legs wider for more. Wanting more. "Mick, wait..." I say, and he stops immediately, bringing his eyes to meet mine.

"Did I hurt you?" His worried tone makes me smile.

"Not at all. I just." I look down, suddenly feeling a bit shy to tell him what I want.

"Hey, eyes to me, Marissa, yeah?" he says, and I meet his gaze.

"I, umm," I stutter. "I want you in my mouth, too," I tell him almost in a whisper.

"Baby, you never have to be shy with me. Ever. You hear me?"

I nod my head at him.

He rolls to his back alongside me as I get up to my knees. I don't even know how long it's been since I've done this, but I know that I want to try. He guides me to straddle his face, and I feel a bit awkward at first. I take him in my hand, his girth so wide that my fingers don't touch when they encircle him. I twist my hand as I stroke him from root to tip, eliciting a hiss out of Mick. Noticing the pre-cum gathering in his slit, I lean over to lick it up, circling the head with my tongue. Mick's hands come to my hips as he pulls me down to his face. I feel his nose nudge my clit and then his tongue running the length of my slit. I double my efforts, taking him as deep as I can while stroking up from the base of his cock to meet my mouth. All the while, he licks my clit and alternating with nips to my lips, tugs on my piercing, and spearing his tongue into me. I'm practically smothering him with my pussy as I grind down on his tongue. The feeling of his barbells running over my lips each time I draw him in feels so good, I just know it's going to feel even better when his cock is inside of me.

I take my other hand to cup his balls, giving them a little tug then massaging them gently. I pick up the pace and suck harder on the head, giving a little squeeze to his cock on the upward strokes with my hand. My thighs start to tremble as my orgasm barrels down on me. He plucks me off him and plants me on my back. He moves off the bed, and I hear the rustle of clothes and the crinkle of a wrapper. I look up at him as he settles between my thighs on his knees and works the condom down his cock.

"Fuck," he says, looking at me as he settles between my thighs.

"My pussy, my pleasure to give. From now on, you come on my fingers, on my tongue, on my cock," he says as he thrusts into me. His cock hits that soft spot inside of me, and those barbells move against my walls in the best possible way. He snakes his hand between us, and his thumb flicks at my clit ring.

I reach up and pull on my nipples, giving them a little twist, and I can feel my orgasm building.

I know it's coming, and I know it's going to be huge. I feel my pussy start to tighten, as those telltale flutters start low in my belly. He finally pushes me over the edge, and my toes curl into the sheets. I come with a load groan, full of his cock, while he races to join me.

Eighteen

Mick

The minute I came into the room and saw her sitting on her bed, the sheet covering her breasts, everything else around me stilled. She is so beautiful, but the look she gave me when I dropped my towel told me all I needed to know.

Gone was the sheet, her mouth open. I knew I wanted to fuck her mouth more than I wanted to feast on her sweet pussy.

Her tongue licking my cock head was the straw the broke the camel's back. Holy shit, I wanted to fuck her face so hard, but I had to pace myself. The way her pussy sucked in my fingers I knew it would be a tight fit with my cock.

"You ready for this?" I ask her, tearing open a condom wrapper and slowly adjusting it over my piercing before rolling it down to the base.

She sits in the middle of the bed, her back to the headboard and hair in a braid. Feet on the bed while her knees are bent, and her pussy is open for me. Glistening. Clit diamond sparkling in the dim light.

"Come here, Marissa." I motion her with my finger. She gets on her knees and crawls to me, her tits hanging low, making me want to fuck her doggie. Next round. This round will be missionary.

I'm standing at the end of the bed, and once she makes it to me, she gets straight on her knees. I lean down to kiss her lips softly, licking her bottom lip before going to her ear and licking the lobe. The motion sends goose bumps all over her. I use that second to slip my finger into her pussy lips, gathering the wetness and rubbing her clit with two fingers. "Love this clit ring." My finger goes down, circling her opening before sliding in. "I want to fuck you with my tongue every day," I tell her before taking her nipple in my mouth, biting it twice, then twirling my tongue around it. Her hips start moving toward my finger, so I add another one, moving them in and out a touch faster while I feast on her other nipple. I rub her G-spot every time my fingers pull out, curling them a little.

I know it's the spot because she moans every single time I touch it. Her pussy starts to tremble, getting a touch tighter. I know she's right there, so I take my fingers out, rubbing them on her nipple then licking her clean again while she tries to rub herself to orgasm.

I look at her, her cheeks pink, her eyes dilated and eyelids hazy. Her pussy puffy and ready. "Lie back, baby." I don't have to ask her twice. She lies back, spreading her legs wide. I lean down, taking one more long lick before climbing on the bed, positioning myself between her legs. "Going to go slow for you, okay?" I tell her while I take my cock in my hand and rub it up and down her slit, getting her wetness on me.

I do it again till I get to her clit and rub it with my cock head. She takes her hands and starts playing with her breasts, squeezing them. I finally bring my cock back to her entrance, placing it inside her. Going in just the tip, her tightness squeezes me. One slow push, just a touch more.

Finally my head is inside her, coming in and out just till the head is in, slowly moving in her. She starts to become frantic because she is pulling her nipples and then rolling them.

"So fucking perfect, my dirty, dirty girl." I enter her a little more. I hiss through the tightness, my knees digging into the bed.

I look down at us. Looking at her pussy taking my cock, at how we fucking fit. "Look at us," I tell her, thrusting a touch more.

She opens her eyes and looks down at us, watching me go in and out of her.

"Like my cock was made for you," I tell her, and then I push all the way in. I'm balls deep in her and I have to stop moving because her pussy is quivering, pulsing.

She closes her eyes and moans out. Her feet move to my waist, her heels digging into my ass. "Fuck, Mick, move. Fuck. Move." She groans, trying to get me to move.

Sucking my thumb into my mouth, I make a pop sound, having her open her eyes, which are now looking at me. I take my thumb and press down on her clit the same time I come out and slam back in all the way to the end. "Fuck," is the only thing I can say before I thrust in and out again. My balls slap her ass as I try to go as deep as I can.

I close my eyes, taking in the feeling. Her wet pussy making me slide in and out is like touching fucking heaven. I know she is about to come because her heels dig deeper, her pussy starts to pulse, and her moans start to come out.

"I'm going to come," she says while she looks down at us, watches me pound into her, watches me come all the way out then disappear again inside of her.

"Come on my cock, Marissa." My thumb starts to move on her clit in circles. Her hips rise up off the bed. One thrust, two thrusts, fucking three, and she goes off like fucking fireworks. Her moaning drowns out mine. The minute she comes on me, I fucking let go. Her tight hot pussy takes everything that I have to give it. I continue fucking her, riding it out, waiting for her pussy to stop pulsing, waiting for her to let my cock go, but she doesn't. Instead, she sets off on another orgasm.

"I'm coming again. Holy fuck," she hisses out while she raises her hips higher and higher.

I don't move. I make her fuck herself. Make her ride out her wave, and fuck, it's the hottest fucking sight in the world.

When she finally stops moving, I pull out of her, my cock still hard like it didn't just come the hardest that it's ever come in a pussy. "Be right back," I tell her, right before I get to the washroom where I get rid of the condom and clean myself off, bringing back a wet cloth.

She is in the exact position that I left her in, legs spread, pussy open. If I didn't give a shit, I would put another condom on, flip her over, and fuck her really deep. But the soft snores stop me. I wipe her down, making sure to go softly as to not wake her.

I throw the rag on the floor before I get into bed next to her, pulling the covers over us. She turns toward me, throwing her leg over my hips before throwing her arm over my chest, pinning me to the bed. I've never been one to cuddle after sex. Sometimes it's fuck and run.

Sometimes I'm just too smashed to leave, but now, fuck no

I throw one arm over my head while I place my other hand on top of hers on my chest before I follow her into dreamland. I've never fallen asleep with a smile on my face, but I could get used to this. Totally get used to this.

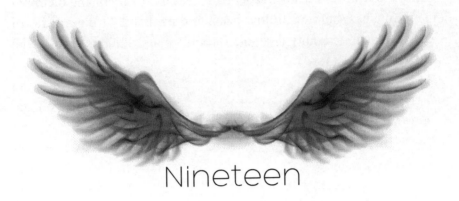

Nineteen

Marissa

I'm dreaming, or at least I think it's a dream. I don't open my eyes yet. I just bask in the heat of my cocoon. I'm wrapped up in his arms, my cheek resting on his chest. His heart beats a lullaby, prolonging my rest. When I finally open my eyes, his hard chest fills my vision. I try to stretch, but I'm immobile in his embrace. I arch my back a little and feel the soreness between my legs. A delicious soreness, proof of the passionate night we shared. Two months ago, I had never heard of Mick Moro. Now I can't go a few hours without thinking about him.

"I can practically hear the wheels in your head turning," he says right as he drops a kiss on my head. "Morning."

I lean back to take him in. His hair is sticking up in places, his eyes soft with sleep. He is a fucking mesmerizing sight.

"Morning to you." I kiss his neck right near his Adam's apple. With my body flush against his, I can feel his very hard cock pressing into me. "Good morning to him, too." I smirk while he chuckles.

"How sore are you this morning?"

"It's not like I was a virgin, Mick. I just haven't had a human in there in a while," I tell him with a giggle.

"A human?" He pushes away slightly from me to see my face.

"A vibrator, Mick. I have a vibrator, and that's the only action I've seen." I turn in the bed to reach into the bedside table to take out my pink vibrator with the rabbit ear clit stimulator. I turn it on to show Mick, who promptly plucks it from my hands and tosses it out the bedroom door. I watch it sail through the door, landing right in the middle of the living room with a big thump. I look at him incredulously. "You're going to owe me a new vibrator if that one doesn't work."

I barely get the words out before he's on me. Using his knees to spread my legs, he settles between them. He pulls my hands over my head, pinning me down. "You need to come, baby, it'll be me who gives that to you," he says right before his head dips and takes my nipple deep into his hot mouth. Just like that, my sleepy body comes alive. I wrap my legs around him and grind my center along the ridge of his erection. "Fuck, she's going to kill me."

I think he's talking to himself, but I don't get the chance to dwell on it when my attention is diverted by his mouth on my other breast. I want to reach down and twine my fingers into his hair to guide him to my pussy. A ride on his face sounds pretty much perfect right now. But he still holds my wrists, keeping me in place, while he plays with me.

His mouth pulls, nips, licks, and sucks as he works me into a frenzy.

"Oh, God," I say, throwing my head back into the pillow, awash in the sensations he's creating. I can feel the stirrings of an orgasm. I'm almost there when he just stops. My hands suddenly free. I open my eyes and see him reach over to grab a condom from the bedside table.

"Don't move your hands," he tells me, but I can't move anyway. I'm too entranced by watching him shield himself with the condom. He rolls it down his thick cock and, even having seen it already, it's still a breathtaking sight.

Once he is covered, he leans down and kisses me softly on my lips. "Guide me into you." He doesn't have to ask me twice. I move my one hand between us and line him up at my entrance. He pushes my knees back to my chest, tilting my ass up and then slides all the way into me in one slow and steady thrust.

We both moan at the same time. My hands, moves back up in place above my head, tingle with the urge to touch him. But I don't have a chance to because he distracts me by deepening the kiss and slamming into me. His mouth and his hips are in sync as he fucks me. His piercings glide so relentlessly over my sensitive spots, and I've never felt anything like this. The girls at the club were right. There is nothing like fucking a guy with piercings.

He rotates his hips on an inward thrust, his pubic bone presses into my clit, and I see stars. My pussy starts to pulse, and I know I'm very close. "I'm going to come, babe," he says, letting go of my mouth. My lids come down as my eyes roll back. He pounds into me so furiously, the headboard slaps against the wall. My back begins to bow, a deep moan escapes, and I fly over the edge. He pumps into me once, twice, three more times, and plants himself as he explodes inside of me.

I take his weight for a moment and then he rolls us to the side, still deep in me.

"Now that's the way to start a day," he says to me, trying to catch his breath.

"You won't hear me complain," I tell him, placing a soft kiss on the underside of his chin before I slowly peel myself from him. "I need another shower." I peek around him to look at the clock. "Jesus, it's already eleven a.m. I've got to get myself up so I can get in and help Phyllis." I make my way into the bathroom and take a look at myself in the mirror. Fucking hell, my braid is a frizzy tail hanging to one side of my head while the other side is plastered to my skull with the ends curling upward.

I try to turn and lock the door, but his hand stops me. "Kinda late to be modest now, Marissa. I've spent most of the last eight hours either lying naked with you or in you." He laughs while walking in and starting the shower.

"What are you doing?" I cross my arms over my nipples, which started to peak as soon as I heard his voice.

"I figure we can shower together. It'll save time." He smirks at me.

"Okay, then what's up with the condom?" I point to the unopened packet that he put down on the back of the toilet while he took care of the used one.

"Shower sex is even better than morning sex."

"Is that so?" I've never had shower sex. I've always rushed through my morning shower, doing my thing, and getting out. When the water is warm enough for him, he steps into the tub and holds his hand out to me.

"Let me show you."

I look at him, this naked god, holding out his hand, wanting to show me the goodness of shower sex. I almost blurt out that maybe it isn't a good idea, but my good sense takes over, and I walk over to the shower, take his hand, and let him give me my lesson.

An hour later, the hot water has turned frigid, I've had more orgasms than I can count on one hand, and I can agree as I walk out of the bathroom on wobbly legs that shower sex is so much fucking better than morning sex.

"I need a power nap or I won't last tonight," I tell him, heading over to my bed and throwing myself into the middle of it.

"I thought you had to help Phyllis?" he says from his position standing beside the bed where he is still naked.

"Wake me in an hour, please." I turn my head, throw the cover over myself, and close my eyes. I fall asleep with a smile on my face and a well used vagina.

I take my one-hour power nap, waking up semi-refreshed but still sore. I look around for Mick, finding him dressed and on the couch watching television.

"You don't have cable?" he asks.

"Nope, got bigger things to worry about than an extra forty-dollar cable bill each month. Besides, we have Netflix, and you don't need cable when you have Netflix," I tell him, gathering my shoes from the front closet. "Will you be okay here or did you want to leave at the same time?"

He gets up, coming to the door to put his shoes on. "I'll drop you off, go to the gym, and then swing by to pick you up after. We can eat at the diner."

"Okay." I follow him down to his car and get in while I do a quick scan to make sure my car is still there and that no one has vandalized it. "I have to move my car tonight so no one thinks I abandoned it."

He doesn't say much on the ride to Phyllis's, but then neither do I. Once we get there, I unbuckle my seat belt and go to open the door when I'm pulled back to him. "Last night was everything," he tells me in a whisper, "everything." He kisses me on my cheek, then my nose, then my other cheek, and then finally on my lips. Soft, delicate kisses. "I'll be back in a couple of hours." He rubs his thumbs on his side chin.

"Okay."

I get out of the car, closing the door, and then start walking into the diner, but turn around and go back to the car where I knock on the window. He lowers the window, and I lean down to look into the car at him. "Besides giving birth to my daughter, it was one of the best nights of my life, too."

With that, I leave him, turning around and walking into the diner where Phyllis is standing behind the counter with a coffee in her hand. One look at her and I see that she is snickering.

"Walk of shame or walk of a new woman, which one is it?" she asks, taking a drink of her coffee.

"No shame in walking out with that man. I can tell you that for sure."

I shake my head and head into the back where I put away my purse, put on my apron, and start my routine. A routine that I started just a couple of days ago, but it's a routine that I'm finally proud of.

Twenty

Mick

I open my eyes for the second day in a row and look over at Marissa, who is still sleeping. Fuck, I can't believe that this woman has been put into my life. She's a fucking angel. And the fucking sex, I've never had sex like that in my life.

The replay of the sex we had last night in my head is interrupted by my phone buzzing on the nightstand. It's Chris, the new recruit, fresh out of boot camp.

"Hello," I whisper, trying not to wake Marissa.

"Hey, Mick, I didn't know if I should call you or Jackson. Some girl came in late last night, early this morning. I think you should hear her story."

As he continues to relay her story to me, the hair stands up on the back of my neck. I don't waste any more time and tell him, "I'll be there in ten. Don't let her leave. Don't let anyone else get in there with her." I click end and call Jackson. It rings twice before he picks up.

"Hello."

"We got a lead," I say to him as I move around to get my clothes and get dressed. "Some girl came into the precinct last night, spinning a tale about meeting a guy and being creeped out by him."

"Okay. You think it's connected?" he asks while I hear rushing on his end as well.

"Not only do I think it's connected, but I also think he's the guy. She kept saying he tried pushing her to take a pill to relax. When she fought him on it, he got pissed off and started yelling at her." I look over at Marissa, who is now sitting up with wide eyes.

"Where was this?" he asks almost in a whisper, afraid of my answer.

"At the fucking mall. It must be their playground. Scan the area, pick out a girl, and then approach her." I look at Marissa and see one tear roll down her cheek.

"Getting in the car in five. Meet you there," he says, and I disconnect and look over at her.

"Babe, we might have something. I can't get into it now because time is of the essence. I need you to trust me to handle it. I promise, if it's something, I will let you know." I want to reach out and hold her, but there isn't time.

She nods her head in agreement. "Be safe." I hear her saying as I rush out the door to head to the precinct, praying that this is the break we need.

I get into the precinct before Jackson does, so I grab the file and start reading the notes. Jackson comes in a couple of minutes later and leans over my shoulder to read it, too. "What have you got?"

"Same MO as Lori. I fucking smell this shit. I feel this in my gut," I tell him, shaking my head. It was right in front of us the whole time.

"Where is the girl?" he asks, looking around.

"Room one. Her parents are on their way," Roger, the desk sergeant, tells us as he walks into the office followed by Chris. I give him chin up.

"What's her story?" I ask him.

"Maya, sixteen, pissed at the world, hangs at the mall with her friends, bitches about her parents, bitches about school, bitches about other people breathing from what I could tell. Guy approached her when her friends left. Started flirting with her. Clean-cut guy, maybe seventeen or eighteen tops. Kept talking about his friends having a party and how he wanted her to go. Something about him was off, she said."

"Finally, bastard got sloppy." I cross my arms over my chest.

Jackson looks over at me, watching Roger walk out. "You okay to do this?" he asks me, knowing I'm emotionally involved even if I want to deny it. I haven't told him that things with Marissa have progressed.

"What the fuck are you asking me, Jack?" I use his nickname to let him know not to fuck with me right now.

"I'm asking you right now if you are okay to do this."

"I'm getting her back. You can do it with me or you can watch. Either way, you let me know what you are going to do."

He nods his head, letting me know, without words, that he has my back.

"Okay, man. Let's get what we need so we can bring her home," Jackson says, following me into the room.

I enter the room and immediately take in the hot pink-tipped, blonde-headed girl. Her brown eyes are bloodshot and puffy from crying. She has a blanket wrapped around her, and she's rocking back and forth. Her adrenaline is finally crashing.

Jackson sits down across from her. "Hey, Maya. I'm Jackson. This is Mick. I know someone was in here earlier asking you questions. Mind if we go over a couple of things?" he asks.

She nods her head yes.

"Can you tell me this guy's name?" he asks her.

"Called himself Ryan," she whispers.

"What did he look like? Any scars? Tattoos? Anything special about his appearance?"

"He had brown hair, brown eyes, shaved sides and longer on top. He was wearing cargo shorts and a plain white T-shirt." She closes her eyes like she is trying to picture him. "Oh, and he had a tattoo." She opens her eyes. "I just remembered. It was a diamond with the word Peace under it on the inside of his right wrist. I remember it now. I saw it when he grabbed my wrist and squeezed me."

Jackson looks over at me, and I turn and walk out of the room, going to the computer to run the tattoo she described through our databases.

It takes a few minutes for the computer to do its thing. It finally spits out a name and address. I barely restrain myself from my fist pumping, because I know better than anyone not to celebrate till we have a successful identification. I pick up the phone and call down to send a patrol car out to pick him up.

Right before I return to the room, Chris stops me. "Maya's parents just came in." I nod and head to the waiting room.

"Hi there, I'm Detective Moro. My partner, Detective Fletcher, is in with Maya right now asking her some routine questions. I'll take you to her. I'm sure you're both anxious to see her."

The mother lets out a quiet sob while her husband wraps an arm around her shoulders to steady her. I hear him whispering to her that everything's fine, that she's okay.

I walk them to the room, knocking before entering. I don't say anything as Maya's parents both rush over and hug her. I tilt my head toward the door to indicate to Jackson to follow me out.

We step into the hall to give them some privacy. He looks at me, waiting to hear what I've learned. "What did you find?"

"Name's Ryan King. Calls himself Diamond Boy. We have an address, and an undercover is heading there now to see if we can pick him up."

"So we wait?" he asks.

"We wait." I walk to my desk as Jackson sits in front of his computer to see what else he can find on Ryan King. Nothing pops up that I haven't already seen. Normal blue-collar family, the kid's got a couple of misdemeanors, but as a minor, they'll be sealed as soon as he turns eighteen, which is in three days.

The phone on my desk rings, and I pick it up. Chris lets me know that they got him. Hanging up the phone, I smile at Jackson, feeling the familiar surge of adrenaline when a case starts coming together. "We got him."

Jackson nods at me and begins getting ready for when they bring in Ryan King. It takes about twenty minutes to bring him in and install him in a room on the other side of the building so Maya won't see him.

When Jackson looks over at me, I'm practically bouncing on the balls of my feet like a boxer getting ready to enter the ring. This kid is going to lead me to Lori, I just know it.

"I think it's safe to say I'm going to be the one doing the talking. You should sit back and listen. Yeah?" Jackson tells me, opening the door, and coming face to face with our first real lead in these cases.

He sits there in baggy sweats, tight T-shirt, and one of those stupid flat-billed baseball hats with diamond logos all around it. He looks like the punk that he is.

"Hey, Ryan, thanks for coming in." Jackson will start easy with him.

"Well, I didn't really have a choice since they cuffed me, put me in a car, and brought me here." Jackson sits back in his chair and throws the pen on the table. It's the first sign that this kid is pushing him to his limits and we've only been in here for five seconds.

"All right then, let's cut the bullshit. Where were you yesterday afternoon?"

"Out and about," he answers with a smirk.

"You go to the mall yesterday?" His voice is calm and I wait for him to dig his own hole.

"Yesterday? I don't really know. Maybe I should check my calendar." Such a wise-ass. I can feel my blood pressure ticking up.

"No need to check your calendar. You see, we have video." It's a stretch. We haven't seen the video yet, and we have no idea what's on it, but Ryan's expression immediately changes.

His smirk gone, the vein in his neck starting to pulse faster.

"What video?" His face pales as he asks the question.

"Come on, Ryan, smart guy like you? You have to know there are cameras all over that mall. It's all going to be there, my man."

He swallows, his leg starting to bounce. "I was told they weren't working," he mutters.

We fucking got him.

"Who told you that? Dude, you got played. It's all there. Gotta say"—he shakes his head at him—"you had us going there for a bit, but it was only a matter of time."

"I didn't do anything." He pushes himself forward, placing his hands on the table.

"See, Ryan, that's where you're wrong," he tells him and when he doesn't say anything further, he continues. "I gave you a chance to tell us your side of the story, but you think you're smarter than us." He leans back into his chair while I lean against the wall with one foot folded over the other.

"I did nothing wrong." He looks at both of us, trying to convince us.

"That isn't what the video shows. You know it." Jackson points to me. "We know it."

"Listen, I don't know what you have, but I did nothing wrong."

"You baited them." Short and sweet. "The video shows you even slipped them something."

"That's bullshit! I didn't give them shit till after we left!" And just like that, he buried himself. He knows it now just like I know it.

"Really? Then it's my mistake. You drugged them after you left, took them to wherever it is you took them, and now you are going to go down for drug possession, kidnapping, assaulting, and I gotta be honest with you, Ryan, no one in jail likes someone who drugs helpless women. Let alone sex offenders. They get the worst treatment in jail."

"I didn't kidnap anyone. They came with me willingly."

"Where are they then?" Jackson asks him. "Give me a location."

"I...I..."

This is when Jackson snaps. "You what? Did you kill them?" He raises his voice.

He just shakes his head no.

"You drugged them, lured them out, raped them, and then killed them." His voice gets louder. "Then you disposed of their bodies. Where are they?" He slams his hand on the table, making him jump. "Pretty boy like you in prison, going to be rough keeping the boys at bay. Tell me what you did with them. TELL ME!"

"I get paid to find the girls and drop them off. That's it!"

"Who pays you?"

"No clue. Calls himself Chucky, like the Chucky doll. I bring them to him. He pays me ten grand per girl."

"How many?" Jackson asks him, and I hope to fuck he doesn't clam up now.

"Three so far." He looks at us. "I wanted to stop, but he wouldn't let me. He kept calling, said he'd dump them off at the cops and all they'd have was my name."

"Where did you drop them off?"

"Some cheap motel off the interstate. I walked them in pretending we were going to a party, and then once we were inside, I just left. He had his guy waiting for them there."

"So you brought those three innocent girls to the devil's doorstep."

"I did nothing wrong."

That's the final straw before I fucking snap. "You lured three young girls away from their families through the use of an illegal substance. You then brought them to someone who rapes and probably beats them, while you walked away with thirty grand. And you think you didn't do anything wrong here, Ryan? If any of those girls are dead, you will be charged with accessory to murder."

I lean over the table, looking him in the eye, and say, "And you better fucking believe I'll be the one to put you in there. I'll lead you in there like you led them in there. How is that?" I have to reel in my anger before I reach over this table and grab this punk by his neck.

He doesn't get to answer before Jackson's cell phone rings.

Getting up, he answers the phone. "Hello?" I don't hear who is on the other end but by the look on his face, I know it's not good news. I don't even have time to ask what is going on before he storms out of the interrogation room, heading for his keys.

"Mick," he yells for me, and I'm out of the room, slamming the door shut behind me.

"Silent alarm was just triggered at Bella's. Someone is on the scene, but I'm waiting for an update from Brian." He puts him on speakerphone so I can hear.

"Jackson, where are you?" His voice is tight. It's curt and angry.

"Give it to me."

"They have an ambulance going there now. Brenda has been beaten pretty badly. Lilah was the one who ran and hit the alarm."

"Where the fuck is Bella?"

"Jackson." He exhales a deep breath. "She's nowhere to be found." And just like that, his phone flies across the room, his knees buckle, and he almost falls down.

"We will fucking get her back." I grab him by the shirt, shaking him, trying to get him out of the haze that he is in. "You need to snap the fuck out of it and help me find your woman. You need to lock your shit down and fucking focus here, Jackson."

We both know who took her. Now we just have to find him before Jackson kills him himself.

I do the driving, and we make it to his house in record time. By the time we get there, two cop cars, their lights still flashing, are already parked at the curb along with an ambulance.

I run inside right behind Jackson, taking in the sight before me. It's like a scene out of a fucking horror movie. The EMTs are working on Brenda, their neighbor, who is lying lifelessly in a puddle of her own blood.

I scan the room, looking for anything that seems to be out of place, a broken window, busted door, something, but nothing seems to be out of place. I see no signs of a struggle. I continue scanning the room, stopping when I notice that Lilah has seen that Jackson arrived. She immediately jumps off the police officer's lap and runs right to Jackson, crying.

He scoops her into his arms, holding her close as she wails out her terror. "Ackson, they take Momma," she says between sobs.

"Who, baby girl, who took Momma?" he asks her. "Who?" This little girl has woven herself into his heart, and there is nothing he wouldn't do for her. I haven't even met Lori yet, and I feel the same way about her. I pull up my phone, texting more security detail to come and watch the house again. Jackson doesn't even have to ask. I just know since it's what I would do.

She hiccups, her sobs, her breath coming out in choppy pants. "Daddy and his briend."

Brian arrives and comes straight to us. "So, he came in the side gate from what we could tell by the sensor times." He looks at his phone. "Front door sensor indicates it was disengaged and reengaged twenty minutes ago. The silent alarm was activated about twenty seconds later."

Jackson looks down at Lilah. "You did so good, baby girl. Just like we showed you." He then kisses her stain-streaked face. "So brave, my baby girl."

"I want Momma, Ackson," she says as her eyes start to close as the trauma of today finally hits her.

My phone starts beeping in my hand with the address of the hotel. "We got the name of the hotel. We are sending two cruisers there right now."

He looks at me, about to ask questions, when his mother runs into the house.

Her eyes are open wide with fear as she scans the area. Tears start falling when she sees Brenda being lifted on the stretcher.

She finds him sitting on the floor holding Lilah. "Jackson." She gets on her knees next to me, stroking Lilah's hair softly.

He looks at her straight into her eyes. "He did this." He doesn't have to say his name because we all know it's Adam, Jackson's long lost addict brother.

Her hand covers her mouth, and she gasps in horror.

"He came here, into her home, and he took her. He beat Brenda, badly as you can see, to get to her. And he did it in front of Lilah."

"Jackson." That word is ripped from her, pained, but it's all she gets out before I step forward, drawing his attention away from his mother.

"Jackson, Bella has her phone on her. We have a location."

He hands Lilah to his mother before he gets up.

"You aren't going to like this," I tell him.

His fists clench at his sides. "Tell me," he says through gritted teeth.

"Same motel Ryan sent us to." It's all I have to say.

He looks at his mother. "I have to know if you will keep her. If anything happens to us, to me, to Bella, you will keep her."

"Jackson, get Bella and just bring her home. Both of you just come home to Lilah."

"Mom, I need you to promise not to leave her sight. Do not leave Lilah alone for a second, not even to go to the bathroom. I'm going to have someone staying with you both, but I still want you to promise not to let her out of your sight."

"I promise, Jackson. Go get Bella."

We both nod at her, rushing out of the house, he jumps in the passenger seat of the car since I'm driving, and he immediately calls for backup.

The address they gave us is about twenty-five minutes out, but with the way I'm driving, we should get there in about ten, maybe fifteen minutes max.

There are five undercovers on-site, waiting around the corner, scoping the place out.

There is a black Honda parked right in front of room eight, which is the room we think they are in.

We let the on-sites know when we are two minutes out. I want into the room the minute we get there.

"You loaded?" The question isn't to ask if I'm carrying my weapon, it's to ask if I'm carrying more than one.

"Got two on me. A couple in the back, locked."

He nods, while I'm preparing myself for the war that is about to be waged at the motel.

The moment we get there, Jackson walks in the front door and straight to the reception desk. "Adam Fletcher, what room?"

She looks at us, smacking her bubble gum. "Who are you?"

Jackson takes his gun out and places it on the counter, her eyes going as wide as saucers. "You really want to do that right now?"

She shakes her head. "Room eight."

I don't even wait to hear her finish before I walk back out, talking to the team that has gathered. Jackson opens up the trunk so he and I can grab our vests and put them on.

"Room eight confirmed. We know they are armed. Brenda has a bullet hole to prove it."

I look around at the twenty officers who have showed up, plus the ten of Brian's guys, all waiting for the war to start. The adrenaline is rushing through my body. The blood in my body flowing so fast from my beating heart that my body is starting to radiate and shake.

"We just saw movement," Brian says while looking over at the room.

"It's go time. Seems they know we are here." I turn to walk away from the car to attack the door from the side.

Jackson approaches the other side. We have our guns both drawn.

We're a few feet from the door when we hear a shot fired. My stomach drops, and I rock to a halt as my feet stop moving. Two shots and my breathing stops. Three shots and I brace myself on the wall outside room seven. My body goes from hot to dead cold. Rage courses through me.

I don't even wait for Jackson. I just shout out, "Police, hands where I can see them."

The swat team breaks down the piece of shit door in one measly kick. Standing next to a naked Bella is a man with his gun at his side.

"Drop your weapon!" I command, upon entering the room. "Drop the fucking weapon now!" I warn him again right before I fire a shot at the man's leg. The man cries out in pain as he drops to the floor, the gun still at his side, so I shoot one more time, this time to his shoulder. His body jerks backward, the gun falling from his hand.

I walk deeper into the room, gun drawn, and it's like I'm walking into the devil's dungeon. I look around, taking in the filth of the room. The smell of urine is so profound, my eyes burn. It makes the pier warehouse look like a spa.

The one bed in the middle of the room, dirty sheets askew, half on the bed, half off. Bella lies in the middle of it, her clothes partially removed.

One lone chair in the corner of the room is wet with obvious blood stains on it. Carelessly discarded, used needles litter the floor all around us.

An old television sits on a cheap, dusty stand facing the bed. The television is on, tuned to The Shopping Network.

I continue scanning the room when my eyes land on three teenage girls huddled in a corner of the room and chained to the wall.

All three are wearing sheer camisoles, with no bras and sheer underwear, leaving little to the imagination. All three are filthy with greasy, stringy hair, and it's obvious none of them have bathed in quite a while. Their eyes are puffy and closed, like they are napping.

Their arms show round, fingertip-shaped bruises and swollen, red needle marks along the inside of their elbows. Their hands are clipped with a chain to the wall. I can see the dirt under their chipped fingernails. If that wasn't enough to push me over the edge, I take in what appears to be dried blood crusted over on their inner thighs. Their panties are almost non-existent, brownish reddish stains covering them in the front.

I almost wish that I shot the fucker, who is lying on the floor near the bed with a bullet hole in his shoulder and kneecap, right between his fucking eyes. He's moaning like a fucking pig, complaining about me shooting him.

The girls have all opened their eyes at this point, all of them looking right at me with empty eyes. They are vacant, like they're here but they aren't really here.

Jackson rushes to the bed, checking Bella for a pulse. It's there, thank God. He covers her with the filthy sheet and gathers her in his arms to walk out of the room.

I look down at Chuck, who is being cuffed by Chris in the middle of the room, blood seeping out of his leg and shoulder.

Brian, Hulk, and Roger are all working to remove the chains from the three other girls in the room.

I walk over to the girls, squatting down next to them. Their condition is beyond deplorable. I know right away which one is Lori. She has her mother's eyes. Eyes that are now starting to clear. She starts to shake, and I'm sure she's looking for her next fix even if she wasn't the one who was injecting herself. She is absolutely filthy, and if I didn't know better, I would assume she's a junkie.

I reach out to move the hair out of her face, and she turns her head violently to the side, groaning in pain and pleading.

"Please don't do this. I don't want this. I want to go home." She looks around and starts to take in the SWAT team members with their badges hanging around their necks. "You came for us?" she asks as the realization settles in.

I have a tear running down my face before I wipe it away. "I came for you." I look at the other girls who are being attended to by the other cops. "Your mom has been searching for you since you left." I reach out to her again, and this time she doesn't turn away. She starts sobbing, calling for her mom.

Once they free the chains from her, I scoop her up in my arms. The smell of urine and feces hits me right away. She is almost naked, so I look around for something to cover her. I don't look for too long when Chris walks up to us and throws his jacket over her.

She turns her head to look at Chris.

"There you go, beautiful," he says to her right before he turns around, shaking his head angrily.

I nod to him right before Lori speaks up.

"I want to go home."

I bring her closer to my chest. "I promise you, baby girl, we are bringing you home."

She lays her head on my chest, and her body goes limp in my arms, her head falling back.

"I need help," I say, running from the room to one of the waiting ambulances. I place her on a stretcher, and the EMT goes straight to work. I move out of their way but stay with her.

I look over at Jackson and call out, "It's Lori. We found them."

He doesn't say anything more because the door to the ambulance shuts. "Sir, you need to step back so we can take her in. Her blood pressure is low and dropping," one of the EMT tells me while loading her into the ambulance.

"Where she goes I go," I tell them while I jump in the ambulance before he shuts the door.

Chris runs over to us.

"Take the car," I say, tossing him the keys. "Meet us at county." The doors close, and we are rushing to the hospital where I hope and pray we are in time and they can wake her up.

I take out my phone and make the phone call that I've wanted to make since I got this case.

It doesn't even ring before she picks it up on a sob, almost like she already knows, like she feels it. "Mick."

"I got her, baby, I'm bringing her home." The wails that come out of her sound like a wounded animal howling in pain. "Baby, you have to be strong. She needs you to be strong." I look down at the girl lying on the stretcher fighting with everything she has left. "Meet us at county. Take a cab if you can't drive."

She doesn't say anything, but I hear the phone squishing, so I know she's nodding her head.

"I need to hear the words."

"You found my baby?" she asks in a whisper, and I can't miss the relief and gratitude in her voice.

"Yeah, baby, I found her." I close my eyes, trying to forget the scene that I just walked out of. "Come to her, babe, she needs you."

"Okay, Mick." She disconnects.

I lean forward and take Lori's limp hand in mine. There are track marks running up her inner arm. I trace them with my finger, praying to every god available that she'll be okay and vowing to them that in return I'll protect her from any more evil.

Twenty-One

Mick

As soon as we arrive at the ER, the EMT starts rattling off Lori's vitals to the ER doctor. He runs alongside the stretcher with the doctor as the paramedic fills them in on what he knows and steers it into an exam room. I run along, keeping pace with them.

The doctor stops me before I can get into the room. "Sir, you can't go in there."

The nurse closes the door behind her and comes out to talk to me. "You need to wait in the waiting room. We will come and get you when we know something." She doesn't wait for me to answer, just goes back into the room. When the door opens again, I can hear the beeping of machines and the bustle of them working.

I walk into the waiting room, and the dread and fear I feel is written all over my face. I see Jackson sitting in a chair, and I make my way to him. I drop into the chair beside him before my legs can give out. "Her pulse is weak, man, so weak. At one point, they couldn't find it." I look toward her room.

He doesn't have a chance to ask me anything else before the door bursts open and Marissa comes running in, looking frantic. Her face pale, her cheeks tear-streaked, her eyes obviously scared and worried.

As soon as she sees us in the hallway, all of the fear and worry of the last few weeks and the uncertainty and concern she is feeling now collide and overcome her. She stops in her tracks, and her knees give out as she wails with so much emotion, I'm shaken to my core.

I move faster than I ever have to get to her. The need to hold her is overwhelming. I scoop her up and hold her close as I sit on the floor with her cradled in my lap, slowly rocking in an attempt to calm her down.

"Baby, she's a fighter," I whisper to her. "She is going to pull through. She didn't survive all of that to die this way."

Marissa doesn't reply. She just clings tighter to me like I'm her anchor in this storm, curling in so close to me, like she can't get close enough, her hands fisting my shirt tightly. "My baby," I hear softly between her sobs.

We both sit in that waiting room, waiting for news.

The minutes feel like hours, the hours feel like days. Each time someone comes out of those doors, we all look up hopefully. At one point Chris shows up and asks if it's okay to stay and wait with us. All I can say is thank you.

The other girls have also been brought in, and their parents are here waiting just like we are. They are going through drug screening and rape kits. It's a fucking parents' worst nightmare.

Marissa has calmed down a bit, but she hasn't moved from my lap nor has she loosened her grip on my shirt. Her head is resting in the crook of my neck, and it's like she was made to fit there. I kiss her head every single time she breathes heavy from all of her sobbing.

Her eyes are open, waiting and anxious for someone to come out of the door and tell her something, anything. I finally see the doctor who was treating her come out. I don't have a chance to get up before he's standing in front of us. "Are you the parents to Lori Sullivan?" he asks, and we both nod yes. "I'm going to cut right to the chase. I've never seen someone so stubborn in my life."

Marissa finally sits up. "What does that mean?"

"She flat lined, twice. We had to intubate her. She also went into shock from the overdose of heroin in her system. I have to say, her blood pressure was off the charts. It's no wonder her heart stopped. We are administering methadone to help with the withdrawal symptoms. The good news is that her body went into shock before her heart stopped, so we placed her in a medically induced coma to allow her body to focus its energy on healing. We ran a pregnancy test, which came out negative. We have also run a full workup for STDs that she could have contracted as well as to rule out any infections that may have been spread from sharing needles."

I look at Marissa and see that her lips have started to tremble, and she looks a little faint.

Chris gives me his water bottle that he has almost crushed in his hand while listening to the doctor's report of Lori's condition.

She grabs the bottle from me and looks me in the eyes as she asks, "Was she raped?" She is obviously processing everything that has happened to her daughter a little bit at a time.

I don't get to answer her because the doctor continues.

"She was raped and sodomized. At this point, she has vaginal trauma and tearing that should heal. She also has scarring on her cervix, which will also heal, but she will need to follow up with her OBGYN. Overall, it could be a lot worse."

The doctor almost continues, but Chris speaks out, "A lot worse? Are you fucking insane?" He gets up. "They fucking raped and sodomized her and drugged her! How much worse can it be?" He is standing up now, his chest heaving.

The doctor has clearly seen worse cases because he isn't fazed by his outburst and answers without hesitation. "She could be dead."

Chris looks to the side and walks out of the room.

"Mrs. Sullivan, the next three days will be very difficult. Heroin is highly addictive. Detox is very difficult because the withdrawal process is so intense. The best thing for her right now is to sleep through it. I'm not saying when she wakes, it will be easy either. Symptoms can persist for months, weeks, even years. One thing in our favor is that we found out from Bella that the girls were forcibly given the heroin. So it's not like they came into that situation already addicted and we have those behaviors to overcome." He looks at both of us. "Do you have any questions for me?"

Fuck, my mind is a mess, swirling with all the information that he just gave us.

"Can I see her? I want to see her." Marissa starts to stand up, not waiting for the doctor to answer.

He doesn't, just leads the way. "Perhaps you should wait for us to clean her up a little."

Marissa pushes past him, opens the door, and the sight before her is too much for her. Her legs buckle as she covers her mouth with her hands to stifle the sobs coming out of her.

Lori is, thank God, dressed in a hospital gown now. Gone are the skimpy things that we found her in while she was being held. Her hair is still in need of a wash. Her skin is tinged an almost yellowish color. The track marks marring her skin are clearly visible in that position with her arms lying alongside her body. The machine next to her beeps quietly. The nurse was writing something down on the paper but stopped when the sobs started.

"Baby, you have to be strong," I tell her, taking her hand and guiding her over to Lori.

Her body shakes a little bit, and Marissa looks at the nurse with fear in her eyes.

"That is her body detoxing."

Marissa sits next to her on the bed, taking her hand in hers and bringing it to her mouth where she kisses it and quietly sobs while she holds it to her face. Going closer to her, she holds her face in one hand while the other hand still holds on to her hand. "Baby, Momma's here," she tells her through her quiet sobs.

My heart is ripped to shreds by the pain that is coming out of her.

"I looked for you, everywhere." She scoots closer to her, leaning down and kissing her face. "Every day I would drive down the street looking at all the faces, hoping that one would be yours." She moves herself to lie on her side next to her and strokes her face tenderly. "I missed you so much. I haven't been shopping since you left." She continues to talk to her through her tears. "I prayed for signs and then I prayed for help, prayed for someone, anyone, to help me." She then looks over at me and says, "He answered my prayers, baby. Mick saved you and brought you back to me." She leans in closer to her daughter while she continues to talk to her softly. Telling her everything that she did to find her. Marissa closes her eyes, the events of the day finally catching up with her.

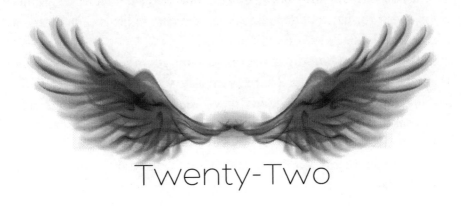

Twenty-Two

Marissa

"I can't wait till you wake up and I can take you home. I got a new job," I tell her while brushing her hair. It's been five days since she was found, five days that she has been in the coma. It was my job as her mother to protect her, and I didn't do that. I did the opposite of that. But I would make it up to her.

I held her while we both slept that first night. When her body would start shaking, I would talk to her till she calmed down. Tell her stories about when she was little. I would just talk so she knew I was here with her.

The day after was the worst, when the lights came on coupled with the sunlight coming into the room, and I could see her skin that was yellow almost like it was jaundiced. Her nails were broken and cracked with dirt under them.

Her arms were barely more than skin and bone. Purple bruises ran along her wrists along with scabs and scars. The hardest thing to see were the puncture wounds. The inside of her right arm was a huge scab. A nurse had told us that her vein must have collapsed, but they still kept injecting into it. Her hair was limp, oily, dirty.

The nurse came back that night to give her a sponge bath. Of course I didn't let her. I bathed her myself. It was almost like I was trying to purge her system. Mick said he would wait outside while I bathed her, but if I needed him to just call for him.

I filled the basin with warm water and started at her feet. I know I should start at her hair, but her soles were black, yellow, and brown. The water had to be refilled after just one foot. Making my way up her legs, my breaking point was the dried blood on her inner thighs. The sight made me run to the bathroom and throw up the breakfast that Mick forced me to eat that morning.

Rinsing my mouth out with water, I looked at myself. "Be strong, be strong." I chanted to myself.

The nurse that had been supervising me stood up from the chair. "If you want, Mrs. Sullivan, I can finish it."

I shook my head. Grabbing the basin, I went back into the washroom and filled it with warmer water. Going back to the bed, I put my hand into the water, wringing the towel and then started washing her legs again. I picked up one leg and quickly washed away all the dry blood. I let warm water soak on her inner thighs before washing it off. The tears mixed with the water and blood. The left over blood and dried semen on her vagina was the breaking point. The sob ripped through me. Mick knocked at the door, opening it and looking down at the floor.

"Marissa."

I looked down and covered her up so no one could see her anymore. "I'm okay, Mick," I said through my hand. Hearing the door shut, I picked up the rag and continued cleaning her. I had to rinse the water ten times before I was able to wash her hair. It took about two hours to wash her from the bottom of her feet to the top of her head.

After I finished washing her hair, I combed through it and braided it like I did when she was younger.

When I finally finished, she looked clean again. I walked out into the hall, and Mick was there talking to Jackson and the other guy, Chris. As soon as Mick saw me, he came right to me, pulling me into his arms.

In his arms, I felt safe, I got strength, I knew I could survive anything. I wrapped my arms around his waist, breathing in his scent.

"Marissa," I heard Jackson behind me. "Bella and I want you to know that if you need anything, you just call us."

I wrapped my arm around Mick's waist. I hated this, people acting like she was dying. "How is Brenda doing?" I asked, wondering if she was going to be okay. It seemed she got shot when Bella was taken. If it wasn't for Bella, they wouldn't have found Lori.

"She's going to be fine," he said, and I looked at Chris, who looked like he hadn't slept in a while. I made a note to ask Mick about him when we were alone.

Now here I am, five days later, about to lose my mind. I just want her to open her eyes. They keep telling me not to worry, that this is her body's way of dealing with the trauma it's been through. It's so hard, though. I just want her to wake her up.

The other two girls who were also taken are having a bit more trouble. I heard them detoxing—the crying, the screaming, the vomiting, the howling—while I sat by my girl's side, praying to take the pain away from her.

I pick up the magazine that Bella and Lilah brought me. The minute I met her I knew I'd made a friend. No words were needed. We just hugged and cried mother-to-mother, victim-to-victim. I'm flipping through the pages of the magazine while Mick sits by the window, playing on his phone, when we hear a low groan. We both look up at each other then look at Lori, who is moving her head from side to side. I'm so stunned I can't move, while Mick is already out of his chair and headed for the door, calling for Dorothy, the nurse on duty.

I get up and rush to her side, stroking her head and talking to her. "Lori, baby, open your eyes, honey." I grab her hand and kiss it. "I'm here, honey. Momma is here, just open your eyes." And slowly, ever so fucking slowly, her eyes start to flutter before they start to open. Once, twice, three times before they open in a squint. Dorothy brushes past Mick, who moves to the end of the bed so she can do her thing.

"Lori," Dorothy says while wrapping the blood pressure cuff around her bicep. "My name is Dorothy. I am your nurse. Can you hear me?" she asks right before the doctor strolls in, looking over her chart.

"Hey there. Lori finally opened her eyes, I see." He puts the chart down on the bed, moving to Lori's side and shining the flashlight into her eyes. Lori doesn't like it apparently because she weakly tries to slap his hand away.

"Mom," she croaks out. "Mom." Her voice is scratchy. "Water," she says, and I rush to grab some of my water that I had sitting by her bed.

"I'm here, baby. Momma is here," I say through tears and laughter that she is awake. I tilt the straw to her mouth, and she takes a big gulp and promptly starts to cough.

"Easy there, Lori, you haven't had anything in your stomach in a while, so you don't want to take in too much all at once, okay? Small sips, sweetie," Dorothy says.

"Lori, do you know where you are?" the doctor asks while he writes something in the chart.

Lori looks at me with tears running down her face. "Momma." She opens her hand out to me. I take it, holding it to my chest as I stroke her cheek and her head while she sobs. "I didn't want to do it." She wails out, her body starting to shake. "I said no. I said I wanted to go home." She closes her eyes and sobs harder.

I cup her chin so that she is looking at me. "I know, baby, I know you wanted to come home. I know."

She looks at me and then her eyes move to Mick, who is standing to the side, his fists tightly clenched. The veins in his arms are bulging, the one in his forehead is ticking, and the anger and rage in his eyes is impossible to miss.

"You saved me," she says to Mick. "You said you'd bring me home."

Tears glisten in his eyes, but he quickly blinks them away, his voice rough when he replies, "Yeah, baby girl, I did. Promised your mom I would do it."

She nods her head, her eyes staying on Mick.

"He found you, honey, like he said he would." I lean down and place a kiss on her head.

"Oh, God, Mom, I didn't want to be there! I didn't want to do any of those horrible things! I didn't want the drugs! Oh my God, the drugs." She looks at me frantically. "No drugs, no more. NO MORE DRUGS!" she screams as she tries to rip out the IV from her arm.

The nurse springs into action and injects something into the IV. "It's the withdrawals," Dorothy assures me.

"Baby, they are going to make it all better," I tell her while she shakes her head.

"No, no, no, no," she says as she fights to keep her eyes open. "No more," she slurs, and it's the last thing she says before she falls back to sleep.

Mick makes it to my side just as I throw my hand over my mouth to let my own sob out, but nothing comes out of me, no sound, no tears, nothing. My eyes fixate on my daughter, who is now sleeping peacefully. I'm shaken by what she said, by her outburst and thinking about what she's been through.

"She is going to be fine," the doctor tells me, shutting her chart and giving it to Dorothy. "It's normal to have outbursts like that in the first week, but because she was unconscious for so long, it won't be as bad. She should be awake again sometime this evening. She is a fighter, Mrs. Sullivan, she's a fighter. Things I've seen, the condition she was in when she arrived in here, she wouldn't have made it another day had she not been found. It's a good day," he tells me with a nod before leaving the room with Dorothy right behind him.

"She's a fucking fighter, babe. You know that, but now she doesn't have to fight by herself. She has us. We fucking fight with her. Sleep," he tells me, holding me close. "It's going to be a long road. You need your rest."

I know he's right, so I just nod and watch her, my eyes never leaving her rising chest. I finally close my eyes but not for too long, because, the next thing I know, she's up again.

Mick kisses my head and whispers, "She's waking up, baby," he whispers, and I sit up and watch her open her eyes.

"Mom," she whispers.

I look around and see that it has fallen dark. It's almost nighttime.

"I'm here, baby." I get on the bed with her and wrap my arms around her. She curls up slightly against me, almost like she did when she was a little girl. "It's going to be okay."

"Hungry." She looks up at me. "So hungry."

I don't even get a chance to reply before Mick gets up. "I'm on it," he says as he walks out of the room.

"Momma, I missed you." She throws her arm over my stomach, holding on tight. "They made me do stuff, Mom." Her voice is soft and quivers. "Stuff I didn't want to do."

I don't know what to say to her or what the right thing to say is, so I just let her talk. "I know, baby, I know."

"I tried to fight," she whispers. "I tried so hard, but it just made it worse."

I feel her tears soak through my shirt as I run my fingers through her hair.

"They gave me drugs, Mom. I didn't want them." She looks up at me, her eyes red and wet. "But then I did want them, so I didn't have to know what was going on."

"You did what you needed to do to survive, baby." I kiss her forehead. "We are going to get you help, okay?"

She continues to nod.

"I promise you that everything will be okay."

She nods, looking at me with all the hope in the world. The door opens and Mick walks in carrying a tray full of food. "Okay, ladies, Dorothy said I couldn't bring anything from outside in, so I had to settle for the cafeteria, which was slim pickings. She also said you could only have liquids, so this is what I got," he says as he places the tray on the rolling bedside table. "Beef broth, vegetable broth, chicken broth, Orange Jell-o, Strawberry Jell-o, Lemon Jell-o, Lime Jell-o." He looks at both of us with a smile on his face.

I haven't looked closely at him in the last couple of days. His face is covered with stubble since he hasn't left my side. His hair is sticking up in places. But his face is soft, his eyes shine, and his strength is there for both of us.

"Why are you still here?" Lori asks, and I look at Mick. We haven't discussed what we are. It's been less than a week.

"I'm here because I want to be here. I'm here because there is nowhere else I want to be." He sits next to his tray on the bed. "And I'm here because of your mom."

That is all he says. He doesn't add anything else and neither do I.

"Okay," Lori says as I help her to sit up on the bed. "I think I'll take some Jell-o."

"You got it, baby girl," Mick says as he positions the rolling table with the hospital tray on it over Lori's lap.

We sit in silence as Lori eats all the Jell-o. She stays awake for over an hour before finally falling back to sleep in my arms. With my daughter in my arms and Mick by my side, I finally let go and fall asleep.

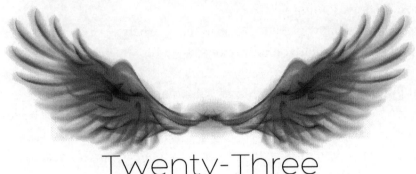

Twenty-Three

Mick

Six days ago, I brought her in. Six days ago, I fell in love with a girl I saw in a picture. Six days ago, I held her mother and fell in love with her. I thought I knew what love was. I was wrong. It's not light and fluffy.

It gripped me by the fucking balls. It made my chest hurt when they cried. It made my heart beat faster when they smiled. It was fucking everything. I knew then and there nothing and no one would ever touch them again. *Ever.*

I finally left them alone to go home and shower. Fuck, did that ever feel good. My next stop would be to call Bella and ask her to stay with Lori so Marissa could go shower. I know she doesn't want to leave her, but she needs to get out.

Right when I walk out of the house, I get a text from Marissa.

Can you get McDonald's when you come back? Lori wants a Big Mac.

Sure thing. What else do you guys need?

Just you ;) and some Big Macs, and now Taco Bell. Pick up whatever is easier.

Send me what you want from there.

The next text is their whole order. Jesus, you would think that there were fifteen people ordering. Who needs ten caramel apple empanadas?

I just laugh it off and drive to my first stop. The phone rings as I'm waiting for the order. It's Jackson.

"Yo," I say to him.

"Hey, how is everything? How are Marissa and Lori?"

"Doing well, finally, all things considered. What's up?"

He breathes deeply before he continues, "We have to come in today and interview her. I don't want to. Trust me, I know you don't want to think about it, but we need her statement. The other girls have already given theirs."

I rub my hands over my face, knowing that it needs to be done, but I'm not happy about it. I don't want it to happen, but I know if we are going to bring Chuck to justice, it needs to be done. She's the one who was with them the longest.

"Okay. Give me an hour. I should be back at the hospital by then," I respond, taking my first order from the Taco Bell cashier and driving toward McDonald's. "What else you have?"

"I didn't want to tell you, but Sandie has been in. Says she needs to talk to you. It's urgent."

"Fuck her. Urgent to her is a fucking broken fingernail," I say, shaking my head.

"Pretty much what I told her. See you in an hour," he says before disconnecting.

I make my way to Taco Bell and arrive into the room with six bags of food. "Who ordered what?" I say to them when I put it all on the bed. Both girls dive into the bags of food. Marissa reaches for the fries, while Lori bites into one of the caramel apple empanadas and moans.

Watching them both eat, I take this time to let them know what is going to happen. "Jackson needs to ask you some stuff." I look at both of them.

Marissa stops chewing, and Lori's eyes open wide in shock and fear.

"I know you don't want to talk about it, but we need to if we are going to put Chuck away."

Lori's eyes fill with tears as she looks at me.

"Will you be here, too?" she asks me.

"Only if you want me to be." She nods her head yes, and I instantly reply, "Then I'll be here."

She then looks at her mom. "Are you going to stay, too?"

"Of course I'm going to stay." Marissa tries to smile, but the tears welling in her eyes give her emotions away. "Now eat, before it gets cold."

She looks over at me, and I nod my head at her. I want to kiss her so bad, give her my strength, and give her anything she fucking needs.

They eat in silence, both of them soon saying that they are full, but we all know it's the nervousness in their stomachs that's making them stop eating.

Twenty minutes later, Jackson walks in with Thomas and Chris following him. Jackson says hello to Marissa, and he introduces her to Thomas and Chris.

Lori gasps when she looks at Chris, and everyone's eyes in the room swing between the two of them. "You were there at the mall," she reminds him. "I saw you."

He looks at her like he's trying to piece the memory together.

"Yes, my friend came up to you and asked for your number. You told her you don't date high school girls."

"Oh my God," he says, everything finally clicking into place for him. "I was there. Oh my God, I was there! I could have stopped it!" he says, his voice climbing.

"No, you couldn't have stopped it," Lori says while she looks down at her hands. "Okay, let's get this over with."

"Lori," Jackson starts, "I'm going to be the one asking you questions, unless you don't feel comfortable with me."

"No, it's okay. Everyone is going to know anyway, right?" she asks us. "I mean, everyone working on the case will read all about it anyway, won't they?" She looks at me, waiting for the answer.

"Yeah, Lori. Everyone working on this case will read the file."

Marissa sits next to her, holding her hand, both of their hands white from gripping each other so tightly. I walk to the other side of her bed to stand there. She reaches her hand out to me, and I take it in mine.

"Okay, let's get this over with," she tells us, trying to look brave.

I give her hand a squeeze, and she squeezes my hand tight back.

"Okay, tell us how this started. From the very beginning, and please don't leave anything out. No detail is too small or insignificant, okay?"

"I met this guy at the mall. Name was Ryan. He came over to talk with me when I was alone, waiting for Rachel to come back from trying on clothes. We sat down and talked about school and stuff. He said he went to Centennial, and well, that was how it started. We exchanged numbers, and we started texting each other. We kept talking. Nothing big at first, though. You know, just talking about friends, school, and home, stuff like that."

Jackson scribbles in his notebook. "Okay, when and how did it change?"

Lori looks at her mother then down at her lap. "I got into a fight with Mom. I went over my cell phone data. It was an extra fifty dollars, and she was pissed. Really pissed. I told Ryan about it." She sucks in a deep breath. "He said I should come meet him, that he would cheer me up. So I, um, just left. Mom was leaving for work. I knew she'd be home later. So I ran out. I didn't even say goodbye." She lets go of my hand to wipe her tears away, and my eyes shift to Marissa, who is looking down at their hands.

"Okay, Lori, doing well. Where did he take you?" Jackson asks.

I know he hates this just as much as we do.

"I met him at the mall and then he said we should go for a ride, so I went with him. We drove around a bit, listening to music. Then we parked near a park. We made out for a bit, and he started getting a little too handsy, if you know what I mean. He offered me some water, and I started sipping it and then I remember my head started to get woozy." Her hands start to tremble now. "I need water, please," she asks, and Chris brings her a water bottle, but she doesn't want to take it. "It's sealed. You can trust me." She nods her head at him and opens the bottle, listening to the click of the bottle opening.

After taking a couple of sips she continues, "I looked at him and told him I didn't feel well and to take me home. He laughed. I still remember that laugh, like it was evil, snickering. I closed my eyes and the next thing I knew I woke up in the motel room. My clothes stripped off and Adam lying next to me." She looks down, and I just know she is feeling ashamed.

I take her chin in my hand gently, raising it to look at me. "You didn't want that," I tell her. "Just remember that. Don't you feel shame for something that happened to you that you didn't want or ask for."

She just nods at me.

"Adam was naked next to me. He was breathing heavy. He looked over at me and said that he loved fucking virgins." She stops talking to take another sip of water.

My body is shaking with anger. I look at Jackson, who just shakes his head. If Adam wasn't already dead, this would be him signing his own death certificate. I hear the sound of the door opening and closing, and I look around to see that Chris has stepped outside.

"Did you try to leave?" Jackson asks her.

"I tried to get up the minute he said that, slowly because my head was spinning, but I didn't even get all the way up when I noticed the chains on my feet. I was chained to the bed. I asked who he was. I asked him where Ryan was, and all he did was laugh. He got up after that and went into the bathroom. I looked around the room for something, anything that could help me. But there was nothing. No phone, no weapons, not even a lamp I could hit him with. I looked back at him in the bathroom. The door was open, and I saw him shoot up." She takes a deep breath and continues, "He was sitting on the toilet, his head against the wall. There was a needle in his arm, and he closed his eyes and moaned. Then the door opened and Chuck came in the room. I didn't know who he was till Adam stumbled out of the bathroom. Chuck called him a junkie and then introduced himself, telling me he was my new boss. I didn't understand what he meant till he opened the door and another strange man came in. He was old, maybe sixty. He was gross. His clothes were dirty. He was almost bald on the top of his head, white stringy on the sides. His teeth were yellow, and he stank like beer and sweat. He was my first customer that night. I begged," she sobbed. "I pleaded with him not to do it." She looks at Marissa then back at Jackson. "I said no, over and over again. He didn't care. He just did what he wanted to do."

My mind is going a million miles a minute. I'm trying to think of any person that I could have met with that description. I know I won't stop till I find him.

"What happened next?" Jackson asks.

"It went on for I don't know how long. The hours turned into days, days turned into weeks. Till someone complained that I was like fucking a corpse. Chuck was pissed. He smacked me right across the face with his fist. The next thing I knew Adam was sticking me with one of his needles. It burned so bad at first. I begged them not to drug me. After that I don't know how long I was out for."

The shaking of the bed draws my attention to Marissa, who is crying openly now. I move to her side of the bed, sit next to her, and curl my arm around her, pulling her into me.

"Do you remember when the other girls came?"

"No. I had no idea what time or day it was. I would come down from my high, they would feed me some crackers, then shoot me up again. The next thing I knew I was chained to the wall while I watched another girl go through the steps. They kept rotating us. Depending on the guys. Some of the guys would come in and choose one of us. We would be untied and then retied to the bed."

I look at her and the tears are gone, her shoulders squared.

"I begged to die. I begged them to kill me. For someone to kill me." Marissa's body stills against mine.

"I always hoped they would give me too much, that they'd overdose me. The days all ran together. Everything was so foggy. The next thing I knew, there were three of us. We tried to help the other one. Two of us were always high while one of us was straight. One time Adam didn't show up for days. Chuck didn't either, and he had no idea that Adam wasn't there. For days, we detoxed and sat there, chained to the wall, with the shakes, with the shivers, with fevers, shitting, and pissing ourselves." The tone of her voice switches from sadness to anger the more she dives into her ordeal.

"Where did Adam go?" Jackson asks.

Lori shrugs her shoulders. "No idea, but when he came back he was all beaten up and bruised." The pen in Jackson's hand snaps. He gets up and walks out the door. Lori looks at me questioningly.

"Okay, I think we need a five-minute breather," Thomas says while he walks out into the hallway. I get up, kissing Marissa on the head and doing the same to Lori before following Thomas and Jackson outside.

I take in my team. Chris is squatted in front of the door, his eyes void of emotion. Thomas is standing by him, hands in his pockets, looking at the floor, and Jackson is standing with his back to the wall, his head back and his eyes closed.

"That was when he was in the hospital. He left them in that room to fucking rot," Jackson says with his teeth gritted together.

Chris looks up at him with question in his eyes. I nod at him to wait.

"Fuck me. That girl lived in his fucking motel room chained to a bed and wall while he pimped her out. I hope he is rotting in hell. I hope worse than that."

"You want me to finish?" Thomas asks, knowing that Jackson is battling his own guilt.

Jackson sighs a deep breath. "No. I have to do this."

"Guys, I hate to rush you, but I want this over. She wants this over."

We all look at each other before I address Chris. "Are you going to be okay?"

He shakes his head no.

"I'm going to get up. I'm going to walk back into the room so she doesn't think I can't stand to look at her. I'm going to pretend I'm okay with it all. I'm going to pretend that it's not killing me, then tonight I'm going to get so drunk I'm hoping to burn the images from my head," Chris says while he gets up and puts on his face, but his eyes tell you that he just died inside a bit. It's a look that he would kill to protect her. It's a look that a man who is caught under a spell looks like. I know because I have the same look except mine is for both of them.

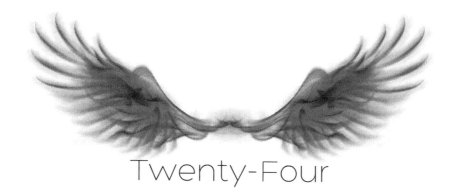

Twenty-Four

Marissa

As a mother, you always wonder a couple of things. Milestones we call them. Her first word, her first step, first day of school. The first time she gets her heart broken, the first kiss. Never in a million years did I think I would sit down and have to hear about the first time my daughter got raped. Not only raped but her virginity stolen from her.

Sitting there listening to the hell she went through was the hardest thing I ever had to do. Being unable to do anything to help her is like living in your worst nightmare and not being able to open your eyes.

Her strength, her determination, her courage is something you could only imagine your child to be. But seeing it with my eyes, I know that it's not going to be easy. It's going to be the hardest time in her life, but she will prevail. There is no doubt in my mind.

"Mom."

I finally snap out of my daydream. "Yeah, honey."

"Mick is right, you should go home, get a shower." She looks at me. Only twenty-four hours ago, she laid out her nightmare for us all to hear and she survived.

"Babe, you need to shower." He looks at me with a smirk.

I shake my head no when there is a knock at the door.

"Can we come in?" Bella sticks her head in.

We don't have time to answer before her daughter, Lilah, pushes the door open.

"I bwing pwesnts, Ukle Mick!" she says, running in, holding a bag bigger than herself. She jumps up into his lap, and he leans forward to blow kisses in her neck. I look at them, at the softness he has with her. Look at the way his hands hold her.

"Hi, sorry to interrupt, but I'm Jackson's girlfriend, Bella, and this is my daughter, Lilah," Bella says while reaching out her hand to shake Lori's. "We wanted to just stop and see if you need anything," she says softly, looking at Lori, tears in her eyes.

"Ukle Mick, you spit on my neck." She giggles. "I got pwesnts but not for you, for Looriii." She looks at him and gets close to his face and whispers, "She's the bwavest."

"Oh, I know that, Lilah chinchilla, go give her the present. Do you want me to carry it for you?" he asks.

"No, I strong, look," she says while trying to put her arms up and flex.

"Lilah, don't do that." Bella shakes her head. "I told Jackson to stop teaching her these things." She laughs.

"Hi," Lilah says while she climbs on the bed. "I'm Lilah and I'm four," she says, holding out her five fingers.

"Hi, Lilah, I'm Lori." She smiles at her and ruffles her hair.

"I bwing you something." She lifts the bag on the bed. She looks at her mom and then back at Lori, whispering, "If you need help I can unwap it for you."

Lori bends even further into Lilah. "My hands really hurt. Can you open it for me?"

Lilah's eyes almost bulge out of her sockets. "Mama, I open pwesnts for Looori."

She rips the tissue paper apart, pulling out a small pink teddy bear with a white heart in the middle. "I chose that." She points to her. "Smell the belly. Strawberry." She leans forward and smells it. "See, berry." She smiles at Lori and then opens the next one, which is pink pjs. "Mamma chose that. They's boring." She holds the teddy bear, smelling it again.

"These are my favorite pjs in the whole world. I'm going to change into them right now," Lori says, getting up and going into the washroom.

"Thank you so much." I grab Bella's hand and squeeze it.

She looks at me with tears in her eyes. "I'm so, so sorry."

We don't say much else because Lori comes out of the bathroom wearing the pjs. The pants have hearts all over them and there, in the middle of the top, is written 'You're a whole lot of lovely'.

"You so beautiful. Hey, Ukle Mick?" Lilah asks.

"Yes, she is, baby, she is really, really beautiful."

Lori just smiles at them and then walks back to the bed.

"Okay, Lilah, time to go. Say goodbye, love," Bella says to Lilah.

"Bye, Looori." She bounces on her bum and then Mick reaches out to help her off the bed. "Bye, Ms. Marissa." She grabs Mick's face between her hands. "Bye, Ukle Mick." She kisses his cheek and tries to whisper in his ear, but her whisper isn't low. "You got candy?"

It makes Mick throw his head back and laugh at her. "No, baby girl, I don't have any, but next time I'll bring double."

She settles with that and wiggles herself down to grab her mother's hand, turning around and waving before walking out, telling Bella that Jackson said she could have ice cream before dinner.

"She was there," Lori says quietly from her bed. "I remember her."

I look at Mick, who starts, "Yeah, she was there. Adam kidnapped her. It was because of her we found you guys early. She had her phone on her."

Lori shakes her head, wiping tears from her face. "I want to go see her and Lilah when I get better."

I nod my head yes.

There is another knock on the door.

"Jesus, it's like a revolving door around here," Mick says.

The doctor walks in with the chart and the nurse. "Hey there, Lori, how are we doing today?"

"I'm okay."

"How are we doing with the urges to get high?" he asks.

"Sometimes I think about it. More so my body wonders. I start having the shakes and my stomach aches."

"That is a perfectly normal thing to go through. I'm going to set you up with a doctor for therapy as well as get you a sponsor to talk things through. I know that you said you didn't want to go into rehab, but I will leave you these pamphlets for you to think about and weigh your options." He drops them on the bed between us. "I'm also going to give you happy news. You can go home. There is no reason to keep you here anymore. But if you get home and have any symptoms of relapsing or your fever gets high or the shakes are uncontrollable, I suggest coming back."

"We can go home?" Lori says with tears in her eyes.

"You can go home, Lori." The doctor nods at Mick and then at me before walking out.

"Mom, we get to go home," she says with a smile. "I get to sleep in my bed."

"Let's blow this popsicle stand," I tell her, getting up, looking at Mick, who is still sitting down in the chair, his feet bouncing on the floor. "What's wrong?"

"Promise not to freak out?" he says with worry on his face.

"What happened?" I ask, my heart pounding, my hands getting clammy.

"There is no way to say this, so I'll just say it. I moved you guys out of your apartment."

My mouth opens and closes, no words coming out.

"Okay, before you freak out just listen. Jackson's mom is moving into his house and out of hers. She was looking to rent it out," he says.

"You moved us into a house?" Lori asks.

"The rent is the same as the apartment, so there isn't anything extra."

"I can't afford that. I have so much debt, and I had a deal on that rent because I owed him the extra." I start picking up the tissue paper that has been torn all over the place by Lilah.

"It's finished," he says, and I look up at him. "It's over. You're free."

I don't think it registers right away till Lori starts sobbing in her bed. "Mom, you're free."

"What?" I look at him. "How?"

"Finished. Over. You owe him nothing."

I sit on the bed, my heart beating so hard into my chest I hear it echo in my ears.

"I offered him a deal that he couldn't refuse."

"Oh my God, he totally just God Fathered that. Mick, I thought you were badass before, but now, now you are legit a badass," Lori says while she packs the tissues into the bag. "Mom, we get to live in a house. No more crack addicts blocking the door. No more gunshots in the middle of the night. No more creepy neighbor trying to show us his dick."

I'm still in shock. "You paid off my debt," I whisper to him while he nods his head yes.

I get up, walk over to him, and grab his face into my hands. "I love you." I kiss him. "I know it's been maybe seven days that we've been together, but no one, no one has ever done what you do. You take care of me. You brought my baby home and now you make us safe." I kiss him again while squeezing his face. "Right down to my soul, Mick."

He starts to say something, but I put my finger on his lips. "You don't get to take this moment away from me."

He smiles under my finger.

"Thank you."

"Mom, can you stop making out with Mick so he can bring us home?" she says, throwing the magazine in a bag, clearing out the room.

"Let me bring you home, angel," is all he says.

I grab his hand and let him lead me home.

Twenty-Five

Mick

It's been three days since I drove Marissa and Lori to their new home. Three days of sitting down and having meals with them, sharing my day with them. It hasn't been all smooth sailings. There have also been three nights of nightmares, nausea, sweating.

Last night I sat on the couch with Lori. After she woke up whining, I carried her downstairs to the couch, giving her warm water with honey. I watched her roll into a ball from the pains in her stomach.

"How long does this shit last?" she asks between cramps.

I shake my head because I have no idea. I couldn't even begin to tell her. "I haven't a clue, but I think it gets easier every day. At least that is what I hope," I tell her while I go wet a cloth to put it on her head.

"You love her, don't you?"

Her question doesn't catch me off guard. You would be blind to not see the signs. I'm sitting here at three a.m. making warm water with honey and chatting with a sixteen-year-old while she detoxes so her mother can sleep.

"With everything I have," I tell her while taking a sip of the warm coffee that is in my hand.

"She never had anyone put her first. Ever. From as long as I can remember she was the rock. She..." She closes her eyes, her body shaking.

I wait for the tremors to pass. "Yup, it gets better." She laughs out. "Told you," I say with a smile.

"She deserves happiness. She deserves to be spoiled. She deserves to be put up on a pedestal because no one has done that for her. My father used to come and go, just bringing more drama and shit to our door." She shakes her head. "I hope he never finds us. I hope he doesn't come here," she says while she closes her eyes, breathing deeply.

I wait for a couple of minutes to pass before walking over to the couch and putting a cover over her. She doesn't stir. I make my way upstairs. I've never slept in the bed with her since I've been here. I usually sleep on the couch, but I have to hold her. I have to feel her.

Walking into the room, I see her curled up with her face looking at the door. The softness of her breathing lets me know she is out for the count. I crawl into bed next to her on top of the covers in case Lori comes upstairs.

Gathering her in my arms and molding my body to hers, I breathe her in. Strawberries. I kiss her neck softly, trying not to wake her. Obviously not soft enough since she stirs and opens her eyes.

"Mick?" she asks, confused.

"It better only be me who crawls into bed with you," I tell her.

She grinds her ass into my cock, which wakes up, thinking it's playtime. I groan out.

"Yup, definitely, Mick," she says with a laugh. "Where is Lori?"

"On the couch."

She immediately goes to get up, but my arm around her waist holds her down.

"She's sleeping, babe. Leave her be. If she calls out, I'll hear her."

"Okay, Mick," she says, laying her head on the pillow. "I love you." Two seconds later, her soft snores fill the room.

"I love you, too," I whisper to her and fall into slumber right next to her with a peace that has seeped into my body.

I don't even feel her get out of bed, nor do I hear them downstairs making breakfast and chatting away. I wake only when I feel her crawl onto the bed to give me kisses on my face.

"Baby, Jackson is on the phone."

I open my eyes and look at her. The sunlight from outside fills the room right behind her, making her brown hair shine, making her look like an angel. I drag her down to me, kissing her lips.

She pushes off me. "Jackson is on the phone." She laughs, handing me my cell and then walking out of the room, shaking her ass all the way there.

Thoughts of turning her pink run through my mind. My morning hard-on gets even harder.

"Yeah," is the only thing I say while one hand rubs up and down my face.

"Is sleeping beauty ever coming back into work?" he asks jokingly.

I haven't been in since I found Lori. I know I have to go in and write my report. They say you should finish your report in less than twenty-four hours so the memories are still fresh. Well, almost two weeks later, I still can't get the memories out of my head.

"Yeah, yeah. I'm coming in today. What time is it?" I ask, unaware of how long I slept.

"Almost noon."

I sit up, throwing the cover that Marissa must've put on me when she got up. "I'm going to shower and then head in." I walk over to my bag that sits on top of the dresser, grabbing a change of clothes before making my way into the en suite bathroom.

I disconnect the phone, throwing it on the bed from the doorway. Once inside, I close the door but don't lock it. I open the water, testing to make sure it's warm enough. Peeling down my boxers, I kick them off with my feet. My cock is still hard as fuck.

I make my way inside the shower, the warm water cascading around me. I place my hands on the wall under the stream of water, letting the water fall on my neck and flow down. I close my eyes, making the heat of the water seep into me.

I'm in there for maybe a couple of minutes when I feel a draft come in. Standing up, I see Marissa naked getting in the shower. I take her in. She has lost weight if that is even possible. Her body was always tight but with no fat on her. Her tits are still the same size, her pussy bald with a pink diamond sticking out. "Where is Lori?"

"Downstairs with Bella and Lilah, who came by to visit," she says while she advances to me. "I needed to take a shower." She grabs a hold of my cock, my head thrown back.

She jerks it twice, twisting when she gets to the top. She gets on her tippy toes, and I bend my neck, meeting her lips halfway. My mouth opens instantly as does hers, our tongues rushing to find each other. My hands reach out to palm her breasts, squeezing them hard. I use my thumb and forefinger to roll her nipples. Her moan is lost in my mouth. Her hand is still working my cock, but her thumb flicks the ball at the top every time her fist comes up.

I take one hand and move it down to her pussy. My finger runs down her slit, finding it wet from the water yet sticking with her juices. Moving my mouth from hers, I make my way to her earlobe, where I suck it at the same time, and I slam a finger inside her hot, wet pussy. She lifts one foot, placing it on the ledge of the bathtub to give me better access. Her moans echo into the room.

"Baby, sshhh." I look at her eyes, half-mast and lazy, almost staying closed while I finger fuck her with one finger then adding in another. Her fist never gives it up, matching the pace of my finger fucking her.

I move down to kiss her neck, sucking it and biting while I assault her pussy, her juices running down my hand. I use my thumb to press her piercing down, rubbing it up and down while pressing down. The minute I do that her pussy starts to throb. She bites down on her lips while she gets up and down on her tippy toes while she meets the thrust with her pussy. I watch her come apart on my hand, and it's almost too much. "I'm going to come," I whisper, and in two seconds, she is down on her knees, taking my cock to the back of her throat. She flips my piercing with her tongue twice and then puts it between her teeth, pulling up, the sensation shooting straight to my balls. It's the last straw before I grab her head. "Fuck," is all I say, and she swallows me in her mouth, sucking everything I have to offer her.

I stop thrusting my hips, but she doesn't stop working my cock with her mouth till I go a little soft. "That was..." I grab her face, kissing her lips. "That was so fucking hot."

Her nipples graze my chest. I moan out, but she pushes me away. "We really need to hurry up before they actually think we are having sex up here," she says, pushing me out of the way so she can get some warm water on her, but the water has turned cold, so she turns the knob to hotter, the water turning a touch warmer.

I watch her take a quick shower, soaping up her body. She must see I'm one second away before having breakfast in the shower when she points at me.

"You have to go to work. I have to go to the doctor with Lori." And she rushes out of the shower before I pounce.

Soap suds are still on her body while she dries herself off. She sticks her head out of the bathroom door, looking to see if the coast is clear before rushing to get dressed.

I follow her out a couple of minutes later, dressing in the bathroom in case Lori comes upstairs.

When I get back into the bedroom, I notice that she has made the bed, folded my clothes, and left them by the bag, not in the bag but next.

I don't have time to think about it before my phone starts ringing again. This time I miss the call from Chris. I don't call him back since he sends a text asking me to pick up lunch on my way in.

I put the phone in my back pocket and make my way downstairs where I spend five minutes listening to giggles before kissing all the girls on the cheek and heading out the door on my way to work with a smile plastered on my face.

Twenty-Six

Marissa

Washing the dishes in the sink, I look out into the yard. I have a yard. Bella and Lori are sitting at the table talking about school options, while Lilah sits in the living room playing with her dolls.

"What time is this group therapy at?" Lori asks, taking a bite of the cookies that Lilah baked for her.

We sat down yesterday and decided that rehab would be out of the question. She doesn't want to be away from me. Although it would kill me to be apart from her after everything, I would do it if she wanted to.

After attending a session with a therapist after we got out of the hospital, we were sold on the idea of group therapy mostly for teens. So today is our first day. I'm lucky that Phyllis is giving me the rest of the week off and didn't fire me, so I have a couple more days before I have to go back to work.

We also have to decide if Lori will go back to the school she went to. We aren't in the same school district, so she has to decide if she wants to switch or do the commute.

"Three o'clock," I tell her, wiping my hand on a dishtowel, walking over to the table, and sitting down. "Are you nervous?"

She looks down at the cookie in front of her, nodding. "What if they look at me and judge me?"

Bella reaches out to grab her hand. "Then fuck them."

I gasp out loud while Lori smiles.

"I don't think anyone sitting in a group therapy session should be judging anyone. You all ended up there. You just took different roads to get there."

Lori nods and goes upstairs to get ready.

"Thank you." I manage a smile.

She waves her hand my way. "Thank you? Please. I owe you two more than I care to think about. If I hadn't been a coward and turned Adam in a long time ago, none of this would have happened. That's on me." She clamps her hands together. "Okay, Lilah, time to rock and roll," she says while Lilah starts to gather her dolls in her arms, bringing them over.

"Rok and roll, Momma," she says with a smile.

I walk her to the door, waving at her once she gets in the car and drives off. I return into the house, watching Lori come down the stairs. She is dressed all in black. It's something I haven't mentioned to her, but since she got back, the only colorful things she has worn have been the pjs Bella bought her. "You look so pretty," I tell her, hugging her. She has long since passed me in height.

"You, too, short stuff." A nickname she used to call me before all this happened.

"I can still ground you." Was always what I would come back with.

I walk around, making sure the doors are all locked before we leave. While we are in the car, she takes her ear buds and puts them in her ears, closing herself off. I turn up the radio, hoping to settle the butterflies in my stomach.

I look over at Lori and her hands are going a mile a minute with her texting. I tap her leg. "Who are you texting?"

"Mick." She doesn't look up, just continues typing away. Once she sends the message she looks over at me. "He wanted to wish me luck and tell me that this doesn't define who I am." She shrugs her shoulders and looks out of the window. "He never once looked at me like I was dirty," she says while quickly wiping away a tear that has fallen out of her eye.

"That's because you aren't dirty. Did you ever ask those men to do that stuff to you?" I ask her, but she just shakes her head. "Then you're not dirty, and even if you did ask all those men to do that it doesn't make you dirty."

I don't continue talking because we have reached our destination. From the outside, you would never tell what it is. There is a Starbucks two doors down, a Subway next door to it. On the door is just the name "Footprints in the Sand."

We both get out of the car and stand here watching. Lori reaches out for my hand and that is how we enter, hand in hand.

Once we make it inside, it looks just like a medical office. There is a receptionist at the front to take our name and usher us to one of the rooms in the back. Each room has the same thing.

There are chairs set in a circle, and there are poems surrounding the walls. I hear Lori read one.

"Peach is said to be offered on the wings of a dove. Prayers can bring peace along with hope, faith, and love." She traces the writing with her fingers. "Mom, can we put this saying up in my room?"

I nod, afraid to talk and she hears my voice ready to crack. We aren't alone for long. Slowly people trickle in. Two girls I think to be Lori's age come in. Both go to sit down next to each other. Next a boy walks in. He's about six feet, his sandy blond hair long and flipped to the side. His blue eyes are almost crystal blue like the picture of the ocean from Bora Bora. He spots us and raises his hand to say hi then proceeds to go sit next to the girls who came in before. They both exchange pleasantries, and a couple more kids come in, filling in the empty seats.

"I think we should get a seat before they are all taken."

Right before we go to the chairs a man comes in. He looks to be about forty, dressed in khakis, his hair cut in a preppy way. His glasses sit on his nose. He sees us and makes his way over to us.

He smiles at us before introducing himself. "Hi there, my name is Daniel. I run this session. You must be Lori and you must be Marissa." He reaches out his hand to both of us. He looks around at the room. There are about twenty people now that have sat down. "I know it's overwhelming at first, but you could just sit back and listen. We are not here to judge anyone or point fingers. We are here to make you see that you aren't alone. That even if you think no one knows how you feel, I'm sure we have all been through it."

He puts his hands in his pockets while Lori speaks to him. "You're an addict?" she asks, wringing her hands.

"Recovering. Twelve years, ten months, four days, and a couple of hours. My rock bottom was watching my two-year-old son drown before my eyes. I was too high to even comprehend what was going on." He must see the shock and sorrow on my face because he goes on. "That is what I have to fight each and every day. So I can assure you, Lori, there is someone here that feels what you do."

She nods her head at him, looking around.

Daniel speaks to the group now. "Okay, everyone, if you haven't found a seat now is a good time. We will be starting in a minute."

We walk over and sit down in the two empty seats. I sit next to Daniel, and Lori is sitting next to me with the guy from before next to her. I squeeze her knee before the group starts, to let her know that I'm here in case she needs anything from me.

"Hey, everyone, I'm Daniel. I'm a heroin addict. Today is my son's or would have been my son's birthday. I got up this morning and the first thing I wanted to do was go back to bed. I wanted to get high. But instead I got up and ran on the treadmill, listening to the lullabies that would play through the baby monitor." He takes off his glasses and wipes his eyes. "Today I'm going to be strong. Today I'm going to beat this."

Everyone around the circle repeats his last sentence.

The rest of the circle filled us in on their name and how long they have been sober. Cocaine addicts, alcoholics, eating disorders. You name them, there was someone here suffering from it.

When it came time for the boy next to Lori to speak, he did it with his hands on his legs, looking at the floor. "My name is Trevor. I'm nineteen. I was born addicted to crack. My parents were crack tweakers. I didn't even know it was a thing till I was old enough to understand what was going on. My father came from a really religious family who crossed him off the list the minute he got his girlfriend pregnant out of wedlock. Forget the fact that they were both on crack when they did it. We lived with my mom's family till they kicked us out of the house, because shit just started disappearing. The good news is they kept me. Well, good news for me, till their dealer came to collect their debt and shot my grandparents in front of me. I was fourteen when I was put into foster care. No one wanted me. It started with weed. Smoke a little weed, take the edge off. Then moved up to cocaine at parties, then the first time I shot up heroin was like I was finally free. I could fly. I really thought I was the shit on it. Till I turned sixteen and got raped and beaten for the first time. It was a never-ending cycle. Till I finally hit rock bottom. Till I finally looked into the eyes of my father, or at least I know it was my father. He, on the other hand, had no clue who the fuck I was. When I called him Dad he laughed at me, his rotten green teeth sticking out. I looked around for my mother, asked him about her, and he said she died. He didn't even fucking remember when she died or where. Just shrugged. I walked into church that night and prayed for help. I fell asleep inside the church till the priest woke me and asked me my name. The only thing I knew was my name. He got me help. He got me into rehab. So my name is Trevor, and I haven't used drugs in two years, four months, and nine days." He finally looks up, his eyes red with tears. "Today I'm going to be strong. Today I'm going to beat this."

Once again, they repeat it after him. It's Lori's turn and she looks over at me. I give her a nod, letting her know that either way it's going to be okay.

She grabs a hold of my hand and starts. "My name is Lori and it's been almost two weeks that I've been off heroin. I was kidnapped." A gasp runs through the group while she wipes her cheeks. "And they gave me heroin to stop me from escaping. Along with other sick, sick things."

Trevor looks over at her while she looks at him and gives her a smile of support.

"I sometimes wake up and think if I get high today I won't have to remember the memories. I don't want to remember some things, and I think if I get high again I won't have to face it. But then I open my eyes and look outside and I am not chained to a wall. I can go outside. I can touch the grass. I can do all that, so I fight it. I guess every day will be a 'today I'm going to be strong. Today I'm going to beat this'."

I repeat after her. I introduce myself, telling them all that I'm Lori's mom but not an addict.

The group lasts more than two hours. Once it's over, Daniel says he will be right back, so we get up and walk over to the water machine in the corner.

Trevor walks up to Lori. "Your story blew me away. I know I haven't been sober long, but if you ever need me just to talk or anything, here is my number." He hands her a paper with his number on it. She thanks him, and he walks away.

Daniel comes to us with a booklet of different courses and therapy sessions that they offer. He also suggests her enrolling back in school, maybe see if she can take some online courses. He gives us both his cell number to reach out to him with any questions.

We walk to the car right when the phone rings. Looking down, I see it's Mick.

"Hey," I say while unlocking the car doors.
"How did it go?" he asks with a worried tone.

I look over at Lori with a smile. "I think it went really, really well."
"Good. I can't wait to hear about it. I'm about to leave for home. Want to meet me there? We could eat outside."

I look at Lori and ask her if she wants to go. She nods her head yes then tucks her ear buds in her ears.
"Sure, we are on the way. I'll stop and pick up pie from Phyllis's."

"Maybe I can taste your pie tonight," he says, and I quickly look back at Lori to see if she heard anything, but her head is moving to the beat of her music. "What do you say? Can I have some strawberry pie tonight?"
"Mick," I hiss out. "I'll see you in thirty minutes." I hang up while I hear him laughing in the background.

Lori takes her ear buds out. "Mom, can we stop and get me a notebook or something?"
"Sure, honey, we can stop now."

I make my way to the diner with Lori beside me. The sun is shining, I got myself a kick ass man, and my daughter is safe. Maybe he just might get to eat strawberry pie tonight.

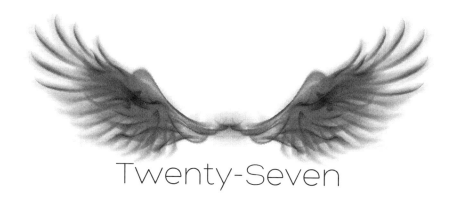

Twenty-Seven

Mick

First day back at the office is kicking my ass. I keep looking over at the time, then my phone, then the time, then the time on the computer, just hoping it goes by fast.

They are attending their first therapy session, and I wanted to be there, but I didn't want to overstep, so I went to work.

Now here I am on my way home to make supper for my girls. I pull up and park deep in the driveway so she can park in the back of me. Walking up the steps, I see a bright yellow note taped to the door.

We need to talk, Mick. It's urgent and important. Sandie

I take the note, crumple it in my hand, and toss it in the trash the minute I get in. I open some windows to get some air going through it. I haven't been home in two weeks, unless it was to get clothes and it shows.

I go to the fridge taking out a beer, twisting the cap off. I grab some steaks from the freezer, throwing them in the sink, and I'm just about to check for some rice when I hear a knock and then the door open.

"Knock, knock," I hear Lori say. "We brought food." She carries a huge takeout tray. "And strawberry pie."

I choke on the sip of beer that I was drinking.

"Are you okay, Mick?" she asks, worried I might choke.

I look up at her and hear Marissa in the background snickering. I grab a towel to wipe the beer off my lips while I glare at her.

"Mick, Phyllis said you better be at her house Sunday to fix the light switch or she will tan your hide," Lori tells me this while taking the cover off the takeout tray. "Oh my gosh, look. It's chicken steak and homemade mac and cheese. Yummy." She lifts her head to look out the window, her mouth opening in a gasp. "Oh, look at the water. Mick, can I go sit by the water while you guys get ready for dinner?"

"Sure thing, there are two chairs down there."

She reaches in a bag to take out a notebook and then walks down to the water.

"What's with the notebook?" I ask Marissa while watching Lori.

"She said she wants to write." She shrugs her shoulders. "Someone mentioned it in therapy, so maybe she will try it."

I walk to her, grabbing her into my arms and lowering my face to meet her lips. She places one hand on my face while the other one goes around my neck. "Missed you," I tell her with my lips pressed to hers.

"Mmmhm," she says while she opens her mouth and slides her tongue along mine, tilting her head to the left so the angle is better. The taste of her makes me come alive. She breaks the kiss softly, pulling away, still giving me little kisses. One hand comes up and rubs her lips.

"Why don't you get the plates and silverware and I'll carry out the food? I, for one, am starving."

She pulls out of the embrace, walking to the counter.

I grab her ass while she walks by me and groan. "Fuck, that ass will be the death of me," I tell her while getting all the stuff to go outside.

Once we make it outside and set up food on the plates, we call Lori to come eat. She walks up to the table, notebook in hand, phone in hand, and a smile on her face. "I love it out here." She places her stuff next to her plate.

"You are welcome to come over any time you want. Even if I'm not home and your mom says it's okay." I start eating my food, scared to ask about their session, but I do anyway. "So how was today?" I cut my chicken and pop a piece in my mouth.

Lori takes a sip of water and then talks. "It was good. We met a couple of people, heard sad stories. Mick, one guy watched his kid die," she tells me, her eyes going wide. "There were mostly kids my age. One guy had parents that were 'tweakers'."

"Did you feel uncomfortable?" I ask her while she chews her bite of food.

"I did at the beginning, but then I heard their stories. I found out that we are all going through the same thing. Sure, I didn't put myself there. It wasn't my choice, but each one of us fights every day not to go back. So they are just like me," she says while she shrugs her shoulders and takes another bite. "I know we have pie, but can we go for ice cream?"

I don't even give Marissa time to think about it. "Sure, you know what? I'll call Jackson and they usually bring Lilah for ice cream. I can still have my pie later." I look over at Marissa, making sure Lori isn't looking and perk up my eyebrows. She is the one now glaring at me and I'm the one snickering the rest of the meal.

We take her car to the ice cream parlor, all of us getting our favorites. Jackson and Bella pass on the invite, so it's just the three of us. We sit down and talk about nothing and everything. I find out about Lori and when she was growing up. The stories that Marissa tells make us all laugh. It's in the car on the way home that Lori asks to be dropped off at home. We look at each other, not wanting to say no, yet knowing she needs to be alone. After dropping her off, Marissa tells her that she will be back soon.

It's crazy that in my mind I've already got her naked and bent over my sofa. Fuck, just the thought has me grabbing my dick. "Whatcha got there, big boy?" Marissa says, snickering from the passenger seat.

"I'll give you a big boy so hard your pussy will be remembering me tomorrow. Can't wait to eat my pie." I look over at her to see her squirm. "You know what is better than pie? Pie on pie. That's right, sweetheart, eating strawberry pie off your pussy. Hmmm, I could just taste it now."

She crosses her legs tight and bites her lip. Her eyes are filled with lust. By the time we make it home, we are both ready to tear each other's clothes off. My mouth lands on hers the minute I close the door, picking her up and walking upstairs.

Two steps up, the doorbell rings. "Ignore it," I tell her between kisses but then knocking starts.

"I know you're in there, Mick. I saw you get home." It's the voice of a bitch. Like nails on a chalkboard.

"FUUUUCKKKK."

"I guess we need to get that?" Marissa says, getting down from my arms.

I make sure she looks okay before opening the door.

Sandie is standing there in her perfect outfit, looking at her nails before pushing herself past me to come in the house. "It's about fucking time you came home. I've been leaving you messages for two weeks now, Mick," she says then finally takes in Marissa standing there in the middle of the room. "Oh, fuck, she's here. Seriously, Mick." She rolls her eyes.

"Sandie, I would watch my mouth if I were you. You left messages. You would get a fucking hint that I don't want your shit or I would have called you back," I tell her, putting my hands on my hips. "Fuck, this is what you came here for?"

"I have something personal to discuss with you." She turns to Marissa. "If you don't mind, you can leave now." She points to the door.

"The only one leaving and isn't wanted here is you," I tell her. "She's not going anywhere. You got something to say, fucking say it. Actually, I don't even fucking care what you have to say." I walk to the door, opening it. "Just fucking leave. Go home, Sandie."

"I'm pregnant."

The two words I've heard before. Two words that changed my life once. Two words that will change my life again.

"It's yours, Mick."

I look from Sandie to Marissa, who is standing there, her face white, her hand in front of her mouth, the tears in her eyes forming, but she blinks them away.

I look back at Sandie, not saying anything, so she opens her purse, taking out a picture, a black and white picture, offering it to me. "I'm four months along. It could only be yours. I left him, Mick."

My hand snatches the picture from her. It's her name on top with dates and shit I don't even understand, but there in the middle of the black paper is a baby, my baby.

"I'm going to go," Marissa says.

I stand here for a second in a fog, my life moving before my eyes. I turn around right before she gets in her car.

"Marissa, wait." I see her back exhale while she turns. Her face shows despair, sadness, her eyes filled with tears. "You can't just leave."

She shakes her head. "Mick, you need to do this." She reaches up and puts her hand on my face. "You're going to be such a great dad. The best dad."

I don't understand what she is saying. I hear the words, but my heart is beating so fast. "These last couple of weeks have been the best ever. I will never ever forget them."

"Marissa, please," I say, begging almost, hoping to fuck this pain in my heart is temporary.

"I can't do it. I won't do it. I won't stand in the way of you having a family. Not now, not ever." She goes to her tippy toes, kissing me on the cheek. "Maybe it just wasn't meant to be."

I grab her face in my hands. "No, no. I'm not letting you go." My heart shatters into pieces. It's a pain that makes you unable to breathe. A pain that if you close your eyes all you see is black.

"You have to let me go. Please, Mick."

She begs me to let her go, but how can I? How can I let her go when I can't live without her? How can I let her go when all my tomorrows have her by my side? How can I let her go when having her is my very own piece of heaven?

She pulls my hands off her face, looking up at me. "Go be a dad, Mick." She drops my hands, getting in the car and driving away.

I watch her till I can't see her lights anymore. I watch her till the memory of her is imprinted in my heart. I stand here looking up, wondering how I could even survive tomorrow when my body is just a shell.

Twenty-Eight

Marissa

The drive back home is a dream of sort. The dream that I almost had it all to the nightmare of it being ripped away from me. Pregnant. She's pregnant with his child.

The thought brings pain to my heart, making it ache. Making it hurt to breathe. Pulling up to the house, I look up and remember waking up with him just twelve hours ago. Watching him sleep. Thanking God for giving him to me. For giving me a second chance.

I blink away the tears. I need to be strong for Lori. She is my number one priority, always. Wiping away the tears with the back of my hand, I walk inside, quietly closing the door. The sound of the click almost makes it final.

"Hey, Mom," she says, and I jump and turn around to look at her. Her hair wet on her head, she's in her pjs, holding the bear under one arm while she carries her notebook in the other. "Mick just texted me. Wanted me to text him when you get home."

A single tear rolls down my face. I don't say anything and just nod my head.

She looks me up and down. "Mom, are you okay?" She advances on me. She must see the pain in my eyes. "Mom, what happened?" she asks. Worry has taken over her face.

"I'm okay, baby. I'm just happy, I'm so happy you're home." I palm her face, bringing her into me. The tears come freely now. She hugs me and kisses me on the head. The roles reversed. Her phone sounds out a beep.

I let go of her to grab a glass of water. "Mom, can I go out tomorrow with Trevor? He's going to the library. He says the peace helps. Can I go? He said he could come and get me."

"Sure, honey. I want you to text me when you leave and when you get wherever you're going, okay?"

She rolls her eyes at me, almost like she did back then.

"Hey, I went a long time without you. I don't want to do it again, okay?"

She looks up at me. "Okay, Mom. Ohh, Bella wants to know if we can go over for supper tomorrow. Can we, Mom? Please? I promised Lilah I would color with her." She looks at me, pleading.

"Sure, um, yeah. I have to work till six, but I'm sure that we can go after that. I'll call her tomorrow. Listen, honey, I'm going to head up and take a shower and go to bed. I have to be at work at six a.m." I walk over to her sitting on the couch texting away, kissing her on the head, turning, and walking upstairs.

Stepping into the room, the first thing I see is his bag with his clothes next to it. Walking toward them, I pick up the T-shirt he was wearing this morning. I bring it up to me and smell it, smell him.

I undress and dress in his shirt, climbing under the covers, his smell is all around me. It's everywhere. It's on my pillow, on my skin, in my memory, in my heart.

I let go of all the tears. They rip through me. The emptiness hurts. The thought of him having a family with someone else is too much for me to bear. The thought that he will love her eventually, the thought that they will raise a baby together. The fact that his smiles will be for her. His heart will beat for her, while mine will just stay still there. No movement, nothing. My eyes close, shut down. The memories of us replay over in my mind till my dreams start.

The alarm wakes me at five-thirty. I peel my eyes open. I know they're puffy even without looking in the mirror. Looking at the phone, I see I missed seven texts from Mick. My heart wants to read them, my mind wants to know, but I do the only thing I can do right now. I block him. I block the number that was my lifeline to him.

Getting up, I go into the bathroom, washing my face with cold water. Looking at myself in the mirror, I see someone who finally let her guard down and lost. Lost. That is what I am, but I'm stronger than this. The pain will linger, the memories will fade, but I'll be okay. I have no choice.

I get dressed for work, going through the motions. I walk into Lori's room and kiss her on the cheek. Telling her I'm leaving, she mumbles and then rolls back to sleep with her bear.

Once I get to work, I walk inside. Given the way Phyllis looks at me and is waiting for me, I know that Mick called her. "Please," I say to her. "Please. I can't do this, not here. If you can't work alongside me without talking about it I'll look for something else, but I can't." I breathe in. "I can't do this."

She doesn't say anything but nods at me.

"You want pancakes today or just eggs?" she asks, walking into the back.

"I'm nursing a broken heart. I want chocolate."

She throws her head back and laughs.

The morning shift goes smooth, lots of people welcoming me back, lots asking about Lori. But most of all, all let me know that I'm treated like family. It's like I'm one of theirs. Finally, I found my place.

The bells ring above the door a little after lunch and Bella walks in with Lilah skipping next to her. Her pigtails started straight but are now lopsided.

"Ms. Marissa, I made you cookies," she says, putting a paper plate on the counter.

"Aww, did you do this for me?" I reach and twirl a pigtail around my finger.

She nods her head yes. "Mamma say Looorri is coming tonight to color with me."

I laugh at the way she always says her name. "She is and she is so excited about coming also." I look at Bella. "Are you sure it's still okay?"

"More than sure. I'm excited for Lori to come over. She mentioned that she would babysit any time I wanted. I may have to break the news to Brenda and Nancy, but I'm super excited."

"What can I bring tonight? Please don't say nothing. Let me." When

I see she is thinking, I tell her I'll bring wine. The visit passes way too fast before they leave and I'm back to filling up the sugar. The bells over the door sound. Looking up, I'm shocked to see Lori.

"Hey, how did you get here?" I ask her when she stops by me and kisses my cheek.

"Trevor. He's parking the car. We went to the library today. It was really cool. I checked online for some courses I might be interested in taking." She sits down.

"Really? That is fantastic news." I sit in front of her.

The bells over the door ring again and Trevor walks in. He looks around for Lori and the minute that he sees her, his face lights up.

"Hi, Ms. Marissa." He sits down next to Lori.

"Please call me Marissa. Do you guys want something to eat?"

Lori looks at him. "Want to share a burger?"

"Sure," he says.

I put in the order and listen to them talk about the books that they looked up and about picking one to read together.

I place the order in front of them with an extra dish. "So what else are you guys up to this afternoon?"

"We are going to a meeting," Lori says while dipping her fries into ketchup. "Can Trevor pass by tonight after we get back from Bella and Jackson's? We want to watch *The Walking Dead* together."

"Um, sure." I look at her and then at Trevor, who is dipping his fries in ketchup also.

When they finish Trevor takes out his wallet to pay, but I shoo it away. I watch them walking out, his hand in the middle of her back, protecting her.

I finish and prepare for the dinner shift and for my plans afterward. Almost one day gone and I only thought of him one million times. Tomorrow, tomorrow will be easier.

Twenty-Nine

Mick

I watch her lights fade. Watch her drive away. Watch her slip through my fingers.

I turn to walk back into the house. Sandie. Fucking Sandie. Sitting at my dining room table eating my fucking pie. I glare at her.

"I usually hate sweets, but since I found out I'm pregnant it's all I can eat."

"How far along are you?"

"Sixteen weeks."

"How are you almost halfway done and you are just coming to me now?"

"I got my period for the first three months and then I started feeling sick and tired. I went in and they told me two weeks ago. I tried to get in touch with you, but you were with that trashy old whore, so—"

I rip the pie away from her. "Let's get this straight. Marissa is off-limits. You do not talk about her, you do not mention her. She has more class in her little toe than your whole body."

She lets out a laugh. "Really, I'm carrying your child."

"How do you know it's mine? You're married."

"He had a vasectomy after Jason Jr. was born because we didn't want any other kids. Surprise, surprise," she says.

"We always wore condoms," I tell her, my head going a million miles a minute. So much to process.

"It's not always effective. Trust me, Mick, I didn't want to do the mommy thing again."

She looks around then back at me. "When do you want to go pick up my stuff?"

I look at her. Like really look at her.

"Pick your stuff where?" I ask her.

"Well, I can't live with Jason while I'm pregnant with another man's child." She rolls her eyes like I've asked her the stupidest question.

"Where are you living?" I ask.

She opens her hands. "I'm moving in here. Obviously, we are going to be together. It's what we always wanted."

"Are you insane? You aren't moving in here. We will raise this child together, but we will never be together again. Sandie, get it through your head. It's over."

"Please," she says, almost like it's the most unbelievable thing she's ever heard. "You can't just toss me out. You love me."

"No, I loved you. Fuck, now that I know what love is, I tolerated you. What we had was nothing. It was a good night. That is what it comes down to in the end."

She slams her hand on the table. "I've had enough of this shit. I'm fucking here. I left my husband for us."

I look at her and laugh. "You didn't leave shit. You got caught with your pants down." Fuck, I get up, shaking my head. "Okay, time for you to go."

She looks shell-shocked. "Where am I supposed to go?"

"Fuck if I know. Where were you staying yesterday?" I ask, crossing my arms over my chest.

"At my parents'."

"Good. Go back there." I walk to the door, hoping to fuck she follows me and I don't have to go back and drag her out.

"MMIIIIICCCCKKKKK, come on," she whines.

"I'll unblock your number. Text me when you are going to go to the doctor. I'll meet you there."

She walks up to me. Her hand goes up to touch my face, and I grab her wrist.

"My kid. That is the only reason I will tolerate you."

She stomps out the door, and I close it before she turns around to moan again.

I take my phone out of my pocket and text Marissa to call me. I then text Lori to make sure she got home okay.

It's five minutes later till Lori texts me back.

Mom's home. She came in crying.

Is she okay? I text back immediately.

She went off to bed. Did you guys have a fight?

You could say that. I'll talk to her tomorrow.

I then send another text to Marissa. And then another and then another. I go upstairs and lie in my bed. The ache in my chest feels like my heart is being shattered. I feel it all through my body.

No way is this the end of us. No way will I let her walk away. No way will I get over her. It's the last thought I have before sleep claims me, sucking me in.

In my dreams, I hear her laughter, see her smile, chase her while she laughs, but the minute I can touch her she disappears, leaving me searching for her. Leaving me empty, alone.

I wake up before the alarm clock. Checking my phone, I have nothing from Marissa. No surprise there. I knew she wouldn't text me back.

I get up and head to the gym where the bag takes all the frustration I have to give. The day passes with no news from Marissa. Not a word. I text Lori, but all she says is her mom is at work.

I start to text Marissa again for the tenth time today when Sandie starts calling.

"What?" I answer.

"Hey, I'm going to the hospital."

I get up, nervous and scared. "Why?"

"I started spotting, so they wanted to make sure the baby was okay. Something about stress. Mick, I'm scared," she says in a whisper.

"It's going to be okay, Sandie, I'll meet you there." I rush out of the office without telling anyone anything and make it to the hospital right before they call her in.

"What happened?" I ask her while walking into the room that has a table in the middle and a huge machine next to it. She gets up on the table that is more like a chair.

"I started spotting this morning. So I called my doctor. He said he would meet us here," she says, and then there is a knock on the door the doctor comes in.

"Mrs. McGuire, you said you started spotting. When was this?"

"It started late last night, then this morning there were little drops and it became more as the day went on."

"Okay, let's see what's going on," he says when she leans back, pulling up her shirt. Her stomach starts to stick out. He pours blue gel on her then takes a wand from the machine, placing it on her stomach.

The next thing I know it sounds like horses galloping with swooshing. He moves it a little and in the middle of the screen, I see my child. The arms moving like it's waving.

He starts clicking things on the machine. "The amniotic fluid is perfect. Her heartbeat is strong."

"Her," I say, looking at the monitor, taking her in. She's perfect.

"You're going to have a daughter." With that, he takes a towel and wipes off her stomach. "I'm going to say that stress might have played a factor in this. We will monitor you at the next month's exam as well. If you have any cramping, you are to come in right away."

"Thank you, Dr. Bray," Sandie says, pulling her shirt down.

The doctor hands me a picture right before walking out. "For you." And then leaves.

I look down at the picture. She is no bigger than my hand, but I love her with everything I have.

"I'm hungry," Sandie says, standing next to me, looking at the picture. "I'm thinking we go eat at the diner. What do you say?"

"No. Choose somewhere else." Just the thought of seeing her makes my heart beat.

She huffs out a big breath. "Fine. Let's go to McDonald's or Wendy's. I just want a cheeseburger."

"How did you get here?" I ask her.

"My mother dropped me off."

"And she just left you here by yourself?"

She shrugs. "I knew you would come." She smiles, and at that moment, I know I've been played.

"You did this on purpose," I state the obvious.

"No. I wouldn't do that." She huffs out.

"We'll go get you drive-thru. I can drop you off. I have to go back to work," I tell her.

She huffs again and walks past me, her heels clicking on the hospital floor.

I stand here shaking my head, holding the picture of my baby girl in my hand. "You've got me wrapped around your finger and you're not even here yet." I laugh to myself, walking out of the hospital.

Sandie and I make it to my car at the same time. By the time I drop her off, she is straight pissed. Steam is almost coming out of her ears. I wait for her to walk up the pathway before I take off.

Looking at the clock, I see that it's almost three p.m. I swing by the diner on my way back to the office. I don't go in. I can't. Just looking at her face from across the street, I see that her eyes have circles under them. She's sitting with Lori and some other kid. She tries to smile, but it doesn't last long.

I watch them. The woman who has my heart and her daughter who holds my other pinky. My three girls. I rub my face, hoping that one day my heart will stop aching. Hoping that one day it beats at the same time as hers.

I pull away from the diner, my chest hurting. I make my way over to Molly's to drown my fucking sorrows.

I stay there till the owner drags me home. I make it up the stairs, swaying right and left. Sitting right in front of my door is my bag from Marissa's house. A bag that I had hoped would stay there unpacked.

I bring it inside and set it on the living room table where it sits and taunts me. Where it holds all my hopes. I sit here till my eyes fall asleep, till I can see her face again in my dreams.

Thirty

Marissa

I rush out of work at six and head over to Mick's house. The bag in my backseat is like a heavy weight on my heart. I put all his stuff back in the bag, except for that one shirt I slept in. I'm really hoping it isn't missing.

Once I get on his street, my eyes scan the cars around. When I pull up to his house, I see that his car isn't there. I wonder if he's with her. I wonder if she will be moving in. I wonder if his child will have his eyes or his hair. Or better yet, I wonder if he loves her. Did he ever stop loving her? Will he marry her? Just the thought alone leaves my stomach rolling and burning.

I grab the bag, running up the steps and dropping it in front of the door. I don't spend an extra minute there in case she opens the door and I have to see her.

I make it to Bella and Jackson's just in time to see Lori being dropped off by Trevor. He watches her walk in, his eyes never leaving her. When he finally turns his head, his eyes find me. He sends a lopsided smile, knowing I caught him watching her and gives me a quick wave before driving off.

Supper is light. They both ask where Mick is, and I shrug that he had something to do. These are his friends. It's his place to tell them. Jackson watches me during dinner. Not openly, but I catch him watching what I do. Like he knows there is something more.

We kiss them all goodbye with the promises to see each other that weekend. Making my way home, I notice that Trevor is already there.

"Oh, are we late?" I ask Lori.

"No. I texted him when we were leaving. He said he was in that area, so he would wait for us."

I stop the car, and Trevor walks over, opening the door for Lori. Her smile shines bright in the nighttime sky. His smile matches hers.

"Hey, Trevor." I walk around the car to lead the way in. "Were you waiting long?" I ask him.

I put the key in the lock and turn it right, pushing it in. When it doesn't move, I turn the lock the other way. "Lori, did you not lock the door this morning?"

"I did, Mom, I even checked it. Trevor saw me do it twice." She looks at Trevor, who nods.

"Maybe you just turned it right and left," Trevor says to me with a shrug.

We walk in, all of us slowly looking around to see if anything has been touched. Turning on the lights, we see that nothing has been touched and everything looks the same as we left if.

I walk farther into the house, opening lights every chance I get while Lori says she will check upstairs. Nothing is out of place, but I have this nagging feeling that someone is watching me. Once I get into the kitchen, I jump when I look into the kitchen window, seeing my reflection and someone standing behind me. I yell out, turning only to see that it's Trevor. "Oh, God, you scared the crap out of me."

"Sorry, Marissa," he says, his face white with fear also from me yelling. "Lori said everything is okay upstairs."

It takes a while for me to feel less nervous, but by the time I'm ready for bed the kids are on episode four of *The Walking Dead*. Making my way upstairs, I tell Lori to make sure she locks up after Trevor leaves.

Going into my room, I start my routine. A routine that I've done alone forever. Once I crawl into bed, I take my phone, going on Facebook to pass the time. A friend request had popped up from Bella, so I smile and accept. I check her page out, looking through all her pictures that she just put on there.

My eyes scan every picture for the eyes that haunt me. For the smile that made me smile. I finally see one of him and Lilah with his face in her neck, her head thrown back. His cheeks puffed out from blowing bubbles in her neck while his eyes look over at the camera.

I imagine him doing that with his child. I slowly drift off into sleep where my dreams are of him chasing a little girl with blond ringlets running through a field of flowers, chasing her till he catches her and flips her over, both of them turning around. She has his eyes but my face. They both wave to me. I sit up in bed, frantic, my heart pounding, tears running down my face. A sob rips through me while I look around, taking in my dark room. The curtains are up so I see the twinkle of stars outside. I lie back down in the middle of my bed, the sheets twisted around my legs, Mick's pillow in my arms. I hold it tight, like I would hold him. I look out into the night, waiting for my eyes to grow tired, but they don't. One hour turns into two and then the alarm fills the silence in the room.

Another day falls into another day. Routine stays the same. My heart beats a little when I hear the jingle of the bells on top of the door. I always look over, wondering if one day those eyes will be the ones staring back at me. Jackson has come in and out, never asking more questions than needed. I know he knows now, so I try to avoid eye contact, for fear he will see how broken I am inside.

I sometimes drive down the road, searching for him or her. Wondering if he is still thinking about me. Wondering if his dreams are filled with the memories of us, filled with the what-ifs. The routine is the same. Work, home, eat, repeat. I attend a couple of sessions with Lori, hoping to find the strength in the stories.

After week one and two, it's easier to breathe. I smile a little more. Joke a little more. Till one day sitting in the driver's side seat is a single white rose. No note, no nothing but the rose.

Every single day for two weeks I walk out, hoping to catch him doing it. Hoping to see him, even a glimpse. One week turns into two, which turns into three and the day I finally see him again.

Thirty-One

Mick

Jackson let me drag my ass for five days. For five days, he ignored me, leaving at noon to go get drunk. For five days, he didn't push me. Till he sat on the stool next to me and I told him Sandie was having my baby.

The minute the words came out of my mouth, he took a shot with me then grabbed me and took me home. He stayed by my side that night while I told him about Marissa, Lori, and Sandie. The next morning he made me shower, sat me down, and placed a picture of my daughter in front of me. Next to that was a picture of Marissa, Lori, and me.

"I let you have your time to be stupid. You have a daughter on the way. A woman who is dying inside," he says, and the minute he says that, my head comes up to look at him to hear what he has to say about her. "Every day I walk in that diner hoping to see her smile, a real smile. But she doesn't," he says then stops. "What do you want?"

His question is simple yet the answer is daunting. "I want my daughter, and I want Marissa and Lori."

"So what the fuck are you doing?" he asks but doesn't wait for me to answer. "You know Lori starts school next week. She and that Trevor kid enrolled in four courses in adult education."

I smile at that I knew she would do it.

"She asks about you. Lori does. Every single time. She doesn't do it in front of Marissa because she knows the answer might hurt her mom."

I nod my head thinking about how far Lori has come, how she was the one being held together and now she is the one holding it together.

"Don't get me wrong. Marissa is the best mother, there constantly, going to meetings. She's surviving."

"I miss her," I say.

"How are you showing her you miss her? By getting shit-faced, by drowning your fucking sorrows? Fucking show her," he yells.

"She doesn't want me," I yell back. "She left me the minute Sandie showed up saying she was pregnant." My chest is heaving.

He laughs at me. "You're not that dumb, are you? She let you go so you could be a family. She did that for you. Moron."

The realization hits me in the middle of my chest like a gunshot. "But I don't want Sandie, I want her."

"Did you tell her that? Did you tell her all of this?"

I just shake my head. No, I didn't. I didn't even try. I just took it and left.

"I'm going to see her," I tell him, getting up, ready to walk out the door to see her.

"You have a visitor," he says and motions to the backyard with his head.

I look past him to see Lori sitting on a chair staring over the water, her notebook in her hand. "She has been here every single day for the last five days. She sits out there till about noon and then she meets that Trevor kid."

I walk past him right to the back door, opening it and walking down to the water. She is holding her pen in her hand, her notebook open, but she is looking out into the distance, the water current soft, the waves rippling onto the rocks. "Hey," I tell her, and she looks over at me. Tears fill her eyes when she sees me.

She gets up, her notebook falling to the ground as she rushes to me and hugs me around my waist, her head under my chin.

"You okay?" she says. The worried tone in her voice slices through me.

I kiss her head while rubbing her back. "Of course I'm okay."

"You told me I could come here any time I wanted. Is that still okay?" she whispers. The wind blows her hair around my face.

"There is nothing I would like more."

She moves away from me, going to pick her notebook, and sitting down in the chair while I sit in the other one next to her. "Mom cries," she says, looking at the water still. "Every night, she tries to hide it, but I can hear her."

I lean forward, putting my elbows on my knees and my face in my hands. "I love her."

"I know," she says. "Is it true? Is someone having your baby?" She turns to me and asks me with tears coming down her face.

"Who told you? Did your—" I don't even finish the sentence when she shakes her head no.

"I saw you at the hospital with a woman. I went there to sign up to volunteer. She said she's having your baby."

"Yes, she's having my baby. But that doesn't have anything to do with the fact that I love your mother."

She shakes her head. "She won't do it. She won't let you back in. She refuses to stand between a family. My father came back four years ago. Said he was a changed man, stayed maybe a week till a woman knocked on our door. She was seven months pregnant. She begged him to come home to her. That night my mother had the locks changed and told him to go back to his family. I asked her why and she said 'sometimes you just need a push to see where you belong and that baby belongs with a mother and a father.' We never spoke about him again. So I know she won't do it."

I let her words sink in. Make it penetrate.

She gets up, looking at her watch. "I have to go, Mick. Can I still come back?"

"I'll have a key made for you so you can go inside whenever you want," I tell her, hugging her and watching her walk out of the yard with her head down.

I make my way inside where Jackson is sitting reading the paper while drinking coffee.

"How did it go?" he asks, putting the paper down.

"She won't change her mind," I tell him, sitting in front of him, my body slumping forward.

"So now what?"

"Now I call a lawyer and find out my rights. I wait for Sandie to fuck up, because we both know she will, and then I hope to fuck Marissa will take me back." I exhale, thinking about the fucking mountain I'm going to have to climb.

I spend the rest of my day on the phone calling family lawyers. I spend the rest of the week interviewing them. Then I finally cave and drive by the diner to see her. Her face is beautiful like the sun after a rain shower. She looks thinner, but she smiles more. Just a touch more. I watch her walk out to her car, opening the door and reaching inside to take out a white rose. She looks around, smiling and smelling it while she makes her way home.

The fear that she has moved on has been on my mind, but to see it. Destroys me.

Thirty-Two

Marissa

For two weeks, every single time I get out of work I find the rose waiting for me. I try to look out all day to see him, to get a glimpse of him, but I never catch him.

Making my way home, I walk into the house while Lori and Trevor sit at the table doing their homework together.

"Hey, guys," I say, bringing the groceries and putting them on the counter.

Trevor gets up to help me.

"You should have called me. I would have brought them in for you." He unpacks them all and puts them on the counter while Lori puts them away.

"It's okay. It wasn't that much. Did you guys eat already?" I ask them, walking to the sink to wash my hands.

"Yup. We just had a couple of burgers with some other kids from school," she says while placing things into the fridge. "Hey, Mom."

"Yeah, honey." I look out into the yard.

"There is this party on Saturday at this girl Farah's house. Is it okay if we go?"

I look over at her. "Do you want to go?" I know it's a big step for her.

"Yeah. I think so. Trevor and I said we should try it. And if either of us feels anything we leave."

I wipe my hands and look over at both of them. "This is a big step for you, guys. Going there. Will there be alcohol served?" I ask them both.

"It doesn't matter if there is alcohol. I'm not drinking and Trevor is driving, so he's not drinking."

I look over at Trevor, who nods at me.

"I don't drink," is all he says.

"Okay, if this is what you guys want to do. Then go. I'm just saying that if you feel out of place or you feel pressured to do anything, I want you guys to call me." I point at both of them.

Lori comes over and kisses my cheek, and Trevor follows, kissing the other, mimicking Lori.

"Okay, guys, I'm going to shower and hang out in my room. Close up when you're done, okay?"

I walk upstairs, closing my door, and go into the shower. Once I'm dressed and ready for bed, I open my door and hear the television playing downstairs.

I get into bed, turning on the TV, switching channels for something good to watch. I'm about to turn it off and go to bed when I hear my phone signal a text message.

It's from Daniel.

I heard the kids are going out on Saturday night. Want to do coffee so I can talk you off the ledge?

I laugh at the text only because I would probably be on the ledge, so coffee with him might be just what I need to do. He can talk me through this.

Sure!

Great. I'll text you Saturday afternoon to set up a time and place.
Have a great night. Is the only thing I answer back.

I close the lights, turning my head on the pillow and looking at the stars outside. It's become my routine. Watching the stars twinkle. Watching them slowly fade into the darkness.

My dreams are vivid and so real. I feel him touch my face, rub my neck. I feel him kiss my lips. The kiss lingers. I want to touch him, but I can't get to him. I can't reach out. I finally stir away, looking around till my eyes land on the silhouette of someone in my doorway. "Lori?" I ask, turning around to open my light. With the light on, I can see that there isn't anyone there.

I get out of bed, going to Lori's room and seeing that she's sleeping. I walk downstairs, checking the front door and the back door. The back door is locked, but the door isn't shut properly. I close the door and make my way over to the window to look out into the dark night.

I walk back upstairs, but my mind is not shutting down. Every single time I hear a crack or a creak I get up.

The minutes turn into hours. Finally at six a.m. I get up and start the laundry. It's my day off and I wanted to sleep in. I put a load in the washer and then start some coffee. Since I'm home, I take out the things to start pancakes. Lori wanders downstairs a little after seven, rubbing sleep out of her eyes.

"Hey, Mamma." She tries to sit on me, curling up, but she's bigger than me, so we almost fall off the chair, laughing.

"You are going to squish me," I tell her, pushing her off me.

She walks over to the couch where she throws herself on it. I get up and walk to the living room, leaning on the doorjamb. "You know that you left the back door open last night?" I tell her.

She looks up from the pillow, her eyes wide. "No, I didn't. I checked them right before I went to bed."

I shrug. "It was locked, but not closed all the way." I take a sip of coffee. "I had a nightmare, woke up, and thought I saw someone's shadow. Must have been my eyes playing tricks on me."

"That is so weird. I thought I saw someone the other night. Now I'm definitely freaking out," she says, sitting up.

I shake my head at her, rolling my eyes. "Okay, well, just from now on make sure that you see if the door is really closed."

I turn around, going to make pancakes. We sit down and have breakfast just the two of us.

"I spoke with Mick," she says while playing with her food.

"Okay," I say while my heart beats fast and my hands get clammy. "Is he okay?"

She nods. "He misses you."

I shake my head at her.

"Mom, I think you should listen to him."

A tear escapes, running down where I rub it off halfway down my face. "No, Lori. I will not be that woman who takes a dad away from them. I will not be the reason the family won't be together. I wouldn't do it back then, I'm not doing it now. Besides, I'm actually enjoying having a good job, loving my job, and being a pain in the ass to my daughter." I laugh at her, trying to make light of the conversation.

"So what are you doing tonight while we go to the party?" she asks me, dropping the subject of Mick.

"I'm going to go have coffee with Daniel. He texted me last night." I get up to go put my dish in the sink. "Wash the dishes for me. Did you want to go out and get a new outfit for your party?"

"No, it's not that big of a party. I spoke to Farah. There are only about twenty people coming. Mom?"

"Yeah, baby."

"I'm scared," she says, her voice low.

I walk to her and hold her. "Baby, it's normal. This is a huge step. But you know that you have Trevor there and you have me, a phone call away."

She looks up at me, wiping tears from her eyes.

"The minute you think or feel out of it, you call me and I will fly there if I have to." I kiss her nose. "On my broom stick no less."

She smiles at me, and I take her cheeks in my hands, kissing her all over her face till she giggles. It's music to my ears.

Later that night she dresses in her tight jeans and sweater with her black Chucks. She kisses me on the cheek, running out the minute Trevor gets there. They both look at me and wave.

I get up to dress and get ready to meet Daniel. I decide to wear tight jeans and a black ruffled shirt with black wedges. I choose my gold loop earrings, putting on just lip-gloss.

My eyes are still sunken in from the last three weeks. I've lost about ten pounds, which I'm trying to gain back. Right when I'm about to walk out the door, I get a text from Lori saying she has gotten there.

I get into the car, driving over to the coffee shop that Daniel wants to try out.

We sit down, telling each other stories of the past. It's a carefree conversation. Till my phone rings three hours later, Lori's name showing up on my phone. My heart stops. My back shoots up.

"Mom, Mom, please. I'm scared. I'm locked in the bathroom. I can't find Trevor. He left to drive someone to the store. But, Mom, people are drinking, and some are getting sick. Mom," she sobs out. "Please."

"Where are you? I need to know where you are." I get up, running to my car, Daniel fast on my heels.

"I'll drive," he says, getting into the car.

"Lori, baby, you need to share your location with me so I can come find you, please," I beg out, the fear of not seeing her again overwhelming me. The phone beeps with an incoming message from Lori. "I'm coming. Okay, baby? It says we should be there in twenty minutes. Okay, you can keep talking to me on the phone." I take my phone from my ear, looking at the screen and it says call failed.

"Fuck. Fuck. Fuck," I yell out, wanting to smash my phone. The frustration of not being about to get there fast is too much for me.

For twenty minutes, I sit and watch the world go by while I hold my breath.

Thirty-Three

Mick

I'm standing in the meat section, deciding if I should do T-bone or rib eye. I should just throw this back and go to the diner, but the fact that I would come face-to-face with Marissa and maybe a boyfriend is too much for me.

I throw both steaks into my basket, walking to the checkout line when the phone rings. Once I look I see it's Lori. A smile comes over me.

"Hey, beautiful girl."

"Mick," she whispers, and I hear the fear and trembling in her voice. My blood turns cold, my basket falls to the floor, and I'm running. "Mick, I'm so scared."

"Okay. I'm going to link you with the station, okay, baby?" I put her on speakerphone and add a call to the conversation, calling into the precinct. Thomas answers on the other line. I link the calls. "Talk to me, baby girl, where are you?"

"I'm at a party. But then people started drinking, so I started standing more and more in a corner. The guy who I came here with went to the store with another guy. But now people are getting sick, Mick, so I ran to the washroom. Mick," she cries out. "I'm sitting in the tub," she wails out. "Mick, please."

"I need the address, baby girl. Give me the address. I'm in the car."

"I don't know it. I don't know it, I just shared the location with my mom." she whispers then we hear banging on the door. She wails out even more.

Thomas breaks in. "We just got a call for an ambulance at a house in the Newtown district. They are saying that numerous kids are sick and one is convulsing. The owner's daughter is called Farah. Is that where you are?"

"Yes, Farah, that is the one who is throwing the party," she says out loud.

Thomas shoots me the address, and I see I'm four minutes away.

"Lori, Lori, are you there?" I look down at the phone. The phone is dead. I smash it on the wheel. "Piece of shit."

I arrive at the same time as the ambulance and a police car. I take out my badge, running in, yelling for Lori. I walk into the room where four kids are throwing up, while another five I count are passed out on the couch. There are a couple of girls crying in the corner. I do a fast sweep of the room, yelling her name. I walk over to a door that is closed and locked, and bang on it, calling Lori. The door swings open and she runs into my arms, collapsing in them. She fists my shirt in her hands, holding on for dear life. "I have you, baby," I say, carrying her outside and sitting with her on the grass. I see Marissa arrive with tears in her eyes. She looks around frantically, so I yell for her, and she sees me and runs to us, falling to her knees in front of us while she holds on to Lori, who is holding on to me.

She keeps rubbing her head, looking at her face and kissing her.

"Marissa," I hear and look up to see a guy who is standing there wearing fucking khakis and a sweater vest. "Lori," he says, getting on his knees also next to us. "Where is Trevor?" he asks, looking around.

Marissa looks up at him and then looks around for Trevor. I see Thomas arrive with Jackson right behind him, followed by Chris.

They see me, so they start walking over to me. "What do we have?" Thomas asks while Jackson takes in the scene. Kids being brought out on stretchers, frantic parents arriving as well as Farah's mother followed by fucking Sandie. What the fuck is going on right now?

Jackson sees Sandie then makes sure I'm okay. We don't have much time to say anything before there is a kid running over to us yelling for Lori. Her hands don't let go of my shirt. He falls down next to us.

"Shit, Lori, I'm so sorry. It took longer at the store than I thought. What happened? What is going on?" He looks around, his eyes trying to get everything that is going on.

"You left me," Lori says, "and then people started to drink that punch. They tried to give me a glass, but I didn't take it. They called me a prude, so I just stayed by myself. I texted you." She lays her head on my chest.

"I'm so sorry. I forgot my phone in the car while we went into the store. Then I tried to call you, but you didn't answer. I told you to come. You said you would be okay. Marissa, I would have never left her if I thought she was in danger." He looks like he's about to cry. The sweater vest dude grabs his shoulder and squeezes it.

"Why don't we give them space, Trevor?" He looks over at Lori. "Do you need anything?"

She shakes her head no, still not letting go of me. "Okay, Trevor, let's get you home."

"We are going to have to take his statement before you leave," Chris chimes in. "We have six kids on their way to the hospital. We need to know what went on here tonight." He leads him to the side where he starts asking him questions, but his eyes never leave Lori.

"It's okay, princess, I have you." I squeeze her, Marissa is still rubbing her hair, watching her. Her eyes finally move up to meet mine. If I thought I was living through hell before, it's nothing compared to the hell I'm going through not to reach out and touch her. Not to be able to hold her at the same time. Not to reach out and kiss her lips and promise her the world.

"Oh, well, isn't this a picture perfect family." I hear and I look up, and by the time I look back down at Marissa, her face is white and pale. "It's good to know where your priorities are for me and your daughter," she continues.

Lori finally lets go of my shirt with a sad smile. "Mom, I want to go home."

She nods her head, getting up to hold her hand. Jackson steps in.

"I'll take you home. Bella will come get me."

She nods, puts her head down, and walks away, leaving me sitting with Lori's tears wet on my shirt but that have seeped into my skin.

I put my hands on my knees, looking around at the scene. Thomas starts walking out of the house with Farah's mother, Maci, high on his heels.

"What do you mean I can't stay here? This is my house." She's yelling and throwing her hands up in the air.

"Ma'am, I've told you this before. This is now a crime scene. You have kids that were underage and drinking. Four have been admitted to the hospital and one is in a coma," Thomas says, keeping his cool.

"Well, where the hell am I supposed to go?" she asks with her hands on her hips now.

We don't have a chance to hear the answer because Jason, Sandie's husband, is huffing and puffing walking up to us. "Nice, very nice, Sandie. This will look lovely in court," he says, smiling.

She looks at him and rolls her eyes.

"I thought you were a negligent mother before. My lawyers are going to have a field day with you in court. Junior has been over at this house how many times, and now it's busted for drugs!"

I get up to my feet. "It's not the case, Jason."

He finally sees me.

"Isn't this great." He points at me. "I'm so glad you're here. Saves me a trip."

I look at him with confusion on my face. Sandie's face has gone white, and her hand goes straight to her stomach. I spring into action, rushing to her. "Are you okay?" I ask her, looking around to see if there are any other EMTs on the scene.

Jason laughs out. "This is precious." He looks over at Sandie. "You haven't told him yet, have you?"

"Haven't told me what? What is he talking about?"

Her face doesn't change, and her hand starts to shake on her stomach.

"Oh, please, let me do it," Jason says. "She's fucking with you."

I look at him, shock filling my body, rage filling my soul, my mouth now dry and no sound coming up. Thomas must have heard because he is now standing next to me and somehow Chris has moved to my other side.

"Don't feel that bad. She did it to me. Fuck," he says, chucking "She fucked you for seven years under my nose. And I didn't suspect a thing." He looks at Sandie.

"Stop it, Jason, just stop," she cries out. "Why are you doing this to me?"

His head falls back, he laughs out, and then you see the rage in his eyes. "Doing this to you? Doing this to you? You ruined my fucking life." He leans in closer to her. "I married you. I fucking loved you. I did everything to make you happy. EVERYTHING," he roars out the last word. "And what do I get in return? You fuck my best friend. Fuck him under my nose. You probably fucked him in my bed."

Sandie cries out, "It was a mistake."

"A mistake," he yells. "Did your cunt fall on his cock? For over five years?"

I yell out, "What the fuck is going on here?"

"She's having his baby and she's trying to pass it off as yours." He looks at her. "Did you think he wouldn't find out?" He shakes his head.

"What?" I whisper, my body ready to charge forward, Thomas and Chris holding me back. "You fucking bitch."

"It's not what you think," she says, now trying to reach for me.

"Oh my God, you're pathetic. I have the proof," Jason says "I hired a private investigator when she told me she was pregnant so I can go for full custody." He looks at her, and her lips tremble.

"You can't take my son from me," she says in a whisper, tears falling out of her eyes.

"Wake up, Sandie, your games are done. You don't get to play the wounded part anymore. You fucked my best friend, your best friend's husband. Who does that? Who?"

She looks at me, tilting her head. "Mick, please, I can explain."

I shake my head. "You explain it to someone who gives a shit, because I don't. I feel sorry for that child you're carrying. Sorry that she is going to have you to look up to. Someone who lies, cheats, steals." I shake my head. "You were going to ruin my life, without a second thought."

"Mick." She reaches out to touch my arm. "I love you."

I shake my hand away to make sure she doesn't touch me. "Love." I laugh at her bitterly. "You don't know what the fuck love is."

And with that, I walk away in a daze, looking for my keys in my pocket.

Thomas grabs my shoulder. "Keys are in the car. But how about I drive you home, yeah?"

I don't say anything else. I get into the passenger side. The sound of the baby's heartbeat playing in my head, the picture of her is the only thing I see when I close my eyes. I get home, crawl into bed, and mourn a child I loved more than anything, a child that isn't even mine!

Thirty-Four

Marissa

I get in the backseat with Lori while Jackson drives us home. With my hand around her shoulder and her head on my shoulder, she sobs the whole way.

When I got to the house, I was already a sobbing mess. My hand shaking in fear, my heart beating so fast I thought it would beat out of my chest. Then to see her on the grass with Mick holding her I knew, I just knew she would be all right.

By the time we make it home, she has fallen asleep. When I move to shake her awake, Jackson stops me and instead picks her up and brings her in, walking her to the couch and putting her down. She doesn't stir. "Do you think I should take her to the hospital?" I ask him, worried that she hasn't woken up.

"No, I think her adrenaline finally quit and she knocked out." He takes his phone out, sending messages out.

I sit by her head on the couch, lifting it up and placing it in my lap, while pushing her hair away from her face. "I swear I thought I was going to die if I didn't see her once we got there. The minute she called and I answered I fucking knew." I shake my head, the tears coming again.

I hear a knock at the door and look over at Jackson.

"That must be Bella. I texted her when we left." He opens the door and grabs her in his arms. He picks her up while he buries his face in her neck. She whispers in his ear while holding him. He kisses her on the lips. Their moment is private, but you can't help but be drawn into watching.

He places her down on her feet, and she walks toward us, falling on her knees beside the couch. "How is she?"

"She's okay, I think. Shaken up, but other than that okay," I say to her while she puts her hand on my knee and squeezes me, reassuring me.

"How are you?" she then asks.

"Me, I'm a fucking mess," I tell her. "The only thing that kept running through my head was her smile when she left tonight. The kiss on the top of the head that she gave me when she called me short stuff." I lower my eyes to watch her chest move. I look back up to see tears falling down Bella's face as well. From one mother to another she knows that feeling.

Jackson comes over. "Babe, I hate to rush you, but I've got to go back to the scene." He squats down near her.

She nods her head. "Okay." She looks at me. "If you need anything, and I mean anything, please," she says, and I finish her sentence.

"I'll call you."

She gets up and places a kiss on Lori's forehead.

Jackson's voice breaks the moment. "Come lock up, Marissa."

I gently move her head from my lap to go over and lock the door. I make my way to the back door, checking it just in case. Once I see it has been locked I open the freezer, taking the vodka out, pouring myself a shot. The cold liquid burns as it runs down my throat. Putting the shot glass in the sink, I close off the lights, going into the living room to see that Lori is awake. Her phone is clutched in her hand as she types away.

"You okay?" I ask, sitting down next to her feet.

"Yeah. Kind of. I don't know." She shrugs her shoulders. "I'm sorry I called Mick first, Mom," she says, wiping a tear away. "I just knew he would come and save me. And he did, Mom. He came in that house like the hulk." She smiles. "When I opened the door I thought he would be green." We both laugh at the picture that is in our minds.

Her phone vibrates on top of her. "It's Trevor. He's sorry he let me down," she says. "But he did ask me to come with him, but I was having fun talking to girls for once, so I said no. I should have gone." The what-ifs play in her mind. "Can I sleep in your bed tonight?"

"Sleepover party?" It's something we do when we put our pjs on and watch Netflix all night while eating junk food.

She smiles big. "Sleepover party!" She fist pumps in the air.

We spend the night watching 'chick flicks' while eating chips, ice cream, Oreos, and frozen pizza. The last time I look at the clock, it's four a.m. when sleep finally claims me.

The sound of buzzing wakes us both up the next day. I groan out loud. "What time is it?"

She doesn't move from her position, the buzzing noise clearly not bothering her. Looking at my phone, I see that it's almost three p.m. "Holy shit, we slept eleven hours." I get up to go pee. She just mumbles something. The buzzing still continues "Lori, get the phone," I yell from the bathroom, looking over my shoulder while I wash my hands.

She blindly reaches out, grabbing it, and bringing it to her ear. "Lo," she grumbles.

I don't know who is on the other line. I just hear her say, "Sleeping later." And she hangs up.

I laugh at her, throwing my pillow at her head. "Get up or else you won't be able to sleep tonight." I head downstairs to get some coffee. I open the blinds in the kitchen, looking outside at the sunny day. My phone rings from somewhere upstairs. I hear Lori answer it and then five minutes later she runs downstairs. "Mom, can we go to Bella's for dinner? Please, Mom, please." She runs into the kitchen, pleading.

I grab the phone from her and chat with Bella, who won't take no for an answer.

We make plans for us to go over at around six and to not bring anything as she was up early baking with Lilah. Lori and I both shower and slowly get ready to go.

Driving over there, she sticks her ear buds in and starts a texting marathon. The sun is starting to set. When we arrive, we barely make it inside before Brenda, their neighbor, runs over to Lori, grabbing her face and kissing her cheeks while Lilah hugs her leg.

"I so worried you get lost again, Looorrii," she says, looking up at her.

Lori bends down and picks her up, her legs wrapping around her waist. "I promise to not get lost again, okay, Lilah?" She kisses her nose. She puts her down, and Bella hugs her next. "We were so, so worried about you."

"I'm okay," she says to everyone.

Jackson comes into the room, hugging her as well and whispering in her ear.

We have never had a family, never had anyone who generally cared for us, and now, now there are people who love my daughter like they have known her her whole life. The feeling brings tears to my eyes.

Bella grabs my hand, dragging me into the kitchen. "I've been chilling wine," she says as she pours us both glasses of wine.

She motions us to go outside and sit down before the sun sets. We sit down and Jackson comes outside. I look behind him, wondering if Lori is coming.

"They are watching *Frozen*. Don't ask," he says while he sits down, grabbing Bella's hand and kissing it.

"Did you speak with Mick?" he asks, and I shake my head no. He looks at Bella, who says, "You need to tell her." Those four words make my heart stop.

"What happened? Is he okay?" I say, sitting up in the chair. "Did he get hurt?" I look at both of them, my eyes traveling back and forth. Regret fills me.

"He's fine," Bella says, leaning forward to grab my hand.

"Well, he isn't fine, but he will be," Jackson says while I look at him. "Sandie lied. It isn't his baby."

My hand goes to my mouth to stop the gasp from coming out. "What do you mean?" I ask, confused. How can she lie about a baby? "She's pregnant. I saw yesterday."

"Oh, she's with child all right, just not his child," he says while picking up Bella's glass of wine and taking a sip. "She was playing him."

My heart breaks for him, knowing how much he loved that baby even if he didn't know it. It's his nature to love with all that he has. "Where is he?" I ask, not sure why.

"Probably at home, drunk on his ass. That's where I would be."

I stand up and before I even realize it, my feet are working before my head. I turn to look at them. "Lori, can you—" I stop speaking when

184

Bella raises her hand.

"We got her, don't worry. She can even sleep over."

I nod, walking inside in a trance. I stop when I see Lori twirling Lilah in her arms to "Let It Go."

She sees me and stops. "Mom?"

"I have to go see Mick."

She smiles at me, nodding.

"I don't know what time I will be back," I tell her.

"Lilah, can I sleep over?" She looks at Lilah, who raises her hands in the air.

"Yeah, sleep over. But you can't go in Momma's bed because Ackson is there and he sleep in his undies." She leans in and whispers, "Is pribate."

I hear Bella laugh and Jackson groan.

I nod to both of them while I walk out and make my way over to him, hoping he will still want me, but knowing I have to try.

I pull up to the curb turning off the car, looking at the house that is pitch-black, not a light in sight.

My hands still clutch the steering wheel. I lean my head down, wondering if this is the right thing to do.

My heart is telling me one thing, but my head is telling me something else. This time I'm going with my gut.

I step out, making my way to the front door. The wooden heeled sandals make clacking sounds in the quiet of the night.

The minute I get to the door right before I'm about to knock, I notice that it isn't closed all the way.

I knock softly, hoping maybe he is sleeping and I came here for nothing.

But the minute my hand touches the door it opens more. I take that as a sign from above.

"Hello, Mick, you home?" I peek my head in the door, listening to see if the television is on.

I tiptoe more into the house, looking into the living room. The television is off and the place looks the same as it did last time. The only thing different is the frame that is sitting next to the television.

It's a picture of the three of us taken when we were out for ice cream. The smiles on all our faces are lit up even brighter than the sun in the background. I'm on top of Mick and Lori is on top of me. He joked and called it a chain reaction, which is what made us burst out laughing.

I can't believe he had it framed. Turning my head, I hear something coming from the kitchen.

When I enter the kitchen the man I've been dreaming of, chasing after, and trying to forget about is sitting on a chair, looking at pictures in front of him. The bottle of whiskey right next to him is almost empty, the shot glass tipped over.

"Hey," I whisper while I lean into the doorframe, crossing my arms in front of my chest.

He looks up at me, his eyes dazed, the white pink and bloodshot.

"You're here?" he asks, and I'm not sure he knows that it's me.

"I thought you might need a friend."

He lets out a little laugh. "Is that right? You look like you were out on a date." He looks me up and down.

He isn't wrong, yet he isn't right. I was out, but not on a date. At least not the way he thinks. I was having dinner with Bella when I got the news. Although from the short jean skirt and flowery tank top, you would think I was actually on a date.

"I was out with Bella," I tell him just to make sure he knows.

The picture in his hand slides through his fingers, showing me it's an ultrasound picture.

"Jackson told me." I don't think I have to say anything else after that.

"So you know?" he asks, looking at me.

I nod my head, letting him know.

"She fucking lied to me, to you, to us. She fucking tried to play God with my life." He picks up the glass, filling it with a shot of whiskey and then downing it. "She fucked with me for the last seven years." He laughs, looking at his hands. "Seven years of promising me things and letting me down. I finally fucking move on, finally fucking let my heart feel what a normal heart should feel, and she comes in here and rips it away."

He pours another shot, hissing while he swallows. "She's a bitch."

I walk to him, watching him turn in his chair, opening his legs for me to walk into.

I'm not sure what we are doing here, but I know I need liquid encouragement to take this next step and hope he doesn't send me away. Taking the glass from his hand, I pour a shot for myself, downing it. The liquid burns right from my throat to my stomach.

He rubs his hands on my back thighs, up and down. Goose bumps fill my body. "Tell me I'm not dreaming." He looks up at me.

I put my hands into his hair while his hands grab my hips. "If you're dreaming, it means I'm dreaming." One of my hands falls from his hair to the side of his face where my finger traces his cheekbone. "You're in my dreams always."

He pushes me away from him so he can close his legs and have me sit on him. My skirt rides way up, my chest rising and falling with every beat of my heart. I haven't been with anyone but him, and it's like my body knows it's home.

His hands cup my face, the thumbs rubbing my cheeks. "You're everywhere. You're in my dreams, in my thoughts, when I shower, when I eat, when I breathe."

My forehead lands on his, a tear coming out of his eye. "I prayed for the first time in my life for you to come back to me."

"Mick, you don't."

"I do. I fucking do. I have to tell you. You have to know. I never touched her while we were together. You have to know." His hands pull the hair away from my face. "Never wanted to touch her, never wanted to taint what we had. But that night that Lori called and she showed up, you left. I thought there was no way in hell you would give me another chance, no way would I be that fucking lucky to get my own piece of heaven. But I still never fucking touched her. I kicked her out and came to your house and watched you from my car."

"Mick," I whisper, my own tears falling now.

"I wore a condom each and every single time. I was stupid to not question it. I was a fucking fool to believe her, but why would she lie to me, right?" He exhales a deep breath, my hands clutching at his shirt now. The tears won't stop.

"Mick, please," I plead with him.

"I love you. Never knew love like this before, never knew it existed. Saw Jackson fall in love and fuck did I want that, wanted to feel that feeling, craved it. Then you looked me in the eye, and I saw what everyone was talking about. They said when it happens you'll know.

Baby, I fucking knew."

"I love you." I don't wait for more. I take charge. I lean in, placing my lips on his. The taste of him is like going home.

The taste of the whiskey on his tongue mixed with mine is like finding a missing piece. The way our tongues dance with each other, it's like they have been doing this for their whole life.

His hands in my hair pull a little, my own hands wrapping around his neck to pull at his hair. The kiss is needy, greedy, and rough.

"How drunk are you right now?" I ask him when we finally leave each other's lips, but he has started to attack my neck. Licking, sucking, biting, making my heart soar and my panties wet.

"Not even close to drunk," he says while he gets off the chair, my legs wrapping around his waist, the skirt rising up till you see my ass. "Tell me you'll stay," he asks right before he takes one more step into the living room right to the steps that lead to his room.

"I'm never leaving. No more, Mick."

"Fuck, not giving you a choice anyway. You left once, fucking killed me when you did. Not doing that again," he tells me right before walking to the door, slamming it shut and locking it.

"Where is Lori?" he asks before we make it up one step. This man not only loves me, he actually loves my daughter.

"Left her at Bella and Jackson's. She's spending the night."

"Good because what I've got planned is going to take all fucking night and tomorrow as well."

I don't get to say another word before he slams his mouth on mine, making me get lost in him.

Thirty-Five

Mick

Sitting at that table tonight drowning my sorrow, I bid my time till I can go to her. Nothing is standing in our way now. Or better yet, no one.

I take one more look at the ultrasound picture before I place it away. I loved that little girl for as long as I thought she was mine. It's a shame she'll end up with a mother like Sandie, but that isn't my problem. Not now, not ever.

So when I look up and see Marissa in my kitchen, it's a gift from God. It's like the heavens are answering my prayers.

But nothing could prepare me for when she comes toward me. I hold my breath, hoping that it isn't a fucking illusion or that I'm dying.

Her hands on me break me. Her touch. I was fucking hers. She owned me, she just didn't know it. But for the rest of my life I'm going to make sure every fucking morning, noon, and night she knows that she owns me.

I have to tell her what I couldn't these last couple of weeks. I have to make sure she knows that what we had was so much more than what I had with anyone, that what we had was *everything*.

Now we are here, in my room, finally back where she belongs, with me.

"Baby." I kiss her neck, ready to get her naked. "Let your feet down."

"No," she says right before pulling me closer to her, wanting to get inside me, and fuck if I didn't want the same thing.

"Baby, I need to get you naked," I say while my hands find her ass, kneading them, pushing her core straight on my jean-covered cock.

"Hmmm, okay." She unfolds her legs, sliding down on her feet, walking to the bed, and getting on it on her knees. In the middle of my bed, in the dark, the light from outside streaming in directly on her like an angel.

She pulls her top over her head, leaving her in a cream-covered lace bra, pushing up her tits nice and round. I start to walk to her, but she shakes her head no, so I stop.

"I wasn't with anyone since you," she says when she unclasps her bra in front, letting her tits hang free. The barbells in her nipples catch on the light, also shining in the night. My mouth waters. I rip my shirt over my head.

"One for one, baby," I tell her, and her eyes hood over in lust.

I rub my cock through my pants, letting her watch me. She unbuttons her jean skirt, pulling the zipper down slowly. She has the matching lace underwear on. She peels it down her hips, lying back on the bed and kicking her skirt away.

Her legs fall open, her finger rubbing down her slit all the while her eyes are on me. I open my own button and bring the zipper down. Pushing the pants down over my hips, my cock springs out. I'm not wearing any boxers, so her eyes go wide as she takes me in. I kick them off my legs.

"I'm naked, baby." I fist my cock, pulling my barbell, the sensation going straight to my balls.

I get on the bed with her, grabbing the panties in my hands, shredding them by pulling. "Oops, my bad," I say right before I bend down, taking her clit into my mouth. She groans out, pushing her pussy more into my mouth. I lick her from her clit to her opening, my tongue licking her all the way inside.

Her head rolls to the side while her back arches up. I push her legs back, opening her up while I eat her pussy like it's my last fucking meal. I look up from her pussy to see her staring down at me, her hands on her tits, playing with her nipples.

I place a finger inside her and slide in to my knuckles. She is so wet I add another finger. "Fuck, I can't wait to sink into you." I pump my fingers in and out, my tongue circling her clit, which becomes bigger. "Missed you so much." Pumping again, I rub her clit with my thumbs, flicking it right and left. "You going to come for me?" I ask her, curling my fingers inside her, rubbing her G-spot three times till she comes all over my hand. She sucks me in so deep, I attack her clit the same time I continue fucking her with my fingers, her legs falling off my shoulders.

I reach over to grab a condom from my drawer. I'm on my knees in the middle of her legs when she sits up. Grabbing my cock in her hand, she licks the tip.

"Mmm," she says, and then she pulls me deep into her throat till I hit the back.

I reach down, grabbing a nipple while she takes my cock. Her moan vibrates right through me. I pinch her nipple, and her ass moves into the bed.

"I really want your mouth, but right now I want your pussy more," I tell her, tearing the condom open. Right before I put it on, she takes it from me.

"I'm clean. We had to always get tested at work. And I'm protected," she says, looking at me.

"I'm clean. I've always worn one," I tell her also for her to know.

She hands me the condom back. "The choice is yours." She leaves it in my hands.

I look down at her rosy cheeks, lustful eyes, perfect tits, swollen pussy, and I throw it over my shoulder.

I've never done it without one and just the thought gets me harder than before. I run my head up and down her slit, getting it wet, my piercing teasing hers.

Bringing myself to her opening, I push my cock in her. Just the tip. The heat fills me up, her wetness smooth, slippery.

"Fuck," I hiss out, pushing another inch in. There is no other feeling than skin on skin, her tightness gripping me till I slide all the way in. Balls deep. I have to take a minute and not think of the amazing feeling this is or I'll blow my load like a virgin.

She pushes her legs back, locking them in the middle of my back. My eyes close as I take in the feeling. Hot, wet, tight. "Mick," she moans, and she tries to move her hips up and down to get me to move, but with the way I'm planted in her, she can't move.

I pull out again all the way out and then slam back home. Fuck, I tilt my hips so my piercing grazes her. I know I've hit the spot when her hands grip my ass, pushing me deeper into her while the heels of her feet dip into my back.

I open my eyes to look at her, finding her staring at me. "I love you," I say to her while I pull out and back in again, slowly torturing both of us. "Lost without you," I say again, following the same torture.

Her chest rises and falls, her nipple rings grazing my own chest. "Missed you," she says in between pants, her breaths becoming more frantic than the last. "You were everywhere." She lifts her hips to meet me.

I pull out of her, and she groans out. I lay down next to her. "Ride me," I tell her, and she gets up, swinging a leg around my waist. She places my cock right at her entrance and then she slowly, fucking slowly descends. She takes her time going down so she can adjust to my size. Once she is all the way down, she throws her head back, moaning out. I push up to get in even deeper. My hands find their way to her tits, holding them, kneading them.

She rotates her hips in a circle, making her clit rub on me. I pinch her nipples at the same time. "Give it to me, baby."

Her head falls forward while she places her hands on my chest so she can move up and down on me. She rises all the way to the tip and then comes down hard. I go deeper than I've ever gotten before. She does this one more time but on the third time, I place my hands on her hips and slam her down the exact moment I thrust upward, pushing her over the edge. Her pussy squeezes my cock as she grinds her clit on me. She doesn't move while her pussy pulses around me. Instead, she falls forward on me.

Her hair falls around my face as she looks at me. She lowers her face, licking my bottom lip. I grab her face in my hands and attack her mouth with mine. My tongue slides into hers, and her hips start moving up and down on me. "I love you," she says in between kisses. We continue to kiss while she slowly works my cock in and out of her. Our mouths connected, her heart beating on mine, my hand in her hair, my cock in her. This is heaven.

She comes again, this time not as powerful as the first, but still her pussy clenches one, two, three, all the while her moans are drowned in my mouth, our lips still sealed together.

I flip her over, never breaking our connection. My hands now by her head, the kiss goes deeper, my thrusts go harder, our tongues mimicking the movement of my cock going in and out of her. The faster I go the harder we kiss. The more frantic we become. A sheen of sweat has covered our bodies. Every single time I'm about to come I slow it down to make it last longer. Till I can't do it any more. My lips come off hers while I take one leg, putting it over my shoulder. The way her hips are tilting, I go deep. So deep she screams out in ecstasy. "Show me how you rub yourself," I say while I pound away twice in her, my balls slapping her ass.

Her hand works its way between us and rubs it through her folds, collecting her wetness. Bringing it back up, she rubs her clit in little circles. Every single time I bury myself in her, she squeezes me harder and harder. "Fuck, I'm going to come." As soon as I say that, she rubs her clit fast and then presses it down while she comes on my cock, her cum leaking out of her. Her moans fill the room, and in one more thrust I plant myself deep as I shoot my cum in her. While I fill her, I roar out her name. We come together, we come long, and we come fucking hard.

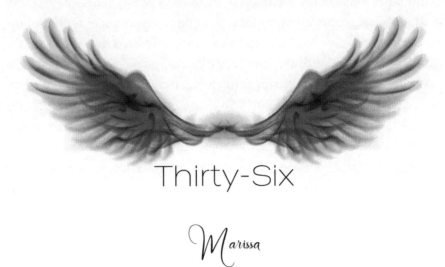

Thirty-Six

Marissa

The warm cocoon that I'm snuggled in can't stop the phone from ringing. Why is it that this is the second day in a row the phone wakes me?

Wiggling my ass into him, I call his name. "Mick," I grumble. "The phone."

"Keep wiggling your ass into my cock, I'll answer it while fucking you." He turns over to grab the phone from his nightstand.

"Yeah," he gruffs out. I hear a man's voice and get up to use the washroom. My body aches in places I had no idea could hurt. The amount of orgasms he gave me I can't even put into words. Once I wash my hands, I walk back inside on my tippy toes. His phone is still at his ear, the cover on his waist. He has one hand lying on his chest. I lift the covers, climbing back into bed. He moves his hand from his chest so I can cuddle into him.

My head on his chest, my chest flush against his side while his hand rubs my shoulder. His phone call lasts a minute more till he throws the phone back on the nightstand. He turns into me.

"Morning," he says while bringing me closer to him, my face going straight into the crook of his neck.

"I have a hickey on the inside of my leg right near my vagina," I tell him, and all he does is agree with a "hmm." I lift one leg over his hip, bringing him in closer. "And one right near my nipple, a couple bites on my hips." All he does is groan. "How am I going to explain this?"

He pushes me away and glares at me. "And who the fuck are you explaining anything to?" His jealousy is very much apparent.

I laugh at him and try to pull him closer to me, but he resists me.

"No, answer the question, Marissa."

"Are you serious right now?" I ask while he continues to glare at me. "Um, you know I have a daughter who is seventeen and who comes in and out while I change."

I see the moment it dawns on him, and two seconds later he pulls me back into his arms. "Oh, no, you don't." I try to stay strong but the moment his face finds my neck and he starts licking it and kissing it. I set off into a fit of giggles.

"Who was on the phone?" I ask him once I finally settle down.

"Jackson. I have to go into work today."

"Shit," I say, reaching over him to get his phone. "I have to call Lori." I look down at his phone. A picture of Lori and me laughing is his home screen. "What's the code?" I ask him. Entering the code, I find a picture of Mick and me on his wallpaper. It was taken by Lori when we went for ice cream.

"She's gone out with Bella, Brenda, and Lilah, something about girl spa day. Jackson said Bella will drop her off at home when they are done."

"Oh, okay, what time do you have to go in?"

"Now. We need to go over the toxicology report that came back from the hospital. Plus, the kid that was in a coma is awake."

I kiss his chest right in the middle.

"I'll make you coffee to go." I turn to get out of the bed. Looking around, I see that my panties are destroyed. Picking them up in one hand, I show him. "Nice, very caveman of you. Now I have to go home with a skirt and no panties. Smart."

He grabs my wrist, yanking me back in bed and covering me with his body. My legs open to him automatically. "If you go out without anything covering your pussy, I'm going to make sure you can't sit for a week." He presses his cock into my core, outside.

My body becomes alive. My nipples get tight, my pussy gets wet, and he hasn't even touched me. "You have to go," I tell him, but it's too late, he has already slid inside me.

"Then I better make it good, and I better make it fast," he tells me while pounding into me.

"And hard," I pant out between thrusts. "Make it hard." That is all I have to say as he fucks me harder, faster, and better than he did yesterday, and he does it so good my toes curl, and I come again and again and again.

We leave his house at the same time, him dressed for work and me wearing his basketball shorts that I had to tie on the side and his T-shirt. He kisses me on my lips then my cheek then my neck. "You sure you don't want to stay here in my bed all day? I don't mind if you pleasure yourself if you send me pictures."

I laugh out, pushing him away from me. "Thanks for the offer, but I'll be fine. I'm going to go home and start dinner. I have to work tomorrow, so it has to be an early night for me."

"Okay, I'll text you when I finish and I'm heading home." He walks away, but I have a nagging feeling in my stomach.

"Which home?" I ask him before he unlocks his door.

"Wherever you sleep, that's my home. So if you're at your place that's home. If you're here this is home." He winks at me, getting in, leaving me standing here with butterflies in my stomach and my heart soaring. I'm his home. The good thing is he's my home.

I wave at him as he drives away and get into my car. Making my way home, I call Lori, but it goes straight to voice mail. I leave her a message to call me.

I go over a list of things to do in my head. By the time I finally get home, I have a plan in my mind. I unlock the door and walk in, dumping my purse on the couch. I then walk around the living room, dining room, and kitchen, opening the blinds. They have been shut for almost two days. I stop in the kitchen to open the back door as well and the window above the sink.

I turn around and yell at Trevor, who is standing right behind me, his face sad. His eyes look tired, almost like he hasn't slept. "Oh my God, you scared me." I put my hand on my chest to stop my heart from beating out.

"I knocked. I guess you didn't hear me," he says while coming into the kitchen. "I waited all night for you guys to come home. I was worried. No one answered my texts," he says while advancing on me.

My mouth goes dry, and right before it looks like he is going to grab me the front door swings open.

"Mom, I'm home."

I choose this time to walk past him.

She sees me walking in with Trevor following me. "Hey, I didn't know we were hanging out today." She looks at Trevor while taking off her shoes and sweater.

"I texted you, but you didn't answer," he says to her in a soft voice. "I was worried."

She looks at him. "Oh, I'm sorry. My phone died yesterday, and I didn't have my charger. But now you're here. Want to continue watching *90 Day Fiancé*?" she says, going to get the remote and turning the television on. He walks past me and throws himself down on the couch.

"Yeah, let's watch that. I want to see if Nicole and Azan actually get married." He gives me a sad smile. "Sorry if I scared you before, Marissa," he tells me before turning his head and watching the show.

Two hours later, they are still watching the show, but he has dozed off. Looking at him from the kitchen table while I look through the fliers, the hair on my neck rises, thinking about him outside all night waiting for us. I make a note to ask Daniel more about him and his story.

Thirty-Seven

Mick

I drive away from her with a smile on my face. Life is fucking good. By the time I get to the precinct, I'm fucking whistling. Jogging up the steps, I see Jackson already at his desk with Thomas at his and Chris typing away.

"Morning, guys," I say, whipping my sunglasses off.

"Morning? You mean afternoon," Thomas says, smirking at me. "I see you got over that bullshit." He leans back in his chair.

Jackson, who is also leaning back in his chair, snickers at his desk.

"Assholes." I sit at my desk, opening up the case file on my desk. "Okay, boys, what do we have?" I ask, reading through the notes.

Chris looks up. "What do we have? A fucking clusterfuck. I can't believe that Lori was caught there. I told her it was not a good idea." He opens his drawer, taking his keys, then slamming it back, and walking out.

"What the fuck was that?" Thomas asks, and Jackson just looks at me with questions in his eyes. Questions we will ask later.

"So the toxicology came back. The kids were slipped Flakka."

"What the fuck is Flakka?"

"According to the reports online Flakka, also known as gravel, the drug is a mix between potent hallucinogens like LSD and stimulants like ice," Jackson says.

"So how strong is it?" I ask, confused.

"It can be as strong as crystal meth and cocaine. It's a new drug just hitting the street. Called the cheap man's crack. Actually, crack smokers are now buying this because it's a five-dollar insanity. That is what the kids are calling it." Jackson rocks back and forth in his chair.

I look over at Chris, who just walked back in with a coffee in his hand. We look over at him, all of us asking silent questions. He looks at us and shakes his head no. I nod at him, hoping he knows we are going to definitely have a talk about this.

"So the kids are either smoking it, snorting it, or drinking it. From what we suspect it was slipped into the punch that Farah made. We took a sample and forensic toxicologists have said it's a match to Flakka," Thomas throws in.

"We need to get a statement from Anthony, who is the last kid in the hospital. He just woke up yesterday. His body had a reaction to it, and it almost shut down. Two other kids ended up having delusions at the hospital. One thought if he went on the roof he could fucking fly. Got on his bed to show the nurses and fell flat on his face. Broke his nose and his cheekbone. Another kid thought the machines were talking to her. She said they were putting ants into her brain," Chris says. "We are missing one statement and the kid hasn't called me back. Trevor White."

Jackson and I both look at each other, but I speak first. "That is the kid that brought Lori to the party. They go to school together."

Chris moves the papers on his desk. "Yeah, I have nothing on him. I heard he was in the sobriety meeting. He has a juvie record, but it's sealed, so we are trying to get a warrant to get it opened. But till then I want to speak with him."

"Okay, first thing first, let's get to the hospital and speak with Anthony. Thomas and Chris, you can see if there have been any other Flakka outbreaks recently in the area. If this shit is hitting the streets it'll be just a matter of time till it's in the fucking schools," Jackson says, getting up.

I get up, grab my glasses, and stop by Chris's desk. "We need a minute later. Yeah?" I tell him before following Jackson out.

When we get into the car, I slip into the passenger side. There's an envelope on the seat. "What is this?" I ask him.

He looks over at me. "That's from Jason. Dropped it off this morning. I didn't think you would want to open this with everyone around."

I look down at the brown manila envelope, my heart beating a little bit fast. Opening it up, I pull out pictures of Sandie and who I assume is Jason's best friend. Jason's best friend, who is clearly not Caucasian. I laugh and show Jackson the picture of both of them in a park with no one else around while he holds her stomach and she laughs at him. "She's a fucking idiot. Did she not think I would realize that this isn't my child?"

He looks over, his eyes bulging out, and then starts laughing. "Not the sharpest tool in the shed." We make the rest of the ride in silence.

Once at the hospital, we check in with the doctor about Anthony. From what they said his brain activity is back to normal, but he's stuttering, which is new. They are watching to see if things change. When we knock on his door and go in he's sitting in the bed with both parents on the side of him. The feeling of dread and fear is marked all over their faces.

"Hi, sorry to interrupt. My name is Detective Fletcher. This is Detective Moro. I'm here to ask Anthony some questions about the party," Jackson says.

Anthony looks at his parents and nods his head. I see some fear on his face, so I tell him, "Would you feel more comfortable just the two of us?"

His father starts to get up objecting, but Anthony stops him. "It's okay, Dad. I want you guys here." He looks over at us. "I mean, how much worse could it get, right?" he says.

"Did you notice anything out of the ordinary?" Jackson asks.

Anthony shrugs. "Not really, no. Not in like a circle or anything. There were different conversations going on."

"Did anybody stick out?" Jackson asks, trying to get a lead to find out who brought the drugs in.

"Not really. I didn't know many people. Farah is dating one of my friends, and he invited me. Um, Marco said it was just going to be a chill party. I'm already on probation, so I don't want to get into any more trouble. So he said everything was going to be low-key. Besides, he said Farah was 'a good girl.'"

"What are you on probation for?" I cut in.

"Assault with a weapon," Anthony says, and his father chimes in. "He beat up a kid at school and had a knife in his backpack."

We both nod at him. "Have you ever done drugs, Anthony?" I ask him.

He looks at both his parents.

"It's going to be a lot worse if you lie to us than tell the truth."

He looks down at his hands. "I do weed occasionally. I did 'molly' last year, but I didn't like it."

"Can you tell us how you knew you were high?" Jackson asks.

"Yeah, I was sitting next to this girl Anna. We just met and we were checking out each other's 'snap stories,'" he says and right away I'm lost.

"Snap stories, what is that?" I ask him, and Jackson cuts in.

"I know what it is. What else happened?"

"Noooottttthing really. Farrrrah said she would be mmmmaaking this huge zombie mix. I sssttutter now. She got started mixing the alcohol but was missing something, so Zack and Trevor went to get the stuff. But she added other stuff in it, so we just started drinking it." He looks down at his hands that have started to shake.

"Who added the stuff to the punch?" I ask.

"Not sure. I wasn't really paying attention. There were about ten or so around it, so it could have been anyone really."

"When did you realize something was off?" Jackson asks.

"After Anna took two sips or maybe thrrreee. She started looking around like she was paranoid. She said something was in her head. I laughed at her, thinking she was a lightweight, so I continued drinking her drink till it was like I wasn't there anymore."

Jackson and I look at each other, each of us trying to piece together the puzzle.

There had to have been someone to slip something in the punch. Someone who had access to it, someone who was slick and sly.

"Okay, I think we are good for now. If we have any other questions we will give you a call," Jackson says, getting up and shaking hands with his father and mother while I do the same.

Walking out of the hospital, we don't say anything till we get in the car. "So we have a bunch of kids getting together for a party and someone slips some drugs in the punch. Nothing we haven't heard before except it's a new drug," I say, looking at him.

"It could have been a test to see how they react to it before bringing it on the streets. It could be just to fuck with them, or it could just be a fucking shit thing gone wrong," Jackson says, starting up the car.

"We need to go to Farah's house and ask her more questions on the 'guest list.'" Jackson guides the car that way.

Once we pull in and walk to the door ringing the doorbell, I look around the neighborhood. It's the typically white picket fence area. High-end as they say.

The door opens and Maci, Farah's mom, is the one greeting us. She stands there dressed in her haute glam clothes. "Oh, fuck, are you guys ever going to stop coming by?" she asks.

"I'm sorry to disturb you again, but we would like a word with Farah. Is she in?" Jackson says calmly.

"She better be. She's grounded for life." She moves away from the door, allowing us to walk in. I take in the house. It's back to normal, nothing out of place. "Farah, get your butt down here."

We wait a couple of seconds before a young girl comes down, same age as Lori, or at least I think so. "Hey, Farah, I'm Detective Moro. This is Detective Fletcher," I introduce myself to her.

"I know you. You were the one who ran in here for Lori." She rolls her eyes. "Girl is so fucking dramatic." She crosses her arms over her chest. "No one even cared she was here except Trevor, who treated her like glass. I mean, she spoke to the girls, but the minute a guy went near her she would start panicking," she continues, but I stop her.

"So you decided it was a good idea to serve underage kids alcohol. That would make you the cool kid?" I ask her.

"It wasn't even my idea." She looks at her mom. "I swear, I have no idea."

"So you weren't the one who got the recipe online?" I say while she pales. "You weren't the one who started pouring the mixture into the bowl?"

She licks her lips.

"You weren't the one who sent two kids to the store to buy more alcohol?" I finally say.

"But I didn't want to," she whines.

"But you did." I point out. "Who else had access to the bowl while you were pouring?" I ask.

"I have no idea. I didn't pay attention. There was a bunch of us," she says.

"So did you hand out the cups? Who handed out all the cups?" Jackson asks.

"No one. People just came and got their own."

"Who brought the cups?" I ask.

"No one. We had them in the pantry. It was high, so I had one of the guys get them."

"Who, who got you the cups?"

"Trevor. He was one of the tallest ones, so he got them down for me. He then dropped them all in the punch and we had to rinse them off. That's why he said he would go get more for us."

I look over at Jackson. This is the second time that his name has come up. We need to talk to Trevor, sooner rather than later.

"Is there anything else you can think of?" Jackson asks while I look around. No one sees it, but my eye catches a small plastic bag stuck under one of the kitchen chairs. Going to it, I pick it up and see that it's a small baggie. "Get me a napkin," I ask Maci, who runs to the other side to come back with one. I pick it up with the napkin and see that small white residue is stuck inside. "I assume you don't know anything about this."

Maci's face turns white, and Farah just shakes her head no. "Do you have a ziplock bag?"

She gets me a small bag where I put the other plastic bag in it.

"Okay, ladies, we will be in touch," Jackson says, and we walk out of the house.

"Who is this fucking kid Trevor?" he asks once we get in the car.

"No clue. They met at Lori's counseling from what I understand. Fuck, you probably heard more about him than I did," I tell Jackson.

"I met him once when he came to pick up Lori, but didn't stay long. He made sure to take care of her, opening her door for her and everything."

"I'm going to ask Marissa about him tonight. I know he hangs around there often."

By the time we make it back to the precinct and do the paperwork for the plastic bag it is well over eight p.m. I know that Marissa has to work tomorrow, so I call her before she falls asleep. She answers on the first ring.

"Hey, what's up?" she asks. I hear covers being ruffled in the background.

"Not much, just finishing up at work. I should be about another hour. Did you eat?"

"I did. I made chicken steak, not like Phyllis, but passable. I set a plate aside for you on the stove if you want."

"Oh, you cooked for me. Look at that."

"No, I cooked for me and Lori and Trevor. I just made extra for you," she says with a laugh.

"Is Trevor still there?" I ask her, sitting up.

"I have no idea. He usually just takes off after they finish their show. Those two have watched every single series available on Netflix of any type of reality show. When I came upstairs they were watching *Toddlers and Tiaras*," she says with a yawn.

"Okay, baby, go to sleep. I'll try not to wake you when I get home," I tell her, but I'll be waking her with my mouth.

"Hmmm, okay," she says. "Be safe."

I hang up and type Trevor's name in the system, same thing as this morning. I know Chris is working on getting his record unsealed. It's a waiting game.

I pull up to the house two hours later. It's almost ten, and the house is dark. I make my way up the front stairs, hoping the front door was left open. When I turn the knob, I'm lucky to find it unlocked. The house is dark, but there is a small light coming from the kitchen.

I walk in, seeing that the television is off and there are some pillows left there. I try to walk slowly as to not wake anyone. The light from the kitchen looks like it's moving.

Walking into the kitchen, I see that Trevor is playing with the door. His phone flashlight is the only light in the room. I clear my throat for him to know I'm there, and he drops his phone and turns around.

I open the kitchen light to see him fumbling to get his phone. "Can I help you with anything?" I ask him.

His face goes pale. "Um, no, I'm just locking up for Lori. She was tired and went upstairs, so I was making sure it was locked."

I nod at him. "Thanks for looking out for my girls," I tell him

204

with a smile. The way he's walking and fidgeting, I know he's hiding something.

"No problem. I'll let myself out and text Lori that you locked up for me," he says, walking away from me. Picking up his hat from the couch, he waves at me before storming out. I walk to the window, watching him walk to his car which he parked five houses away. Weird since there is no one parked in front of their house.

When he drives away, I take a picture of his plate and send it to Chris, asking him to get me the owner's name and address.

When I get to the back door, I check the lock to see it is locked but not closed all the way. Pushing the door shut, I warm up my food, eating it standing up in the kitchen, playing the day's events over in my head.

If had known that it would be my last meal in that house I would have savored it. I would have cherished it. If I had known that my life would change in the next twenty-four hours I would have held on tight and never let go.

Thirty-Eight

Marissa

I heard him come in and I'm assuming he's eating. Knowing he was coming, I never fully fell asleep. My stomach is riddled with butterflies, eager to see him again.

I hear him walk to the front door, locking it. Coming upstairs, he checks Lori's room then makes his way into my room.

I'm sitting up in bed, reading a book I long stopped caring about.

He leans into the doorframe while he takes me in. "Hey, there. I thought you would be sleeping," he says. His face looks tired. His body tense, the vein in his neck ticking.

"Gotta say I love seeing you in bed, babe, but not a fan of seeing some other man's flowers in your room," he says, his jaw now ticking.

I look over at the vase of white roses that I have been collecting for the past two weeks. Every day after work, I would get one. I would bring it home and watch it blossom.

"You can cut the act, Mick, I know it was you," I say, sitting up smiling at him.

He looks at me, his eyebrows pinching together. "What are you talking about?"

"You," I say, getting out of bed and going to the vase. "You put one in my car every day." I lean down to smell them. "Every single day I would get off work and one would be waiting for me. I looked around to see you, but I could never catch you." I walk to him smiling, wrapping my hands around his waist. "You're a sly one, Mr. Moro. And a romantic," I whisper the last one.

"It wasn't me," he tells me, and my hands fall from his waist.

I look over at them, my neck starting to get hot and my body cold until I start to shake. "What do you mean it wasn't you?" I almost fall, but he catches me.

"Babe, I never left them. I saw you once I drove by the diner. Saw you get in the car, take one out, and smell it and smile. Broke my fucking heart. I thought you were dating." He walks over to them. Grabbing the vase, he looks like he's ready to pitch it against the wall.

"There was someone in the house," I whisper to him. His body turns around almost like lightning speed. "One night I dreamed you, not just one night every night, but this one night I could swear you were here. You touched my cheek, you kissed my lips. I opened my eyes, and there was someone standing in my doorway, but when I went to open the lights, there was no one there." I start to tremble. "The door, downstairs, it wasn't locked. I thought it was just my imagination. Oh my God." My knees give out. I fall on the carpet, my heart beating so fast I think it's going to come out of my chest.

Lori walks into the room, rubbing the sleep from her eyes. "What's all the noise about?" She sees me on the floor on my knees and she is suddenly awake. "What happened?" she asks, falling down next to me.

"Someone was in the house," Mick says to her, going to look outside for God knows what. He pulls out his phone, texting or calling someone. I have no idea. My eyes are fixated on the roses that are sitting on my bureau.

"Pack a bag. We are leaving," he says while he grabs a bag from my closet. He turns to Lori. "I need you to go into your room and bring stuff you need for the next couple of days."

She nods at him and runs in her room, opening all her lights and the lights in the closet.

I watch Mick run around my room, throwing stuff into a bag. "Babe, you need to get up and get dressed."

But I don't have time because before I know it, we hear Lori yelling from her room.

Mick gets there before I do, with his gun drawn. She's sitting on her bed, the drawer open next to her bed holding all her bras and underwear. All have been shredded. She holds them up in her hands. "Drop it, Lori, don't touch anything."

Her hands shake while she dumps the things back in her drawer. Mick picks up his phone and calls Jackson. "We have a break-in at Lori and Marissa's." That is the only thing he says and then calls someone else. "I'm at Lori and Marissa's. Someone is fucking with them." I hear him say okay four times and then hangs up. Then he calls one more person. "This is Detective Moro. I have a PC 664/459 at the address One Four Seven Grand Road. No suspect on the scene."

I look at Lori whose hands are shaking, and tears are running down her face. "Who would do that do us?" she asks me, and I have no idea what to answer her, so I just hold her while she cries.

I hear a knock at the door and I start to shake, but Mick is gone for two minutes and returns with two guys in uniform. He takes them to my room where he shows them the flowers and then brings them back into Lori's room, showing them the drawer where her things are chopped up.

I hear more people coming up the steps.

Jackson fills the doorway this time. "Hey, Bella is in the car. She can take them to your house. I have Ralph on standby to watch them while we finish here," he says, but we both shake our heads no. The thought of being without him to protect us is something we aren't going to do.

"No, I'm not leaving without you," I say, and Lori nods with me.

He doesn't say anything before we hear stomping coming up the stairs and Chris is there, his hair all disheveled like he was sleeping. His basketball shorts hang low on his waist, and his T-shirt tight on his top. His biceps almost break out of the sleeves. "What happened?" His eyes go straight to Lori, who looks at him with full eyes, in a way I didn't notice before.

"Someone must have broken in and destroyed all of Lori's things," I tell him when he walks toward the drawer to look in.

"Don't," she yells out. He looks up shocked. "Please don't," she whispers, looking down at her hands.

He looks at her, going to his knees in front of her. "We are going to make you safe again," he tells her, squeezing her hands. "I promise you. If it's the last thing I do it's going to make sure you're safe."

She looks at him and doesn't say anything but stares at him. His hand comes up to wipe off a tear that is falling down her face.

He gets up and goes out the door, jogging down the steps. The only thing we hear is the door slam so hard the windows shake.

It takes them over four hours to process and take pictures of everything. By the time we get in the car and drive over to Mick's house, we are all dead on our feet. Phyllis sent me a text, telling me to take the next shift off. I'm so tired I don't even argue with her.

Once we make it inside his house and he has Lori settled, he comes back into his room, climbing into bed next to me. If I had known that this would be the last night I would get to hold him, I would have held him tighter. Spent more time touching him, spent more time smiling with him.

Thirty-Nine

Mick

When the words 'There was someone in the house' left her lips it was the second time in my life my blood ran cold. The first was when I watched my mother overdose in my arms.

It was also the second time in my life I vowed revenge. My main goal is to get the person fucking with them. I wasn't going to rest till it was done.

All inventory was taken from the scene, including the fucking white roses. The minute my eyes flew open the next day I knew the end was in sight. I felt it in my gut. My fingertips almost touching it.

I get out of bed, going downstairs to get coffee. There are questions that need answering, and I know yesterday wasn't the right time.

I look in on Lori, who is sleeping curled into a ball in the queen-sized bed I have in the spare room, the white bear in her grips.

When I finally walk back into my bedroom with two coffees in my hands I see that the bed is empty, the bathroom door opening right after.

"Morning," I say, giving her one of the coffee cups.

"Thank you," she grumbles, taking it from me. "What the hell is going on in my life?"

"I have no idea, but we are going to find out. And it's going to be soon," I tell her, watching her eyes close while she nods again. "We need to have a talk."

Her eyes open with fear.

"I understand that this is too much to have in your life. I get it. Trust me, I do." She puts her coffee cup down, hugging her stomach.

"It's not that kind of talk." I look at her. "I need to know what you guys know about Trevor."

She sits on the bed, wrapping her arms around her legs, close to her chest. "We met him in therapy. He has no parents. He was born addicted to crack. He says that his grandparents were killed by his parent's dealer, he got the insurance settlement when he turned eighteen, which is why he has a car and an apartment and can afford not to work. He spends most of the time with us. He doesn't give up much, and it's not like we ask him questions. Do you really think it's him?"

"I have no idea, but my gut is pointing in his direction. So I'd be more than happy to cross him off the list. For Lori," I say, crossing my hands over my chest, leaning on the bureau in my room.

Lori walks in, rubbing sleep from her eyes. Marissa opens her arms so she goes into them. Both my girls are in my bed. Dream come true. But not this shit that lingers over them.

"Lori, what do you know about Trevor? Anything, anything you think can help cross him off the list."

She looks at both of us, turning her head back and forth. "You really think Trevor did this? But, why? I don't understand. Should I ask him? Should I text him?"

I answer her right away. "You don't have any communication with him till I know it's safe. Nothing, Lori. I don't have any answers right now, but you can bet I'm going to find out even if it kills me." Maybe those were not the best words to say because they both gasp out loud. "Ladies, it's a figure of speech." My phone rings at the exact moment.

I see that it's Jackson. "Yeah?" I ask.

"We got something. I'm going to three way Thomas in. He's been at it all night," he says while putting Thomas on. "Okay, I'm with Mick. What do you have?"

"Fuck, what don't I have? First thing, the license plate you took yesterday. The car is registered to a dummy corporation. I'm trying to get who owns it, but it's all fucking criss-crossed. One name leading to another till you get back to square one. Two, this fucking kid Trevor... his prints are all over your girl's house."

"I know he's there all the time." I look at them both, watching them watch me. "All the fucking time."

"Yeah, well, is there any reason we would have his fingerprints all over Marissa's stuff? Like all over her drawers, her fucking shower soap?"

I look down, trying to keep my rage intact till I can get out of here. "What else you have?"

"His apartment that he has on file is a fake one. No such address. But get this, the fingerprints that we picked up aren't Trevor's."

"What do you mean? You just told me they were."

"Oh, they're 'Trevor's' but that isn't his name. His name is Tim Bennett," he says, blowing out a huge breath. "Both parents dead and so is his younger brother, Trevor."

I hear Jackson curse out. "He's been using a fake name. So I pulled Tim's record. Not a lot off of it. Some small shit selling and stuff but nothing extreme. I also have an address for him. Get this, in a ritzy high-rise. Now how does someone with no family, no money, nothing afford that shit?"

"We need to hit up that apartment," I say, and Jackson agrees.

"I just called Chris in. We do this, we do this now, and we do this fast. My guess is that he knows we are on to him, and we don't want him leaving town before we get him. I say twenty minutes we meet at his place, pack your heat. I'll also pass this with captain in case we need backup."

We all agree. I hang up, rushing around the house, getting my clothes and dressing. I take out my gun box, opening it up and taking an extra two just in case. I look up. The fear on both girls' faces has gotten them to sit there pale and shaking. "It's just in case." I go into the bathroom to put on my bulletproof vest. I'm not taking my chances. He might be a loose cannon.

I walk out, looking at both of them. "Brian, a security guy is downstairs, and he's going to be guarding the house. You do not leave under any circumstances, unless you hear it from me," I tell them, knowing it's a lot to take in. "I need to go, but I need to know that you hear me."

They both nod at me. I go in, kiss Lori on the head, and then go to Marissa. "I'll be back later." I kiss her lips softly, letting the kiss linger.

"Promise?" she says, and I nod at her.

"Promise." And with that, I walk out of the house.

We all meet at the corner of the high-rise that Tim lives in. Jackson and I get there first, but not a second later Chris and Thomas climb out of their cars. "Okay, I got someone on the inside to give me the scope. There are two ways in, elevator and stairs. Now his apartment is in a corner right next to the stairs."

"I'll take the stairs," Jackson says. "With Chris." We look over at Chris and see him shake his head.

"I want in first." We all look at him, Thomas speaking first.

"You need to lock down whatever shit you have going on in your head. This isn't practice at the academy, this is real fucking life."

Chris whips his head to Thomas. "You think I don't fucking know this? I want to get to this bastard first. I'm fucking ready." He finishes the sentence, looking at me.

"I go in with Chris," I say, looking at them then back at Chris. "But I go in first."

"Let's do this."

We take the elevator to the floor level, walking out two at a time, our guns drawn. We walk past the apartment where we hear loud voices. Jackson motions he's going in the stairwell while Chris and I take one side of the door each. Before we knock, we listen to the voices inside.

Two males' voices. I recognize Tim's right away. The other is deeper, raspier, older.

"I paid you to fuck up these girls, not to fall in love with them, you stupid little twit," the strange voice says, and I look over at Chris, questions all over his face.

"You paid me shit. I got closer than you thought I could," Tim says. "You fucking push me, old man, I'll go straight to them and tell them everything. EVERYTHING," he screams, and in a blink of an eye, we hear him groaning and a thump to the floor.

I look at Chris, making the decision to kick in the door. I kick it, and it opens in one kick.

I take in the scene. Tim is on the floor holding his side, which is bleeding out while he chokes on his own blood. And then the man holding the knife that is still leaking blood down his hand.

My eyes make it to his. And in a blink of an eye, my life changes. "Hello, Son," is the last thing I hear.

Forty

Trevor/Tim

I've been up all night. Fucking cocaine is wearing out. I look in the
kitchen drawer for more. Finding another ten packages, I take another
three hits before it finally reaches, and my heart starts beating a little
bit faster.

I fucked up last night, getting caught in the fucking kitchen fucking
with the door. I wasn't expecting that pig to come in. From what Lori
said he was working. Which gave me enough time to fuck with the
locks. I had to wait for her to go up to bed.

All I needed was another second and I would have been home free.
Now I've made a mess of things.

I got back home and started my plan into motion. I was going to
kidnap them both. I could do it. Lori would come willingly, but Marissa
might give me problems. But once she saw that I loved them, both more
than anything they would stay with me.

What I wasn't expecting was getting a call this morning from *him*.
He never calls me. I met him twice, and then I've been off his radar.
Till this morning.

When I heard the knock at the door I took another hit, the burning
sensation shooting straight into my nose. Shaking my sweaty palms, I
open the door, not expecting to see both of them.

"What's going on?" I ask them, looking at both of them, my

confidence slowly coming down.

He pushes past me and walks into the room. "Word is you fucked up bad this time, Tim."

I close the door after they both walk in. "I did no such thing."

He stands up, looking out at the view. "I loved this fucking apartment. You know this is where I used to bring my whores? Your mother included. She used to suck my cock while I looked over the skyline."

My fists clench by my sides. I don't know why my mother messed around with this guy, but money pays the bills. "I've heard this story before."

"Did you know she was one of my favorites?" he says, still looking outside. "Well, not counting Mick's mother. Now that bitch could fuck till my balls had nothing left. And the best is she believed I was actually in love with her." He snickers like he's a comedian. "Got knocked up with that bastard and then tried to hook another one on me."

He turns now, and I can see his face clear. The face of a devil. "I made sure she didn't have any kids after that. Can you imagine? I married into money, taking over my father-in-law's investment corporation. The perfect fucking son-in-law. Keeps his daughter happy. No one cared that she was like a dead fish in bed. So I fucked her to have kids. When that happened I sealed the deal to take over from him once he retired." He puts his hands in his pockets. "I had it all, till that bitch sent me a letter, blackmailing me. She thought she got the best of me."

He drags his hand through his hair. "You see, she got me good, but then I found out where she was, had her drugged. Watched her whore herself out." He chuckled. "Once when she was so loaded I got into that pussy again, and let me tell you, fucking heaven."

"Why are you telling me this?" I ask him, waiting to see if he will give me answers.

"I paid you to fuck up these girls, not to fall in love with them, you stupid little twit," he tells me.

I snap then. He can't fucking push me around. I have proof of everything. "You paid me shit. I got closer than you thought I could," I tell him, advancing to him, almost nose to nose. "You fucking push me, old man, I'll go straight to them and tell them everything. EVERYTHING," I yell the last word out, and in a blink of an eye, his hand comes out of his pants and he shanks me twice in the side. The burning hitting me the first time causes that I don't feel it the second time. I look into the devil's eyes one last time before I slump to the floor, holding my side. Trying to stop the bleeding, I look over into the corner, wondering if he is going to help me. He is my father after all. Is he going to do anything?

I see the gun in his hand the same time I hear the door being kicked open. I blink and then see Daniel raise his gun and shoot three times straight at Mick. Two hit him in the chest, protected by his vest, but one hits him in the side of the stomach where he has no protection and just like that, he's slumped on the floor.

I close my eyes just to rest for a second when I hear yelling and more gunshots. I try opening my eyes to see what's going on, but it's getting harder and harder to breathe. Till I'm soaring.

Forty-One

Mick

Eyes I could never forget stare back at me with blood leaking down his hands. "Hello, Son," is the last thing I hear before a gunshot brings me back into the now.

I didn't see Daniel standing in the corner with his gun drawn. One shot gets me in the chest, knocking me back, making my breath hitch. Another shot gets the other side of my vest, jerking me that way. By the time I aim my gun he's shot off another round, landing in my side. I look down at my side, the blood coming out. Holding my side, the blood seeps out of my hands. I fall to my knees while I hear yelling all around me.

I hear another gunshot go off, but this time I see the knife fly from my father's hand, his shoulder being hit, and his hand going to the wound while another hits his leg. He falls to the floor. If I had my way, I would put a fucking bullet in between his eyes.

I close my eyes, pressing down on the wound when another shot is fired. I don't open my eyes for that one because I'm just too tired.

I hear Jackson next to me, talking to me.

"Wake up, Mick, open your fucking eyes."

I try, but I'm just too tired. I hear yelling around me.

"Get in here, I can't feel a pulse."

Who are they talking about? I can't hear anyone anymore. The bright light is shining in my eyes.

I open them slowly, and I'm suddenly in a huge flower field, the flowers reaching mid thigh. The sun high in the sky makes the flowers' color bold and beautiful. I walk in the field, my hand grazing over them. They feel like satin in between my fingers. I continue walking, hearing laughing in the distance.

I can see a woman in the distance, so I walk to her. She twirls a baby girl in her arms, her brown curly hair flying with them. I put my hand over my eyes to block out the sun and to get a better view of the two.

When she stops twirling, she looks straight at me. "Mom," I whisper. She's healthy, she's happy.

She smiles at me. The little girl in her arms looks exactly like I did when I was younger. The little girl looks at me, smiling also. "Look, it's your brother," my mother says. The little girl puts her head on my mother's chest. I try to get closer, but my legs don't move.

"Mick, you shouldn't be here," she says with her voice low and soothing.

"Mom," is all I can say because she continues.

"You can't be here. It's time for you to go back."

I feel peace fall over me, a feeling of being free, a feeling of flying through the world. "I just got here." I try to get closer and closer to them, but no matter how much I try to run they just get farther and farther. "Mom," I yell out, and then she waves one last time and turns around to walk.

She smiles over her shoulder. "Go back to your family, Mick." And she disappears in front of me.

"Clear." I hear my body shocked back to life. "We got a pulse." My eyes try to open, but they can't do it. "We need to get him into the OR and stop the bleeding." I hear when all of a sudden I'm flying again.

Forty-Two

Marissa

I'm sitting on the couch next to Lori, trying to watch this show, but my mind is going a million miles a minute. I get up to get water for the fiftieth time.

I look out of his kitchen window at the water. The sun is shining in the sky. Looking to the left, I see a woman standing with brown curly hair, holding a baby girl in her hands. Eyes I've seen before, eyes I've looked into before. She sees me and waves at me the minute that Brian's phone rings, and I turn to him.

I turn back around to search for the woman, but she isn't there. I look back at Brian, and his eyes rise up to mine. The way he looks at me I know the phone call is about Mick.

His face goes hard and all I hear him say is, "I'm on my way."

Then I hear yelling in the background. A shrilling yell that rocks me to my core. I don't even realize it's me making that noise before I see black.

"Mom, Mom, wake up," is the next thing I hear. "Mick, Mom, he needs us," she says, and I blink my eyes till I don't see blurry anymore.

Brian is right there with her.

"Are you okay?" he asks, and I shake my head no. "We need to go. You want me to call an EMT or can you get there on your own?"

I sit up, shaking my head. "Mick needs me." This is my time to be strong for him. I look over my shoulder, glancing at the water, the lady gone.

We walk out and drive to the hospital, getting there in record time. I don't even wait for him to put it in park before I run into the hospital. The sight that waits for me has me stopping in my tracks.

Jackson is sitting looking at his hands. Hands covered in blood. Hands covered in Mick's blood. I hold on to the railing for support. Gasping out, he turns his head to look at me. Sorrow, sadness, and defeat are written all over his face. His eyes are wet with tears. Thomas is sitting across from him with blood on his shirt. A woman is holding his hand next to him.

Then my eyes find Chris's. He's got blood splattered on his white shirt and hands. His eyes look at me for forgiveness. Look at me for me to tell him it's okay.

These men went into a war zone, and they didn't even know it. They went in there, not even knowing that guns would be blazing. That one bullet would get one of them. Lori rushes in with Brian at her heels. She looks around the waiting room, her eyes landing on Chris's.

He gets up and walks to her while she runs to him. Her hands go around his waist, his arms going around her while she places her head on his chest and he kisses her head. He whispers to her, and she cries into his chest.

Jackson gets up and walks to me, holding out his hand. I put my hand in his, and we go sit down and wait for the heavens above to answer all our questions.

We sit here for what seems like days. The minutes creep by. The hours go slower than a snail. As more people hear what has happened, the waiting room becomes fuller.

Bella shows up with Lilah. Brenda shows up with Nancy, and Phyllis shows up with enough food to feed an army. She sits by my side, holding my hand while Lori holds my other hand. Chris is never far from her side.

Jackson sits in front of me. His hands are clean now, and his clothes changed thanks to Bella bringing some for him. Bella holds his hand, whispering things in his ear, but his eyes never leave mine.

The doctor walks into the room, ripping off his mask and cover-up from his scrubs that are covered in blood. He looks over at us. "Mick

Moro's family."

I don't say anything. Instead, it's Jackson who says, "They are right here." He points to Lori and myself.

We both get up, looking at him.

"He's going to make it." Collective sighs fill the room. "He was shot in the side of the stomach. Bullet went right through him, tearing through his liver and kidney. We were able to stop the bleeding. A centimeter more to the right and he would have been a goner. He almost flat lined a couple of times, so we are keeping him in the ICU till I'm comfortable with moving him."

Tears are falling down my face, my hands on my chest, on my heart. The beating finally back to normal knowing he's going to be okay. Lori grabs my shoulders in a hug.

"He's going to be okay, Mom," she says through her tears. "He's such a badass." She laughs through her tears.

"Can I see him?" I ask, afraid they might not let me.

"You can, but it has to be one at a time," the doctor says. "I know that visiting hours are over, but we will make an exception for this one time."

I look over at Jackson. "Do you want to go first?"

He shakes his head no. "You go first."

I don't wait for him to change his mind. Instead, I follow the doctor down the hallway leading to the ICU, leading to my man. Leading to the man who made my dreams come true. The man who saved my daughter from the devil. The man who has given me my own little piece of heaven.

Forty-Three

Mick

Fuck, this hurts like a bitch. I try to sit up, but the pain is just too much. I open my eyes, blinking them while I get used to the light that is coming through the curtains. I hiss through my teeth when I look down at the hospital gown. I raise my hand to see the IV injected. I touch my side, feeling the bandages on the side. Fucker got me good.

I look around the room and see the chair right next to me with Marissa curled into a ball, her head on a pillow that is on one of the chair handles. The way she's sleeping, I know her neck will be hurting like a bitch.

I look around at the flowers that fill the room, nothing like the flowers from my dream. A couple of balloons also with pictures drawn by Lilah are all around the room.

I press the button next to my hand, hoping the nurse comes before I fall back asleep. My lids are already heavy. The nurse walks into the room. From the look on her face, she doesn't expect it to be me who has pressed the button.

"You're awake, Mr. Moro," she says, and her voice breaks Marissa from her sleep, who opens her eyes and swiftly sits up in the chair.

"You're awake!" she says, getting up and walking over to me. Her eyes fill with tears, but she blinks them away. "You're really awake?" She rubs my face with her hand.

The nurse pushes Marissa aside to take my vitals, making her glare at the nurse. I laugh, but the pain just makes me groan. The nurse looks over at Marissa. "If you get in my way again, I'm going to have to ask you to wait outside."

Marissa rolls her eyes at her, stepping back. The nurse leaves my side to write on the chart.

"Is it okay if I hug my fiancé now?" she asks the nurse, and the nurse looks up, glaring as she walks out of the room.

"Fiancé?" I ask her.

"You've been asleep for a week and that is the only thing you have to say to me?" she says. "We had to lie to them to have me sleep here," she says, walking close to me.

"Is that so?" I hold my breath because of the burning that is now going on. "Fuck, this hurts."

"It should hurt, you almost died." She leans down, her face coming closer to me.

I move one hand to her face, touching her softness. Her lips find mine, and her scent invades me everywhere. Softly, she kisses my lips, till my hand finds the back of her head, bringing her deeper into me. When I let her go she doesn't move far from me, this time sitting on my bed, trying not to hurt or move me. "I missed you." She grabs my hand and places it in her small one.

I don't have a chance to respond to her because Jackson comes through the door.

"About fucking time you got off your ass," he says with a smile. "Who knew you'd be a slacker!"

I smile and don't even try to laugh, but I point at him. "Wait till I'm better. I'll show you slacker."

He walks over to the chair, sitting down, crossing his legs. "You waking up is going to kill Chris. He was gunning to be my partner. Guess that is put on hold also."

Marissa starts laughing with him.

I glare at both of them. "Is everyone else okay?" I ask him, wondering how my team is.

Jackson nods his head. "Only you were hit. It was touch and go there for a second. Fucking bullets flying everywhere."

I look over to Marissa to see if it's too much for her. But she sits there. Shoulders square, head high.

"What the fuck happened?" I ask, trying to piece shit together.

"You walked into a trap of sorts. You heard Tim fall and busted in the door. What you didn't know was that Daniel was loaded and waiting in the corner. Gun drawn."

I look at both of them. "Daniel? The guy that was Lori's 'mentor'?"

"The one and only. Not only was he Lori's mentor, he was also Tim's father," Jackson tells me.

"Shut the fuck up," I say, shaking my head. "How do we know all this? How the fuck do they have anything to do with my father?" I wait for the answer.

"Daniel. The minute we took him in, he sang like a fucking canary. He was on your father's payroll. Seems like daddy dearest was trying to get rid of you."

I look at him. "Why? I don't get it."

"Seems your mother was blackmailing him even from the grave. She has a lawyer send him letters once a month. So every month he had to put ten thousand dollars into a trust in your name. Now, unless you weren't around to collect it..." Jackson looks at Marissa, who nods her head. "They were framing you. The goal was for Daniel and Tim to drug Marissa and Lori, fill them with drugs until they overdosed, and they planted shit around her house with your fingerprints all over it. Like a smoking gun."

The thought of my father hurting them is like a punch to the stomach. "What the fuck?"

"Everything was going according to plan till Sandie came in and took you away from them, fucked it up. You weren't around anymore so then they were going to get Daniel to start dosing them, but then you fucked up there by coming around again. But then Tim thought he could get them to go away with him. The guy was on so much coke I'm surprised he had insides."

"Where is my father now?"

"He's dead," Marissa says. "Killed himself at the scene."

"Bastard," I growl. "Fucking worthless piece of shit."

"Pretty much. We also found Flakka in Daniel's apartment, so we have him on intent to sell, attempted murder, and a whole shitload of charges. Basically, he's going to die inside," Jackson says and then gets up. "I think you've had enough for one day."

I nod at him while he reaches for my shoulder and squeezes it.

"Good to have you back, partner," he says before walking out.

"Tell Chris to get off my fucking desk," I tell him, and he smiles at me.

"How did you know?" He shakes his head, walking out.

I look at Marissa, who returns my gaze.

"Are you okay?" she asks.

"Marry me?" I ask her. I don't have a ring, I don't have a plan, but I know that I can't let another minute pass without knowing she will be mine. That she will be the one holding my hand forever. That she will be the one carrying my kids. That she will give me my piece of heaven.

Her lips curl up into a crooked smile. "I thought you'd never ask."

Epilogue

Mick

I pull up, parking on the street. Toys litter the grass along with three red cars, two tricycles, and a pink electric scooter all thrown in the driveway.

I make my way around them, jogging up the stairs. Opening the door and walking inside what I consider my very own personal daycare, the door doesn't even close behind me till my boy Liam runs to me.

"Daddy, Momma said I can't have dessert because I bad." He frowns at me.

I lean down and pick up my little monster, who just turned six.

He is my clone, just don't say that in front of Marissa. The whole time she carried him for nine months is a sore subject since he has nothing of hers.

"And why are you bad?" I ask him.

He shrugs his shoulders.

"I'll tell you why, because Liam thought it would be a good idea to get worms and put them in Sarah's doll carriage," my wife says, coming out of the kitchen holding one of my twin girls Sierra while Sarah hugs her legs. Where Liam is all me, my two-year-old twin girls are all their momma. Soft blond ringlets fall to their shoulders, but their eyes are all me. They are the bane of my existence, and they play me like a fiddle. All they have to do is smile at me and I'll do whatever they want. Fuck, throw tears in there and I'll fucking go to the ends of the earth just so they don't have those tears.

I look at my boy, who is trying to hide his smirk at this revelation. "Did you put worms in Sarah's stroller?"

He looks down, so I know he's lying.

"Did you clean them up?"

"No, Momma did," Sierra says. "She yell 'ahhhhhahahahah'," she says with her hands in the air.

I look at my wife, who looks just like she did nine years ago when I married her. The day she walked toward me wearing a white lace gown on Lori's arm, both of them walking toward me. To join me. To take my name. Both girls are now Moros. And I couldn't be any more fucking prouder. I walk over to her, bending to kiss her lips. Slipping my tongue into her mouth, my cock stirs.

"Hmmmm," she says to me, wiping my lower lip with her thumb.

"So gross," We hear coming downstairs. Our eight-year-old son Jackson walks down the stairs. "When does the kissing stop?" he asks, walking into the kitchen and opening the fridge.

"Never," I say, and he groans.

"I wish I had normal parents." He pours himself a glass of milk.

We both roll our eyes.

"Did you finish your homework?" Marissa asks him while she goes into the dining room to put Sarah in her booster seat while I put Liam down in his chair and buckle Sierra in hers.

Marissa walks away, and I watch her ass as she walks out. Her shape never changed. She is sexier today than before. The first time she told me she was pregnant I fucked her till we were both raw. The fact that she carried my kid in her was the hottest fucking thing ever.

Then I saw her stomach swell with my child. I fucked her anywhere I could.

I remember being at a restaurant and getting into the car and parking so she could ride my cock while I sucked her swollen tits. Her nipples getting darker and darker as the months passed. She took off the piercings when she fed our children but put them back in the minute she stopped nursing.

She must feel me thinking about it because she still has her back to me when she says, "Out of the gutter, Mick." It's like she feels me place my hands on her. Fuck. I need to sit down before my eight-year-old sees my boner.

It's never a dull moment in the Moro house, especially when their older sister comes to visit. Well, except the time that Jackson took her earring to try to put it in his pecker. That was an explanation I didn't ever want to have. Looking at my twenty-year-old daughter while my son explained he wanted one just like daddy is something I never ever want to do again. The fact that she looked at my junk after, pointed at me, and laughed wasn't great either. Or the fact she high fived her mother.

Marissa comes to the table with the lasagna. The meal goes as smooth as it could be with two toddlers, a boisterous son, and an almost hormonal boy.

Three hours later, we are lying on the couch watching some fucking reality show that Lori has been obsessed with. You would think being a mom to a one-year-old would slow her television time, but not her.

Not one to let the opportunity to grope my wife pass me by, I slide my hand up Marissa's shirt to cup her tits. Fuck, still a handful. I roll her nipple and still after all this time she moans.

My hand slides down her still flat stomach into her shorts, then right into her slit. She's already wet and primed. "So fucking wet for me already," I tell her, shifting so she could spread open for me.

"Hmmmm. I played with myself in the shower," she says, and I know she isn't lying.

"Did you?" I ask, sliding one finger in her and then two. "What were you thinking about?" I finger her harder while she snakes her hand into my basketball shorts, her hand gripping my cock, squeezing it and matching the way I finger her.

"I was thinking about the time you bent me over while I was wearing my five-inch heels with my garter belt on." The memory makes my cock even harder. "You ate my pussy from the back."

I curve my finger up while pumping her pussy.

"Then you got up and fucked me hard," She starts gasping. "Fucked me so deep, remember? You even lifted me up a little. Balls hitting my clit so much it was starting to swell."

I moan in her neck, her hand fisting me fast.

"Then when I was about to come you played with my ass."

Fuck, that was a dream come true to me. My hips thrust up in her hand while I take my fingers out, licking them then sliding my tongue into her mouth so she tastes herself on me. She stops talking but only to suck my tongue into her mouth. She sucks my tongue the way she would suck my cock.

I rip her hand off my cock, pushing her off of me. I get up, kicking the shorts off me, my cock springing out. She falls to her knees in front of me, taking me deep in her throat, all the way to the back while her tongue twirls around me.

I let her have her fun for two minutes then I yank her up, pulling her shorts off. Her pussy is wet and waiting. I turn her around, bending her over the arm of the couch. She puts her knees on the arms and then bends over. I love the sight of her like this, open and waiting for me. I lean down, licking like I did that day she was talking about. From her clit to her opening where I slide my tongue into her. I fuck her with my tongue while she plays with her clit. I join her finger on her clit, playing along with her, dragging it on. Till I feel her muscle start to tremble on my tongue. I get up and plunge inside of her. She grabs the cushion on the couch to scream into. In this position, I'm deep and it's fucking tight.

I grab her hips while I pound into her. It takes two pumps before she comes all over my cock, her juices coming fast, leaking down my balls. My girl can come. I make sure my piercing rubs her G-spot each time I come out. Her pussy quivers again, and right before she comes again I suck my finger and stick it in her ass the next time I go balls deep. Her pussy gets even tighter with my finger in her ass. I work her ass the same time I work her pussy. "Fuck, babe, you're fucking soaking me," I tell her, my balls starting to draw up. "Next time I think I should fuck your ass." The thought of fucking her ass is just too much for both of us because I plant myself deep in her and empty myself the same time her pussy clenches and unclenches. The same time her head falls forward and she comes again and again. We stay like that till our breathing comes back to normal.

"Does it ever get bad?" she says later that night after we locked up and made sure the kids were okay.

I climb in after her, grabbing her in my arms and kissing her neck, smelling the strawberry soap she has on her. "Nope, not when you're touching pieces of heaven."

The Fucking End

Other titles from Natasha Madison

Hell and Back
Something So Right

Acknowledgments

Every single time I keep thinking it's going to be easy. It takes a village to help and I don't want to leave anyone out.

My family: to Tony, Matteo, Michael, and Erica, who have to put up with Mom sitting at the table listening to country songs and serving you frozen pizza or McDonald's. You encouraged me, you pushed me, you support me, and I am utterly and forever grateful for all of that. Well when you weren't complaining you want real home cooked food, which was often. Thank you for going on this journey with me.

Crystal: My hooker. What don't you do for me? You named this book! Thank you for holding my hand. Thank you for cheering me on even when I was overly dramatic. Just thank you for being you and loving me!

Rachel: You are my blurb bitch. Each time you do it without even reading this book and you rocked it. I'm really happy I bulldozed my way into your life.

Kendall: You have become a special part of me. The nice part, of course. You pumped me up when I get down, you pushed me to be better, and you made me cry. Your friendship is better than chocolate.

Lori: I don't know what I would do without you in my life. You take over and I don't even have to ask or worry because I know everything will be fine, because you're a rock star!

Beta girls: Teressa, Natasha M, Lori, Diane, Sian, Yolanda, and Ashley. You girls made me not give up. You loved each and every single word and wrote and begged and pleaded for more.

Danielle Deraney Palumbo: No matter what the universe threw at you, you still managed to read my book. I don't think I could have done this without you. Thank you for taking the time and reading it and sending me your notes. I don't think I could release a book without you!

Madison Maniacs: This group is my go to, my safe place. You push me and get excited for me and I can't wait to watch us grow even bigger!

Mia: I'm so happy that Nanny threw out Archer's Voice and I needed to tell you because that snowballed to a friendship that is without a doubt the best ever!

Neda: Is there each and every single time I have a question, regardless if you're working or not. Thank you for being you, thank you for everything!

Emily, my Editor Extraordinaire: Thank you for not tearing my book to shreds and for loving it with me.

BLOGGERS. THANK YOU FOR TAKING A CHANCE ON ME. EVEN WHEN I HAD NO COVER, NO BLURB, NO NOTHING! FOR SHARING MY BOOK, MY TEASERS, MY COVER, EVERYTHING. IT COULDN'T BE DONE WITHOUT YOU!

My Girls: Sabrina, Melanie, Marie-Eve, Lydia, Shelly, Stephanie, Marisa. Your support during this whole ride has been amazing. GUYS, HOLY SHIT, LOOK AT ME GO!

About the Author

When her nose isn't buried in a book, or her fingers flying across a keyboard writing, she's in the kitchen creating gourmet meals. You can find her, in four inch heels no less, in the car chauffeuring kids, or possibly with her husband scheduling his business trips. It's a good thing her characters do what she says, because even her Labrador doesn't listen to her...

You can find/stalk her here:

Facebook
https://www.facebook.com/AuthorNatashaMadison/

Twitter
https://twitter.com/natashamauthor

Instagram
https://www.instagram.com/natashamauthor/

ReadersGroup
 https://www.facebook.com/groups/1152112081478827/

Goodreads
https://www.goodreads.com/author/show/15371222.Natasha_Madison

Amazon
https://www.amazon.com/Natasha-Madison/e/B01JFFMPP8/ref=ntt_dp_epwbk_0

70560689R00133

Made in the USA
Columbia, SC
13 May 2017